Zhang Xianliang

was born in Nanjing in 1936. In 1952, bankrupted by the communist takeover and unable to attend college because of his 'inferior class status', he went to primitive Ningxia in northwest China to be a farmer. In 1956, he was designated an 'enemy of the people' and for the next twenty-two years he was alternately imprisoned and sent to work in labour camps. He began writing after his 'rehabilitation' in 1979 and he is now a leading figure in the Chinese literary scene. His novels were awarded China's major literary prize several times in the early 1980s but in recent years he has been criticized by the authorities and his work has been banned. His previous novel, *Half of Man is Woman*, was published to great acclaim in the West. He still lives and writes in northwest China.

Martha Avery was born in New York. She has lived in Tokyo and Hong Kong while travelling extensively in China as a manager for a leading scientific publisher. Her translations of Chinese literature include Zhang Xianliang's previous novel, *Half of Man is Woman*.

By the same author

Mimosa
Half of Man is Woman

ZHANG XIANLIANG

Getting
Used to Dying

Translated from the
Chinese and edited by Martha Avery

Flamingo
An Imprint of HarperCollins*Publishers*

Flamingo
An Imprint of HarperCollins*Publishers*
77–85 Fulham Palace Road,
Hammersmith, London W6 8JB

Published by Flamingo 1991
9 8 7 6 5 4 3 2 1

First published in Great Britain by
Collins 1991

ISBN 0-00-654422-3

Printed in Great Britain by
HarperCollins Manufacturing, Glasgow

AUTHOR'S FOREWORD

Getting Used to Dying was published just prior to the events of June 4, when the attention of the Chinese people was focused on things other than literature. As a result, it has received little public criticism or public praise – and this is fortunate, for otherwise I would be in trouble. Internal discussions among those in power in China today have already pointed out this book without mentioning it by name. I am not able to tell you more about this – my apologies; it is, as they say, a 'matter of maintaining discipline'.

I can, however, tell you that this has been one of the best-selling books in modern China. 300,000 copies have already been sold on the mainland, including copies of the literary magazine that first published the work. With the passage of time, I feel confident that this book will have an ever greater influence. First, it gives an acute analysis of the mental framework of China's intellectuals and, second, it is highly prophetic. For example, after reading it one can understand why people were so active, so dynamic, before June 4 and yet why, after June 4, they were so docile, so obediently willing to self-criticize.

The style in which the book is written is new to China. In structure and in voice, it sets a precedent. It is also written in a new form of poetic prose. It can be said that *Getting Used to Dying* has begun a new era in the writing of novels in China.

Zhang Xianliang
April 4, 1990

TRANSLATOR'S INTRODUCTION

The author of this book has spent half his life in the labor camps of northwest China. Much of what he describes in his writing is autobiographical. *Getting Used to Dying* was completed in early 1989 and was originally published in a Chinese magazine in April of that year. After the events of June 1989 and the subsequent tightening of censorship, the work was banned inside China. As of this writing Zhang is under investigation by the Chinese government. He still lives in Ningxia, in the far northwest of China.

There is a term in Chinese which means 'to be made to accompany to the execution ground'. It is common enough to be included in most Chinese dictionaries. The term refers to a person who is taken to the execution ground, believing that he is going to be killed. As people around him are executed by gunfire, he is left alive.

Zhang describes this experience, which forms the central theme of *Getting Used to Dying*. In discussing the theme with the translator, Zhang adds, 'Although the gun may never have been fired, the bullet of fear and repression has lodged inside the brain. Every intellectual in China lives with this kind of bullet in his brain.'

Getting Used to Dying is narrated by two voices of the same person and is a portrait of what, in Western eyes, is a psychosis. In modern Chinese eyes, though, it is a portrait of normality. Communist China has been open to the West for only a decade; four-fifths of the life of the author has been spent in a tightly closed, self-sufficient system. Within that framework, events that occur inside China in these pages are rational and natural. Juxtaposed against scenes in Paris, New York and San Francisco, however, they become terrifying, while the West becomes absurd and surreal.

It is this layering of the surreal and the all-too-real that makes *Getting Used to Dying* so powerful.

Zhang's black humor in the face of 'what is worse than death' is a testimony to his own tenacious will to live. 'If you can cry, you can live,' says one of his characters. Zhang laughs as he cries and, so far, he has stayed alive.

Hong Kong, October 1989

CHRONOLOGY

	Events in the Main Character's Life:	Events in Chinese History:
1936	Born.	
1957	Accused of being a 'rightist', sent to labor reform camp.	'Anti-Rightist Movement' in China.
1958–60	Three years labor reform.	'Great Leap Forward': 1958.
1959	Contemplates suicide.	Famine in China 1959–61.
1960	Almost dies of starvation. Scene in corpse-shed.	
1961	Gets out of camp and goes to see B in Baotou hospital.	
1963	Accused of 'sabotaging production' – sentenced to three years' surveillance.	
1965	Convicted of being 'counter-revolutionary' – sentenced to three years' labor reform. Scene of digging bones.	
1965–68	Three years of labor reform.	Cultural Revolution in China: 1966–76.
1968	Gets out of camp and goes to see mother in Beijing. Is rearrested and sent back to Ningxia.	

1970	'Accompanies to-the-execution-ground' – execution scene.	
1979	Rehabilitated. Meets A in Canton.	Faction of Deng Xiaoping comes to power.
1987	Criticised while on trip abroad. Travels to San Franciso, then New York. Meets C in New York.	Anti-Bourgeois Liberalization Movement in China.
1988	Travels to Paris for several months, writing book. Returns to Ningxia in the autumn.	
1989	Spends Chinese New Year in small mountain village in China. Finishes book.	Tiananmen Massacre. June 4, 1989.
2001	Dies at age 65.	

❊ I ❊

SNAKE

Ningxia, China, a labor reform camp, 1959

IT IS NO longer clear to me when I began to want to kill him. It was, of course, after the two of us had parted ways. When I first began watching him I had no intention of killing him – it was only later that he became intolerable.

In the end his feelings came to coincide with mine, so that as I planned his death he was gladly coming to terms with dying. This saved me considerable trouble. At the moment he died we two joined as one, and it was a coupling that transcended love-making with any woman.

We both achieved what we wanted when the shot rang out. He was obliterated, while I lay dying on a bed, awaiting the soft touch of a woman – the touch of fingers with a ring on them that would gently close my eyes.

He sought death by his own hand once, in the past. But dying is not so simple, it can become quite a feat – we normally achieve it only once in a lifetime. He tried in the labor reform camp, after roll call one evening.

The men were being counted, 'One, two, three, four . . . twelve, thirteen, fourteen.' The moon was not up yet. Sky and earth formed a lacquered sheet of darkness. Pinpricks of stars joined the flickering kerosene lamps of the guards. The camp was arranged in parallel blocks of buildings. Each block had a guard and contained a number of cells. Each cell held between fifteen and twenty men, who now stood outside waiting to be counted.

The shouted roll calls of the block guards seemed muffled by the dark, as though each string of numbers was an eerie signal from another world. The numbers, like the men, bubbled out of nowhere and returned to nowhere, like raindrops sizzling for a moment before being drunk in by a scorched desert.

'The End!' The final call echoed inside him. He felt lifted and rocked by the ricocheting waves of this 'End'. The significance of the word washed over him although it had no real meaning. His search for meaning was something that came later.

Nobody had escaped. Nobody had died. It had been a normal, uneventful day for the camp. The 'End' of it now pressed him back with the other prisoners to his cell.

The earthen walls of this room were studded with irregular wooden pegs. Prisoners had pounded them in so that the wall looked like a miniature upright forest. Years later he remembered this forest as he gazed at the Bois de Boulogne. Lumps of all shapes and sizes were hung from the pegs – a wealth of lumps glowed in the dim lamplight. Prisoners kept their few belongings hung up on the wall – this cut down their already limited freedom to move, but it gave them a sense of owning something tangible.

As the other prisoners groped their way onto their bunks – planks of wood twelve inches wide with a narrow pad made of rice stalks – he sneaked a rope from under his own pad and slipped out.

Shortly after, the lamps in the cells went out. Hidden at the end of the blocks, he watched as the buildings darkened. The realm of men, of reality, receded, like a boat that was slowly drifting away. When the last light went out he thought he had already died. Heaven seemed infinitely high but made of the same blackness as the earth. He had not anticipated that death would be so easy.

Soon he realized that death does, after all, have its obligatory procedures. Eliminating your own body is no easier than killing someone else. The effort involved stopped him many times in the years to come, when in rage or despair he contemplated suicide or murder. The effort was all that stopped him: he was neither a coward nor a saint.

With the energy left in him from his last supper, a bowl of thin rice gruel, he dragged the rope behind him to the threshing ground. The grumbling accompaniment of his stomach reminded him of the sounds of a donkey-pulled water cart.

He had once been quite creative, good at beating any chess opponent with a surprise move, but the limited means provided by the labor camp had circumscribed his skill. He had no choice but to hang himself. It was, in truth, a tasteless way to go.

He sat down on a stone roller by the side of the threshing ground,[1] still gripping the rope in his hand. Before committing suicide, a person should pause to reflect: this seemed to be part of the established procedure. Nobody teaches you how to kill yourself, and yet each suicide unconsciously does the same things. Perhaps this behavior, repeated over thousands of years, seeped into our ancestors' blood and became a part of our genetic code.

'Don't worry about it!' he told himself. Descending to the level of his ancestors in selecting an old way to die wasn't anything to be ashamed of. After all, he had been toyed with by history, manipulated by those in power, and yet not even those powerful leaders had brought anything new into the world. Two tears rolled down his face, but he paid no attention – they were merely another step in the normal process.

The stone roller was cold: his ass seemed the only conscious part of the universe. Everything had been thought out, thought through and through – and once everything had been arranged in his brain, classified and organized, one would have thought it could be set aside. Only later did he realize that he had not thought things through, and that he never could.

The fragrance of threshing extended in all directions, while a dark distillation of it seemed to hover above the ground. A cricket, greeting the faint flickers of stars above, absorbed their tremulous rays and sent them back to the heavens through its own small voice. There was no wind but he seemed buoyed by a floating lightness

[1] A threshing ground in China is a large open square of earth that has been rolled hard and flat by a stone roller around four feet long and two feet wide, pulled back and forth by a donkey before threshing begins.

under his feet. Cast off from grinding hard labor, freed from his 'class background'[1] and his future, he felt the darkness before him seemed to blossom in a profusion of colors.

He rubbed the supple and smooth rope, a well-used rope of hemp. In the bitter night air it felt like a dead snake. As he rubbed it, he felt strands of hate and love in himself coil together. Neither had any object or focus – they were simply a stimulating flavor inside him. He tried to grasp the feeling but it escaped, and he was left with the emptiness that precedes death.

The tears had been the secretions of early spring. He was twenty-three years old that year. By the time I used a gun to pulverize him at the age of sixty-five, he was able to face me squarely with a smile. The smile showed me he was dying willingly, happily. It showed me that he ought to die.

Through a blur of tears he discovered the moon. At first it was not the moon but its clear, cold light that he noticed, which carried a slurping sound as if the parched earth were sucking in its moisture. Then shadows of that light lashed over him, as a flock of crows took off from nearby poplars. Their wings whipped up a tumult of shadows. Some bounded for the earthen wall before him, some pounced on stacks of grain, some even swooped over his own body. The stars had faded but the cricket called with an intensity greater than before. The snake came violently alive. Several minutes passed before he realized that his hand was shaking.

At that moment the moon leapt above the tops of the trees. Its orange orb was enormous – it was enormous. Years later he still could see that wheel of a moon in his mind. It was the kind of moon, the kind of moonlight, that can appear only once in a lifetime. All the moons he later saw were pallid reproductions.

The imperial moon seemed, like the sun, to be filled with a vital force of youth. Each tree in the forest stretched out towards the force, and the moon seemed to grab hold and pull. From beyond the cries and struggles of the trees now came the rolling shout of

[1] 'Class background' is the criterion by which people are judged in China. Those with the worst background come from educated, affluent families and are punished accordingly.

the wilderness, and from the end of the wilderness the shout echoed back, reverberating through the empty firmament.

The cries of the trees awakened him. He whipped his head back, to find that it had sprouted bristle grass. He had been sitting on the stone roller for years. The orange moon now radiated a cold blue light, submerging the wide earth under a light turquoise sea. Small ripples played with his short hair. Like the hands of his mother, or of lovers, the light reached down to touch him from the unseeing sky.

He did not tie the rope around his neck. The broken heels of his cloth shoes slapped the ground as, rope in hand, he returned to his cell. That was the moment he and I parted ways. As I watched him go I saw a cloud of white smoke billowing behind him. It was his cowardice and indecision puffing out from the top of his head. Then he was lost in the white smoke and gone.

This was a rehearsal for dying, one which was to provide the subject for many of his later conversations. The more he spoke of it, the more abstruse and profound it became. As he later sought the reasons for wanting to die, and for wanting to live, he did not realize that he was becoming degenerate. The motivation of his actions would always be beyond his comprehension, certainly beyond his ability to articulate. He spoke in a high manner of life's 'significance', but he excelled in deceiving himself as well as others.

Yet now the words 'The End' began to pursue him, whether he was speaking in public or making love to a woman. He only needed to be greatly moved or disappointed for me to shout these words into his ear.

These two words contain and cover all. I have a pair of eyes that do not know the meaning of exhaustion: at any time or place I am intently watching him. He sometimes wants to speak with me, but I never say more than:

'The End!'

Since we parted ways, we come together only when he is on the cusp of death. Several more deaths followed this first rehearsal. In between, he was infatuated with the so-called meaning of life. He became entranced with the verbiage of mankind and made words the repository of all human wisdom. The reality of life outside of language made him conscious, however, that he did not really want to live. Death became second nature to him, but he lacked the strength or tenacity to die. It was at times like this that I had to help him.

I have often felt that a great number of people must want to die, yet, like him, lack the physical or mental means to do it. To a certain extent living is a mere convention, a form of inertia. If dying were as easy as walking, this over-populated world would soon be rid of two-thirds of its people.

UTOPIA

China 2000, one year before his death at age 65

IN THE YEAR 2000, a newspaper published this article:
'Good news for those suffering from incurable disease! In addition to euthanasia you can now enjoy a new form of dying. Developed from the *qi-gong* and "vital heat force" fads of the 1980s, it is a means of linking life and death. The method is simple, and allows those who are too lazy or too tired to die to enter a new world with a minimum of bother. The physical body dies while the spirit lives on in the soul's imagination.

'Practitioners of this art extract the soul from the body and preserve it — in the same way human organs are preserved for transplant. Once free, the soul roams the universe at will, enjoying whatever life it wants.

'According to informed sources, many are lining up for this treatment. The queues are even longer than those in front of shops selling soap. One way to distinguish a line of people waiting for the link-up treatment is that, rather than a shopping basket, they stand there holding a box for the ashes. Those who want to die early must, as usual, go through the back door.'[1]

When this article appeared, I urged him to pay a visit to a practitioner of this treatment. He had turned sixty-five that year, an age when, according to *The Yellow Emperor's Classic on Medicine* the kidneys deteriorate and the penis withers and the ability to make

---

[1] The 'back door' in China means any illicit means of getting something you want.

love collapses after one shot. In this sorry condition, and having often been crushed by death anyway, he had little reason to let his body go on.

The black walls of the practitioner's operating room were hung with surreal paintings. One was a cross-section of a fault line in the earth's crust. In its center was a blind cow's eye that had been split open by the crack. Entitled *Society*,[1] this painting had been personally selected by the practitioner.

Seated before us, this swarthy man began to intone: 'You must believe me completely. You must tell me everything that is in your mind. Tell me the Paradise you imagine . . . so that I will be able to direct your soul.'

These words revolted me and must have revolted him. Every person and institution in his life had demanded his trust, then turned around and used his own trust to trick him. Each had asked him to 'make a clean breast of it', to 'hand it all over',[2] so that he eventually grew weary of playing the game. Who would have thought that to enter the gates of heaven one had to crawl into the same trap that one had already been through in hell? I now noticed that *Society* was not a blind cow's eye in the earth but a cross-section of layers of epidermis in a split-open womb.

'What kind of Paradise would you like to enter?' The voice of the practitioner was oppressively grave, while the two of us seemed to be sitting inside an earthen jar.[3]

'A Christian Paradise? You would be together with God there, and angels with wings would be flying around. Or would you like to live in an Islamic Paradise? Countless dark-eyed beauties would keep you company. The Buddhist Paradise, on the other hand, would be illusory but also quite real: it would allow you to re-enter human society in another incarnation. You would enjoy a glorious

---

[1] The word 'society' in Chinese has a broader meaning than in English. It includes connotations of 'socialism' and of obligation to an all-embracing social structure.

[2] These are common phrases in China. They imply that in order to be reformed and accepted as part of society one must abjectly confess to wrongdoing. Only then can one be cleansed and start over again.

[3] People's bones are stored in earthen jars in many parts of China.

destiny if you chose this Paradise: this one has eight golden characters shining radiantly at the front gate: "From each according to his ability, to each according to his need." This one is the ultimate communist utopia.'

I pulled him away without waiting for more. All human imagination seemed to have dried up, not just his. The same old chewed-over ideals had ceased to inspire. Without new vision, every Paradise had become tasteless.

Happiness is, after all, a feeling, and the ability to feel was precisely what he had lost. Although many deaths had left his corporeal body intact, they had killed the nerves that allowed him sensation.

When a dentist numbs the mouth, cold, hot, sweet, sour lose their meaning. In the same way, paradise had lost any meaning for him. Rather than find some utopia, his goal was to piece together his shattered soul. He hoped, in the process of looking for its shards, in the wasteland, in the garbage heap, to retrieve a small piece of any nerve that would allow him to feel.

Later he dragged his body and shattered soul all over the world. While others thought he had found happiness, he felt only pain. I learned that his hoped-for happiness was a sham, and his pain was a sham too: I knew at last that his shattering had been irrevocable. He would have to be reborn. So I decided to put him to death.

After long deliberation, I still could not find a suitably ingenious way to do it. Most means of suicide and murder have been used before. The link-up between life and death would not do – it would have allowed him to retain his soul, which was precisely what had to be eradicated, plucked out. A shattered soul could be caught up by the wind, forcing him to float forever in limbo, enduring unspeakable things without a chance to be reborn. To destroy him completely would be his only salvation.

Of all the shops in New York, Paris and Frankfurt, the ones that caught my attention were those that sold guns. I lingered before them, admiring the displays. Their marvellous variety was like that of a children's toy shop. They tempted me to use them more than once. I imagined myself weighing a gun in my hand, aiming, firing . . . This, more than anything, would suit his ideas of masculinity. Since human creativity had evaporated, he couldn't have any reason to belittle such a mundane way to die.

So I induced him to buy a pistol. And after I had the gun in my hands, I selected a radiantly sunny morning. China Pinks were blossoming outside the window. I heard a fresh breeze wrap itself round ancient wind chimes. I peered very gently into the barrel of the gun . . . The blackness inside was impenetrable. The breeze had died but the chimes still sang, their ding-dong chanting my own resolution. Oddly, my hands didn't shake. This would be the first time I had killed anyone, yet I felt like a practiced assassin. I realized that mental repetition can exercise one's skills.

I would never aim at his head. It had been hit with enough simulated bullets already. I also would never fire at his heart. There was only emptiness where his heart should have been. From childhood, everyone he knew had laid claim to his heart and he had generously handed it out. Some of it was scribbled on notepaper in wastebaskets, some was thrown out in the garbage, some lay mouldering in the files of the Documents room. Much more had been given to women. The part that he had fastened to the bodies of women had beaten so hard it frightened them, made them unable to sleep.

Since the method of murder was old, where to aim should at least be new. I have tried to break new ground all my life and, although this has hurt me, I have never regretted it. He had always been trampled on by others but he had, in turn, trampled on women. Owing nothing to anyone else, he did owe a debt of gratitude to them.

So what most deserved punishment was his penis. If he was to be done away with, that was the place to start. I snickered when I aimed down there, thinking how completely society's punishment of him had missed its mark.

I had just taken up the gun when I heard a cock crow in the distance. Before there was time to be surprised at how a cock could crow in the middle of a city, the gun automatically aimed itself at a spot below his belly. In that instant the sound of women's laughter filled the room, each voice with its own timbre and intent, while the China Pinks shook violently, splattering blood-like petals against the wall. All his face registered was a tiny smile, and I felt the same smile on my own face. With an easy conscience, I pulled the trigger.

As the shot rang out, I saw before me a sexy Christ lying on a sheet of white clouds. The high walls of a labor reform prison rose behind him. On the prison walls were written these slogans:

'Change bad to good, the future is glorious.'

'From each according to his ability,
to each according to his need.'

✳ II ✳

INTERROGATION

Flying over the Pacific from China to San Francisco, 1987

In Beijing with A, 1986

'LOVE MUST END in tragedy before it can be perfect.' He must have said something along these lines to A before.

He had found it increasingly difficult in the past few years to remember what he had said to one woman and what he might have said to another. For example, he had told one, 'I know that I promised to write you a letter every week but . . .' and she had shouted, 'God! For heaven's sake don't do that! He just loves to open and read my mail.'

He was absolutely certain that he had said these words to this particular woman, though. The reason was that he could remember her eyes. Her eyes had a look of terror as orgasm approached. He saw those eyes everywhere, even in this airplane.

When making love, she used every nerve in her body to explore her sensitivity, to find the nodes of pleasure coursing through her body. Only when she finally pounced on one would she begin to thrash beneath him. Unlike other women, she didn't cry out before orgasm approached – her stillness before a climax never failed to astonish him. He often felt like a truck driver as she, terrified with eyes wide open, watched him drive a heavy truck over her body. Her orgasms were unsightly and tragic, he thought, and he had laughingly told her that they put him out of the mood. She smiled sweetly, and the next time was exactly as before.

Since he remembered that special look, he was certain he had said the words to her.

Her eyes were before him now, as he flew over the Pacific. The boundless indigo sky streamed in the window. He gazed intently at those eyes for a long time, and suddenly realized that their look was the same as his when a gun pointed at his brain.

Staring at the back of the head of the woman seated in front, he felt the skin of his scalp begin to prickle.

It was shortly before he met A, in 1979, that a cadre in charge of Documents came to visit. The cadre brought with him several pages of material which contained the transcript of a former interrogation. The cadre wanted a copy of a book he had written in exchange for letting him see it, and also wanted his autograph.

The material recorded the proceedings of the interrogation as follows:

Question: Are you X?

No answer.

Question: Are you currently employed as a farm laborer?

No answer.

Question: Your family background[1] is reactionary. You were a teacher. In 1957 you were singled out as a rightist[2] and you did three years of labor reform.

You did not respond to reform, and in 1963 you sabotaged production. You also promulgated reactionary[3] opinions on public affairs and so you were

[1] The Chinese term for family background includes the sense of being born into the status of a certain class. The full meaning of this sentence is that he was guilty from birth of being born on the wrong side of the revolution.

[2] Literally, 'You have been marked out as a rightist', that is, a line has been drawn between you and the rest of society. The Anti-Rightist Campaign began in June 1957. According to John K. Fairbank in his book *The Great Chinese Revolution 1800–1985*, '. . . between 400,000 and 700,000 and perhaps many more skilled people were removed from their jobs and given the devastating label of "rightist" – an enemy of the people.'

[3] In Chinese the word 'reactionary' has specific connotations of being 'against' the Party or, at that time, against Mao.

sentenced to three years of surveillance by the middle court of — town.

Since you continued to rebel and stubbornly maintained a counter-revolutionary stance, in 1965 the court decided you should be hatted with the title Counter-revolutionary Element.[1] You were sentenced to another three years of labor reform.

After being released a second time from labor reform, you not only did not repent, you added to your crimes by using every opportunity to oppose the Great Chairman Mao. You sinfully attacked the Central Committee of the Party.

Do you admit that the above is correct?

No answer.

Question: Do you admit that you oppose the Great Leader Mao?

No answer.

Question (quoting government policy): You are a hardened criminal, you understand the Party's policies on the above matters, stubborn resistance will not benefit you in any way. Do you or do you not admit that you oppose the Great Leader Chairman Mao?

Answer: If you say I oppose then I oppose. *(The criminal admits his crime.)*

Question: Do you know what fate awaits those who oppose the Great Leader Chairman Mao?

No answer.

---

[1] To be 'hatted' in China is to be designated with a 'crime'. A person so designated can be ostracized from normal life, denied basic rights and even executed. The 'crime' of being counter-revolutionary, for example, is not in any law book in China, but is still being used to sentence people to death.

Question: Opposing the Great Leader Chairman Mao means you will be shot to death, do you know that?

No answer.

(Investigator says this three times.)

Answer: If you say I will be executed then execute me.
(Criminal agrees to the verdict of a death sentence, no further appeal to a higher court.)

Yes! That was the look in her eyes – the same as his when the gun was aimed at his head. As he watched for the gun behind her eyes when they made love her look only heightened his passion. The comment about ruining his mood had been a flirtatious phrase – he wanted her as she had always been.

Their very last meeting had been in Beijing, in the small room where she stayed. The clamour of all-night construction across the street covered the murmurs of their love-making. Flashes of a welder's electric arc-light raked through the window, soldering their bodies together in its blue heat. They slowly fused into hot, slippery glass.

After peeling their bodies from each other, they lay motionless, absorbed in their own thoughts. Stultifying air from too-hurried meetings and partings permeated the room. A particularly violent flash of the arc-light raked them again, and it was in the glare of that light that he said those words to her.

Love must end in tragedy before it can be perfect: the sentence was not intended as a promise. What he had actually wanted to tell her was that, 'In the beginning, hand in hand, we ride recklessly wherever we wish, like happy billows splashing on an immense ocean. But ultimately we are bound to be smashed on the rocks. I do not know about you, but what I saw was a sheet of red mist before us, then blood spouted out as though from an artery. The sound was as gentle as the touch of fingers, as it flowed down your cheek toward your ear. Unlike in the past, you had your eyes closed, oblivious to anything but enjoying me; as always in the past, I had mine open, oblivious to anything but enjoying you. But both you and I were conscious that we had come to the end – it was over.'

I did not bother him that time, did not shout in his ear, 'The End!' But hearing him say those words both amused and exasperated me. I pitied the women who were not aware of the evasion and withdrawal in the phrase. The truth was that his heart could no longer accommodate love. So he put the sentence in his pocket and pulled it out like a handkerchief every time the love-making ended. He always said it with an inscrutable face, as if the words were profound and he had raised sex to the level of philosophy. In fact he had betrayed the heart of any woman before he ever began making love. Every sentence he ever said to a woman would ultimately crash to the ground, littering the floor with meaningless black spots.

This woman, however, was clever. When she recognized the impossibility of a life together with this married man, she walked decisively and resolutely in the other direction.

She flew to the West, to California, while he was left behind in China to get his bearings alone.

You walked out into a cold rain.

I did not call a taxi for you, you just ran out. You were always in a hurry, as though always searching for some unattainable patch of your own on this small planet.

You said that you were used to coming and going in the rain, that when you made movies they often had you wandering through man-made torrents. This language of old movies still expressed the solitude of a woman, her disappointment and her necessary self-reliance.

You said that you did not need time to assume your role before shooting a scene. 'I never knew if I was playing the movie or if the movie was playing me.' And then you sighed, one of those silk-gauze sighs that lightly covers old wounds. I was thinking, 'I never know if I am writing the novel or if the novel is writing me.'

Our lovers' meetings reminded me of threshing, years ago in the labor reform camp, when I would secretly run off to the guard's room to warm myself at the stove. I would mesmerize myself with the flesh-colored fire, throwing my existence and everything else into its flames. My nose was encrusted with rice chaff from the threshing. By breathing in the heat I could imagine I smelled the aroma of cooked rice. But before my hardened, splitting hands were properly warm, I would have to go back, to the pitchfork and the knife-edged wind. An eternal weary disgust stayed with me through the temporary comfort.

And then you left.

I was not able to deal with your strength of will, just as I had no answer for your solitude and your disappointment. Later you sent a letter saying that you had caught a bad cold from the rain, but that it was a small price for our moment of happiness. I read the letter, then turned it over and read the other side.

The back was white and empty.

I can still see you as you were that day in the bath. The bathrobe you took off also removed the warmth of your body and hung, like a disembodied ghost, on the back of the door to spy on us. I took your hand and kissed your fingers, one by one, while you laughed and said how like a scene in one of my novels it was.

The scene was the same but the characters had changed. I heard the cock crow from the distance of a rustic rillage – the sound was muted as it came to me through the mists of time. I held you more tightly, wanting to hug the past to myself, but instead you turned me around and forced me to look in the mirror.

I despise mirrors, since I hate looking at myself. Later, in Paris, with mirrors everywhere, I finally found I could not escape. Perhaps that is one reason I have written so many words.

That time, however, the mirror reflected only hazy flesh, an unclear outline which was embarrassing to neither of us. You were shivering in my hands like fine rain, and I thought how the two of us were like a double soap bubble attached to one another: we could not separate, nor could we fuse as one. If you were to break, I too would be lost.

You turned to me and measured the height of your head on my neck. You said it was your 'line', that you wanted me to remember it forever. I felt that you had put a rope around my neck.

I believed that the rope would be there for a lifetime. Yet later, when Natalie took me to buy clothes for you in Paris, the 'line' had become no more than a measure of your height.

The airplane began its descent in the midst of thick cloud. Landing gear was lowered with a metallic grind. White, black and yellow faces showed alarm through their exhaustion, like tired birds trying to keep their perch in a heavy wind. Beijing – Tokyo – San Francisco, she had taken this same route, indeed he seemed to be following her, tailing her. But he knew that what is lost cannot be retrieved. Love proceeds in a straight line or a parabola, it never hops along a dotted line.

Nonetheless, would she be at the airport to meet him?

Pearls of water from outer space were pulled backward on the airplane's window, trembling slightly against a dark sky. The coldness of foreign countries welled up inside him, and he dared to hope she would. Only she could link the two sides of the Pacific. Only she was familiar territory to him.

In the year that he was sixty-five, he looked back on the various stages of his life, and discovered that he had depended on a woman in every one. Each of the stages had also been linked by women. He could not remember a time in his life when he had been without a woman.

He had mailed her a letter from the post office in Beijing. After handing it in at the International Mail counter, he wondered whether he had written the date and time of the flight correctly. He was not in the mood to retrieve the letter and double-check, though; if she had time and the inclination, she would call the airport in

San Francisco to confirm. There could not be that many flights coming from Beijing.

Other questions hovered behind his fear that she might not come. She had written him not to call her. The reason might have been the time difference and the chance of disturbing her sleep, but it was also possible that another man would be by her side. Their original trio might have become an inharmonious quartet. He pushed the thought aside as the airplane landed.

AMERICA'S BEST

Airport in San Francisco, 1987

SAN FRANCISCO WAS as I had found it before. The internationaliza-
tion of airports made me wonder which country I was in. What
struck me first were the many potted plants. Set in low orange walls
was the glare of thick glass, and behind that was a leaden sky. An
airplane was taking off, looking for the sun.

We two were also searching, for each other, through the crowds.
In my imagination I saw your face float toward me through the
leaves of an India rubber tree; I returned your smile and was soon
pressing my face against your cool cheeks. Not to worry! This was
familiar turf. I tightly held the hand that lived in my memory. It
was still tiny, round and moist – everything about you continued to
be round. Strange that life with its hardships was never able to beat
sharp angles into you.

Although the letter you sent said that you had lost weight, the
you in my mind's eye was the you of the past. The characters of
your letter had the same exquisite smoothness as your body. Reading
them, I was surprised at my calm emptiness. Endurance is not a
physical entity which can be demolished, but a sheet of nothingness,
a vacuum.

When we parted in Beijing you resolutely walked away. I hoped
you would at least turn around, give some indication of being sorry
to go. But you didn't, and I never saw your eyes again.

And so I collected rear views of women in my memory.

A long moving sidewalk carried him to the exit. He continued to search for her, in the midst of other searching people. But among all the blue, grey, black, brown eyes, hers were missing.

Flashy ads lined the walls, wooden-faced models looking as if they could walk straight out at him. All the cigarettes claimed to be 'America's Best!' Famous brand-name whiskeys monopolized the taste of mankind, while perfumes made skins of all races of the world smell the same. The unknown world on this side of the ocean was familiar, while the familiar world on the other side had become strange. He felt adrift, squeezed out by the overlapping of East and West.

Naturally, her face, her eyes, were not there, only many others, men with long hair, women with short hair. By the end of the long corridor he realized his premonitions had not deceived him: the wishful thinking of that imagined scene was not to be.

He held out his hand to call a taxi. The driver, a grey-haired black man, helped him put his suitcase in the trunk. Before getting in, he cast a last look over the airport, as though her shadow might by some miracle have been left behind. Two immobile planes were suspended against a distant sky. It was an impenetrable sky which blocked out all movement, all hope. He noticed that the entrance to the airport had eaves of Chinese tiles.

FREEDOM

San Francisco, home of Jing Hui,
wife of his cousin Joe, 1987

JING HUI opened the door to greet him and drew him warmly into the living room.

He had stayed at her house the last time he was in San Francisco. 'Jing Hui' – neither the name nor the person could have come from the mainland. He could smell the difference between mainland Chinese and others. Jing Hui's very way of walking, as she moved into the living room, showed that she had never marched in any communist parade. She couldn't be called pretty, but it was equally clear she had never worked in a production brigade or in the fields. Her long sculpted fingernails toyed with an exceedingly small dog that she had scooped up and was now cradling in her arms.

'Do you remember this little gentleman?' she asked him, so he had to nod at the dog and smile.

'I remember that his name is Fu-lei-dun,' he said. Her polite reception turned to genuine warmth as she began to praise his memory and his unwillingness to forget old friends.

No, my good lady, do not be misled! He was quietly ashamed as he thought of the real reason for remembering the name. Fu-lei-dun means freedom, dear lady, freedom![1] For how many years has this one word struck terror in the hearts of some Chinese, so that even today one does not dare say it out loud.

Last year had been the first time that he had been required to pet this dog, and he remembered thinking then how trivialized its name had become. Freedom meant a different thing here in America

---

[1] Fu lei dun, in Chinese characters, is the Chinese alliteration for the English word 'freedom'.

– even the dog was more adornment than dog. If you were to put this dog out in the wilds, in the village, say, where I spent those years, cats would soon have it climbing walls to save its life. The Chinese system of sending people to the countryside does have its advantages.[1]

Jing Hui left Shanghai as a little girl to go to Taiwan, and then left Taiwan with his cousin Joe as a young wife. She was now describing her first trip back to China, the previous year. Her voice was lilting, her throat had never been made hoarse through the shouting of slogans. He sipped his coffee slowly, as though listening to a nostalgic song. Rain began to fall outside.

As it came down on the leaves of a large elm in the yard, Freedom looked up with pampered distress. The fragrance of the rain shower wafted through the room, filling it with hypnotic desolation. He heard her telling him about her old home in Shanghai and about visiting the grade school she had attended. The home was on Huanlong Road beside Fuxing Park.[2] 'The place looked like it used to,' she exclaimed, 'except that there were so incredibly many people living in it – it really scared me silly!' He put his cup down carefully and expressed his sympathy with a little smile.

The decor of the living room might have been taken from *House and Garden* – even the ashtrays elegantly announced that they were not for actual use. A dried-flower arrangement of the reeds he had seen so often in the labor camp made them look high and mighty, even here, as they arched out of the vase. Progress in the world seemed to be achieved by wringing the juices from every living thing.

Jing Hui was describing what she most admired about Shanghai, and it was precisely what ten million Shanghai residents hated. She liked the 'ancient aspect' of the city.

As he listened to her, he thought back to a recent visit he had

---

[1] An estimated fourteen million young people were 'sent down to the countryside' during the Cultural Revolution to be exposed to the habits and standards of the rural working class. The practice was revived in 1989, for students who 'have grown too divorced from the masses'.
[2] The author says this location in Shanghai was equivalent to living on upper Fifth Avenue in New York.

made to Shanghai. He had stayed at a large hotel on Nanjing Road. When night spread its curtain, a good half of the inhabitants began preparing to sleep in the streets. Because of cramped quarters and the heat of a Shanghai summer, people flowed like water out of their own living quarters. Young women dreamed private secret lives in the open, under street lamps. He remembered an old grand-mother, cradling a child in her arms, sitting beside the revolving door of his hotel. She was greedily soaking in draughts of air-conditioned air. Listening to Jing Hui, he tried to suppress a yawn.

The yawn reminded the mistress of the house that her guest must be hungry. She quickly put Freedom down and ordered the dog, 'Stay.' Then she went to the kitchen to make dinner herself.[1]

This woman judged the palates of all men by the tastes of her absent husband, and as a result the dishes were made without salt. During dinner, Jing Hui explained unhappily how her son had become Americanized. He sent a card every year at Christmas, but other than that had no contact with either of his parents. She lived on the West Coast while Joe, her husband, lived on the East.

Listening to all this, he pinched a tender scallop between his chopsticks, and the image of a Korean woman came to mind. Her name had been Jenny. Joe was his cousin, now living in New York. Two years ago, when he was visiting that city, Joe had been despondent about women from Taiwan: they were not as warm and lovable as they used to be. So he had recently changed companions and was now with a woman from Korea.

'South Korea, or North Korea?' He was still foolish enough to ask Joe the question. The impression North Korea had made on China was that deep.[2]

'South Korea, of course!' Joe had shot back. Later, Joe brought Jenny along for a meal.

At the table, Jenny seemed at all times like a very pretty maid.

[1] Many Chinese assume that people in the West all have maids. The author is intentionally telling a Chinese reader here that Jing Hui does not.

[2] The author says that Korea means North Korea to any mainland Chinese. He adds that the psychological impact of the Korean War on the Chinese was substantial, linked as it was to xenophobia and fear of American invasion.

He remembered that she had dimples at the middle joint of each finger. 'What about it?' Joe asked. 'Would you like me to take you to a place I know – have a taste of Korean girls? Let Jenny introduce you, I guarantee it's absolutely safe.'

Laughing, he shook his head no.

Joe chuckled. 'I've had quite a lot of business contact with you people from the mainland over the past few years. It seems to me you've got the most ridiculous sense of morality – your morality's all limited to sex. In other ways, you're exactly like Chinese from Taiwan.'

Are we the same in a good sense, or a bad sense, or both?

Protected by the low light, he glanced guiltily at Jing Hui as he peeled his fruit. She was clearly unaware of Jenny's existence. He was suddenly moved by her and by her situation. A cold draft moved through the modern house like an emanation from a mossy old well.

Facing a lonely woman, he felt a stronger loneliness build up inside him. The same story seemed to be told in every corner of the world: men playing, women loving, and it was told in such a limited number of ways. What the father did the son does, and what the son does the grandson will do. In the midst of change, the world remains unaltered.

ICE CUBES AND OYSTERS

Bedroom in Jing Hui's house in San Francisco
(What might have been), 1987

ONE PERSON now sat in the dark guest bedroom of Jing Hui's house. Exhaustion had dissolved as desire rose through his loneliness. He began to fantasize what might have been:

How long ago was it? How many weeks, days, hours . . . that I was still in China, waiting for this night.

I finally caught sight of her at the exit to the airport. Of all the women in the world, only this one can move 'like petals stroking willow leaves as they fall'.

The appointment was not confirmed so the joy of our meeting was subdued. We silently kissed each other's cheeks, then clasped hands and let go again. Our feet floated from the airport more lightly than any departing airplane. Our bodies melted into the clear evening of the West Coast. We became two transparent butterflies pirouetting above the steel and concrete of skyscrapers, as the neon lights of America made Shaoxing opera costumes of our colorless wings.

By the time the orange sun had thrust deeply into our native land, we were sitting at Fisherman's Wharf, eating oysters in a romantic glow. The darkness outside was fathomless: the Pacific had become a nameless lake. Its waves lapped harmlessly below us, gurgling out fairy-tales of our homeland.

As we faced each other, candlelight gave a new gloss to the ancient patina of love. We did not need to flirt or show off in order to be understood. We were two boats that had navigated the ocean and had at last reached the other shore. The lashing of the waves had trained us both in the same restraints and rules of conduct.

Sipping whiskey with ice cubes in it, we looked out across the darkness to China. The problems on that opposite shore could not possibly cross the wide ocean. All that was felt here of their enormous weight was the slight whisper of a piece of silk. The thought of that other side was almost a warm recollection in our numbness. Remembering old anxieties in new comfort seems unnecessary at first and then seems silly.

Where did we come from? How did we live before? Our former lives melted away under the languid, sweet strains of a song by Jean-Claude Brialy. The most important thing had become the moment, the second, that we were together.

No needle-sharp eyes were here to keep watch on us, no furtive whispers went around to cause a rush of fear.

We watched desire begin to raise a flush on each other's faces. Cradled by soft light, her eyes and face were all that existed in the world. Those eyes now filled with yearning.

As midnight approached, my own tenacious dreams began to insist on becoming real. I called for the waiter and paid the bill. I was reminded we were in a different country by the tax and the need to pay a tip.

We went to a cheap, clean hotel. The threatening roar of the ocean was merely atmospheric as we stepped out of the car. Gentle light from nineteenth-century lamps at the front door did not admit its waves into their welcome.

She had selected the hotel using years of acute training in frugality in Beijing. Everything in her life was measured, required calculation. She could also take this complex life and make it into something wonderfully simple.

A bellboy helped with the suitcase as we took the lift to our reserved room. The bed was King Size,[1] the room seemed aware of our intentions. Thick purple drapes shut out the outside world. They were so protective and safe that I decided to disregard their color. Two roses in a white vase gave the room a center of gravity.

---

[1] English in the original.

Drawers in the chest were comfortingly empty – nobody but us inhabited this place. It no longer mattered whether this country was ours or not – together, we possessed the land wherever we stood.

We quietly took off our clothes. Anything that needed saying had long ago been said. I hung my trousers carefully in the closet in the wall, we took turns in the bath. As I waited for her I was calm enough to take out my diary and run through the calls I had to make the next day. Among them, one seemed to mock me – it was the telephone number of Jing Hui.

As though we had been together for years, we lay a certain distance from each other in bed. Only our fingers were intertwined. We wanted to stretch desire to the limit. Like wine, the longer it was kept, the stronger it would become.

When I saw that her eyes were again filled with terror, and felt her body brace to meet the high tide, I felt again the erotic stimulation of a gun aimed at my head. Life had not been so mean with me after all.

A SEDUCTIVE PHONE

Jing Hui's house in San Francisco
(What was), 1987, evening

HE LIT a cigarette as he came out of the bathroom and stood before the bedroom window.

Jing Hui's house was built on a hill and he looked over half the lights of San Francisco. The city was so brilliant it seemed removed from the lies of reality. Even the moon appeared unnatural. Car lights buzzed around like fireflies. Without being able to hear it he felt that the world outside was throbbing to music. The pounding of the drums made his heart beat faster, and he felt again the constant terror that lives inside the Chinese.

For as he gazed out, he could not help but wonder what would happen to the world if some calamity befell the West.

He saw his face reflected in the glass. Superimposed on it were the flickering lights of several large buildings. People were madly gyrating on his face, dancing, drinking, making love. If he were to move his face aside, all the demented people in all those buildings would collapse.

Autumn would be arriving soon. The elms had not turned, though, and a streetlight highlighted one at the bottom of the slope. The tree looked like a stage setting, immobile in the light, but in this very second its jade-green color was fading away.

An old man in a flowered shirt was walking a dog in his direction. He saw the white of the man's hair flash like a pale flower amidst the green. The dog squatted on its hind legs and appeared to

---

[1] The implications of these sentences are probably clearer to a Chinese than a Western reader. The precarious nature of apparent stability is clear to Chinese who have lived through decades of psychological trauma.

enjoy the act of shitting while the man stood quietly by. During this performance, man and dog looked at each other serenely.

Such a peaceful corner actually existed in this cacophonous city. The small scene exuded happiness, stroking worry from his mind with the softness of cashmere. The whole world should be like this man and his dog, he thought. Indeed it could survive in no other way.

But I was not content: I was wanting A.

I was remembering how A had said she wanted to learn to drive, wanted to get into the American way of life. I laughed at her for thinking the future would automatically be rosy, told her not to forget that America had more traffic accidents than any other country in the world. Fatalities from the accidents over a ten-year period were at least as many as those who sacrificed their lives during the Cultural Revolution.[1]

I began to stare at the ivory telephone at the foot of the bed. She had once told me the most beautiful skin color a woman could have was 'ivory'. I smiled at her ability to compliment herself, but I also remembered kissing her ivory neck.

The seductive powers of ivory became apparent to me now as the receiver began to turn into her lovely wrist. I needed only to pick it up and call and tell her . . . Her voice could so easily be caught, could be trembling there in my hand.

I thought also how wrong it was to pass this night in a normal way. No matter how normal freedom might seem to other people, it carried multiple layers of significance for me. To spend the first night in a free country sitting on a bed doing nothing, as though being here were the most natural thing in the world, was not only to mock myself, it was also to mock the country.

I picked up the telephone, acutely aware that I was free to

[1] People are not said to 'die' in wars or in the Cultural Revolution in China, they are always said to have 'sacrificed their lives'. Here the author ironically calls them 'sacrificed goods' in the Chinese original.

do so. The receiver was as smooth and as silky as A. After dial-
ling, I felt the uneasy suspense of waiting outside a knocked-on
door.

I heard the pulsing of the electric current as the telephone rang
– the winds off the Pacific seemed to have burrowed into the wires.
I hoped she would answer and at the same time hoped she would
not. She might be racing up to San Francisco right now . . . I saw
an old Buick streaking down the road. Then again, something
terrible might have happened – in my mind the road turned into
the white walls of a hospital.

As I was wondering what to think, I heard a man's voice answer
the phone.

'Hello?'

Somehow I was sufficiently calm to recognize that the voice was
not that of a Chinese. Even more calmly, I used English to ask if
she was there. There was no need to conceal myself – the telephone
was a perfect hiding place. The man seemed slightly surprised as he
said, 'OK.' When she spoke immediately into the phone I realized
that she must have been by his side.

Her voice was as clear as though it were in my hand.

'I read in the Chinese papers that you were coming,' she said.

Chinese papers? Why from the newspapers? This kind of lie was
like the San Francisco nightscape. Could the man at her side
understand Chinese?

I understood what she meant, whatever reasons she might have
for her lies. I could see her situation as though I were standing
before a 'reality transmitter'.[1] I could also hear the beseeching tone
in her voice. There was nothing to do but follow her example and
politely ask how she was. Like a pair of eyes, her voice pulled the
other man into the picture. Hundreds of miles were between us,
but I felt we were sitting in one room. I saw his glances, and felt
my own awkward response.

In the artificiality of the moment, I glanced nervously at my

[1] A fax machine.

watch. Already adjusted for the time difference, it said the time was past midnight. I finally understood that the two of them were lying in bed, and that I was as much an intruder as if I had walked into their bedroom.

I ended the call abruptly, as though staggering out of the door. The only difference was that I hadn't sprained an ankle. I still sat in a most normal way on the bed.

SILVER SCREEN

Jing Hui's house,
after the phone call, 1987, night.

THE FRAGRANCE of soybean meal now spread through the room, that stinging smell which permeates the air each time I make love.

I understood what I should have known long ago. There were things A did, movements so familiar to me when she made love: why shouldn't she rehearse them, one by one, with another man? She might be lying there right now with her eyes full of terror, awaiting yet another high tide – only today it was a foreign truck that rolled over her body. Why should it make any difference to her?

I felt my lips tighten as my thoughts became vicious. Soon I forgave her, however, although I lacked any right to grant forgiveness, and it made no difference whether I did or not.

Before our last time together, the two of us had walked down a street in Beijing and dirty rays of sunlight slipped around her neck to the valley between her breasts. I thought at the time that the much-vaunted white of ivory was nothing more than a city's washedout pallor. She pointed to a newly-built public toilet, and said that she would not leave Beijing 'even if they allocate me a room like that!'[1] Her voice was so bitter that I felt my eyes fill with tears.

I turned to look at her as she said it – the beautiful image of her face was familiar to me from my days in the camps. Back then, they hung the movie screen between two tall poles, over the camp slogan written in large black characters: 'Change bad to good, the future is glorious.' She gave the prisoners plenty of raw material from which

---

[1] Living space in China is allocated by the authorities, normally by one's work unit – there is no free market in housing.

to ferment rich dreams. I once demonstrated to her how we perched with our rumps on bricks on the ground, heads cocked back to see the screen, hypnotized by her. She laughed, saying no actor could portray the posture so well.

The eyes of this beautiful actress, sometimes the valiant leader of a women's guerrilla detachment, sometimes a lady doctor whose 'class alignment' was absolutely pure, now showed their fishtail wrinkles in the wan light of a Beijing day. Dreams, too, must weather the passage of time.

I softly kissed those wrinkles that day in Beijing, and had only to close my eyes to bring back the sparkle her eyes had lost. Kissing her, I lost myself in two different kinds of dreams: was the reality that I, a prisoner in a cell, sleeping among a dozen dirty men, was dreaming of kissing this beautiful guerrilla leader? Or was the reality the dream that I was actually kissing her right now?

When I stared at her on the screen in the camps, I imagined that she was too far away ever to reach. I could not possibly imagine her pressed like me into a smelly room with a dozen roommates. She must live by herself in several large perfumed and exotic rooms. Back then, I believed that she, a guerrilla leader, was capable of pointing a gun at the class enemy, me.

And so it was not just for sex that I hugged her in my dreams in those days. It was not only because she was one of those strange creatures we had almost forgotten after so many years ('What do women look like?' 'They're the ones with long hair in the movies!'). I took her, in my mind, because it gave me the ghastly pleasure of retaliation.

When she floated down from that silver screen and came to me, years later, and when I, with eyes wide open, felt her full lips brush the corner of my mouth, her eyes were already showing fishtail wrinkles. But by that time I was thinking that fate had not treated me badly after all, and I was almost capable of believing that I had been turned into something good.

I took her kiss to be my real rehabilitation.

I knew, in those days, that she had reasons for doing whatever she had to do. So later, I understood my calm when another man answered the phone.

A group of blondes gyrated to a heavy beat, while they shouted to everyone to come and try a new sort of French fries. A man from outer space, arriving in his flying saucer, charged into the group of girls and asked for a particular brand of soft drink . . .

He quickly turned off the TV in the bedroom. Fantasies had their price here, and the more extraordinary the more expensive. He had discovered that the priceless dreams he and A had dreamed – the ideals they had valued beyond any wealth – had been ripped to shreds by the power of money, tattered like a tornado ripping through mist. Neither East nor West allowed an inch of space for a romantic to stand on. Humans had given romanticism back to the gods, and in return had assumed the right to degenerate.

He opened a bottle of whiskey bought from the duty-free sales on the airplane, wishing that all creation could be steeped in its transparent amber. Finding ice cubes was easy, but where was one to find someone to drink with?

He was reminded of her eyes as he looked at the liquid in his glass, and of the time she had looked at him and said, 'Given the time and the opportunity, we will love each other.' He had gazed with alarm into chrysanthemum-studded pupils, but found nothing in her eyes except warmth and honesty.

What A was saying was that without time or opportunity there could be no love. Instead of this time being the last, every time was the last.

He had been amazed at her ability to savor the stolen sweetness of love, the pleasures gleaned from between the cracks of this floating life. Everyone else was madly pursuing opportunities they had missed the past twenty-odd years, to the point that they scratched and clawed for more, even while being kissed.

Sipping his whiskey, he realized that, right now, A had neither the opportunity nor the time. She was pursuing the chance for a home. The rest of mankind had long since emerged from living in caves – how could he blame her for wanting her own few square meters of living space?

He thought back to the last time he had been in America, when an Irish-American professor had taken him to a baseball game. He simply could not understand the enthusiasm for this game, the excitement a white-haired professor showed for a home-run. Similarly, he realized that Americans, who always want to live in the country, could not understand the importance of a city registration to a Chinese.[1] If he, of all people, could not understand her skill with an abacus, then who could?

He could well imagine her new home in southern California. 'No time and no opportunity' did not chill the warmth of the blue sky there. Homesickness slowly thinned and spread out in the wide spaces, until it was so diluted it could be tossed out to water the lawn. New things were happening every day down there which could chew through loneliness like a silkworm.

He should also remember that she was tired of eating for so very, very long with so many other people from the same big pot. She was tired of being squeezed by overpopulation, until the people around her turned into a tribe of caged hedgehogs, until to be alone was something one dreamed about and craved. When the spirit had emerged from a stifling space that is the size of a matchbox, even the smell of fresh air on one's body can be a comfort.

If she loved she loved, and if she did not, she did not, so she must be living quite happily down there.

The air of the bedroom was so still that he felt he was in a void. Fortunately the odor of whiskey was now seeping into the guest room's long-uninterrupted sleep. When he knew that this night would be spent in a normal way after all, he felt a smile of self-ridicule creep up the sides of his mouth. A rustle of midnight wind simultaneously climbed the slope outside – although it could not enter

[1] Every person in China is supposed to have a registered place of residence, from which he cannot move unless he receives official permission. Registration to live in a city is unattainable without influential connections. The countryside is seen as primitive and devoid of culture and stimulation.

the room, its spirit cooled his own. The smell of soybean meal, a heavy fog, had not yet dispersed. He took advantage of being tipsy and fell across the bed.

It was odd, he thought, that he cared so little about all that had happened and had not happened in his life. So it was even odder that he should have these remnants of love in his heart.

The soybean meal was slowly wafting into the night, the air of the room was getting colder and drier. As he pulled the blanket over himself he found he was sinking back to 1961, to Baotou . . .

AMBER MEMORY

Jing Hui's house in San Francisco, 1987

Remembering Baotou in 1961

WHERE AM I . . . What time is it . . . Am I escaping? Am I in a train station or in jail? Or in the emergency room of a hospital? Is this the first time I have come out of the camps, or the second? Have I gone over the walls without official permission . . . ?

He raised his head alertly with the instincts of an escapee, as he awoke to find himself on a bench.

Before his eyes were open, he sensed that there was no danger here. He smelled charcoal smoke and gladly breathed it in, indiscriminately taking in smells of his own body and many others. He felt himself relax – experience had taught him that the more complex the smells, the safer. In prison, the smell is singularly monotonous.

He tasted his mouth as though he were chewing on a piece of candy. Without knowing how long he had been sleeping, he knew from the saliva that his body was strong. He had just had a strange and wonderful dream – he dreamed that time had rolled back to the day he entered the labor reform camp, and that everything since then had happened quite differently.

He dreamed that he was a writer, and that he was travelling in America. He dreamed that he had married, and also that he had fallen in love with a movie star. He dreamed that he and she had eaten dinner in a restaurant on the West Coast, and that the two of them had gone to a small, clean hotel . . .

He sat up. A dim light pressed down on a multitude of people; the air was so heavy he felt suffocated. The waiting room was overcrowded with humanity – the space his head had just vacated was instantly filled by a Mongolian in a sheepskin coat. Squeezed by the stiff sheepskin, he regretted not staying stretched out on the bench. He could just as well have opened and closed his eyes, and continued to occupy the space of two people.

He had long known the value of a piece of bread, a length of rope, a torn blanket. All man's scholarship talks of the inner life and extols ideals, but in reality everything confirms that the important things are what a man can physically hold in his hand. Here was evidence, in the form of a wooden bench in front of his eyes.

Fortunately, dawn was beginning to break. He watched the early light shine on a breast-feeding child, and noticed the flicker of the child's young hope join the sunshine in its eyes. It was as though the child thought that with the arrival of dawn came the assurance that today he would eat his fill. He watched the wind stir dirt and ashes around outside the room, as it waited for the opportunity to sweep them inside. The whole train station seemed to have been built on a pile of trash.

The humanity in the room looked also like accumulated garbage. The ragged heap was filthy, but its rich diversity struck him – it was so unlike the uniformity of the labor reform camp. To his eyes, it was like a pile of old butterfly wings that had been blown together.

'Hot water's here!'

The call echoed like a song through the waiting room. Bodies seemingly buried alive now began to wriggle. Live people began to break out of their sleep through a layer of dirt.

Unlike the others, he had neither a tea mug nor a travelling bag. As he watched the steam of the boiling water that was being passed around, and listened to the sucking of hot sips of water, he swallowed a large mouthful of saliva. He had lived through China's Great Famine[1] in the labor camps, and he knew well that the secretions of the body were precious. Both urine and saliva had their uses in an emergency.

---

[1] According to the author, this lasted from 1959 to 1961. It is said that 20 million people died of starvation in China in 1961 alone. The famine resulted from severe disruption to the economy after the disastrous policies of Mao's Great Leap Forward of 1958–60.

Also, if you did not allow yourself to shit for a long time, you could make believe that there was actually something of substance in your stomach. This allowed you to think that you were fully fed and that you need not, like others, drop dead along the road. This was fully in accord with Mao's great dictum: 'Turn spirit into matter.'

He now reached into the upper pocket of his torn cotton jacket, using the sensitivity of a concert pianist's fingers to avoid the holes. He drew a piece of paper from near his pounding heart and gently and carefully unfolded it.

Only when he had confirmed that it was an official authorization to leave the camp, that he had 'served out his term of punishment' and was now being released, only when he saw his name written impressively on the paper, did he allow himself to believe in his own existence. And then he knew that the people around him, the growing light of the sun, the whistle of the steam locomotive . . . were real. The movie star in a small restaurant on the West Coast of America had been an illusion.

It was only years later that he appreciated the versatility of this paper: it was a marvellous document, furnished by the labor camp, that entitled a prisoner to walk back into society. It was also a document which, by its mere existence, could allow society to lock a man up again.

He folded the paper carefully and tucked it away, then re-tightened the hemp rope around his waist. For this grand occasion he had substituted hemp for the usual grass rope – using available resources, he had done what he could to dress up.

Now he stood and walked to the rest room. Undirected emissions there had solidified to ice, turning the floor into a topographical model of the earth. He stepped over the Himalayas and strode to the innermost latrine pit. He was able to disregard the smell since the same odor permeated the waiting room. He squatted. Instead of pulling down his pants he removed a shoe, then lifted a layer of inner sole and with two fingers extracted a five-*yuan* note. After checking again to make sure no-one was using the neighbouring pit, he was able to fondle the bill in peace. He looked lovingly at it, smoothed and caressed it as though comforting a sniffling baby. He felt apologetic towards the steel worker with a drill in his hand pictured on it.

After a while he sauntered from the toilet, pretending to be fastening his belt, having again hidden the solitary note. He had successfully eluded three different ticket checks on the train, but on the last one he was caught and given a thorough body search. The checker found his release certificate, but not the bill – otherwise it would have been taken from him as a 'fine'. He endured a string of stinking curses from the checker and was forced off the train for having no ticket, but at least he still had his money.

'Long live that old labor reform prisoner,' he said under his breath, giving heartfelt thanks to the secrets of success passed on to him by that man. The secrets surpassed the wisdom of a host of professors. Events had again proved that the realism of the camps was more elevating than the scholarship of any academy.

It had been with some reluctance that he left the train's toilet. This was his port in a storm, his rabbit-hole when the conductor came by. The tiny space was safer than his own dormitory – for it was in his dormitory that they arrested him and took him away. Yes, he thought, the safest and warmest place on earth is a toilet.

With that comforting thought, he lengthened his stride and walked out of the train station. As he went by the large hot-water tub at its entrance, however, he noticed several drops of oil[1] floating on the surface. These rare drops were shining seductively with the glossiness of a peacock. In his hunger, they were positively gleaming with a greed-inducing sheen. They made him start to wonder . . .

Where did the drops of oil come from?

Where did the oysters come from?

Where did the whiskey come from?

The doorman at the Yinchuan[2] Municipal Hospital, a rheumy-eyed old man in old-fashioned pants and a short gown, had said that

---

[1] Cooking oil was then an extremely scarce and expensive commodity in China.
[2] This is the capital city of the province of Ningxia. The main character had been in a labor reform camp around fifty kilometers from this city. Before going north to find B in Baotou, he checked for her at the old hospital.

B might have married already. Nonetheless, I had to find out. He confirmed that she was at a hospital in Baotou, Inner Mongolia, several hundred miles to the north. I had to follow.

The doorman's rheumy eyes no longer recognized me, though the old codger had once spent a long time reminiscing with me about his past. He talked of the 'old society' in Yinchuan, and the city walls, and how the gunpowder he used for the local warlord's weapons had finally ruined his eyes. He no longer knew me and yet I managed to believe that his constant blinking was sending a hidden message: that his mouth was saying she had married but in fact he believed it wasn't true.

When I got to the Yinchuan Hospital, I was aching to see B whether she had married or not. I had met her here, when I was brought in sick once from the camp. When I regained consciousness and saw her, I felt I had leapt from death straight into her bosom. The front staircase, the corridor, the waiting room of the hospital were all just as they had been before. A rope for drying clothes in the yard was still hung with long white doctors' coats – frozen solid, they creaked mournfully in the cold. They seemed an embodiment of the past, cracking up before my eyes in the freezing air.

When I was sent back to the camp from the hospital, I began to think that I could not do without her, in the same way that I knew I could not do without myself. Her glossy hair glistened in my mind, and the pleats of her white uniform stayed crisp. But over the next three long years, all I could visualize was her back.

As I remembered her rear image, doing 'night war'[1] one night in the paddy fields, I imagined her moving towards me out of the moon. I brought the scythe I was using straight down into my leg. The camp doctor, who worked only on labor reform criminals, told me it would have been better to cut a little higher – in fact, it would have been best if I had cut the whole leg off. I did not regret cutting

---

[1] The author says that in 1959 China was 'militarized'. Everything was described in terms of warfare, so that harvesting crops became fighting a war to get the crops in, and so on. In order to speed the pace of the country's development, people were forced to work at night as well as during the day.

myself, however, for in my imagination I was just turning her over to look into her eyes.

Now, in the famine year of 1961, I felt weightless, insubstantial, as I walked out of Baotou's train station to the street. The yellow wind of Inner Mongolia followed at my heels like a dirty but loyal dog.

I sniffed the air of the prairie – it was the air of Siberia. The wind had been dyed yellow by the wild prairie's autumn grasses. Hidden in the wind was the dark song of exiles beside the shore of Lake Baikal:

> *Baikal, our mother!*
> *We come to your side*
> *Struggling for freedom, for equality.*[1]

B and I once sang that song together. We were simply happy, simply expressing a nameless delight. We could have used any song at all to pour out our happiness. Our desire for each other reached out in the form of song, as if singing were the same as making love on a bed. We knew no other way to show love between a man and a woman.

Baikal, our mother . . . Later I went to a place that was more bitter, more grim. It was more Siberian than Siberia.

There were no stalls selling food on the streets of Baotou during the famine, but several stands stood ready to mend and fill the tires of bicycles. It was as though people were expected to depend on pure air to live. I suppose there was some benefit in having not some but all of the people hungry, for nowhere was there the temptation of any food. My lightness was not due merely to a new sense of freedom, it was because my stomach was empty. I had been wise not to defecate just now in the toilet – the digested waste and my long intestines supplied each other with a measure of heat. Since the transaction was taking place within, I could count on twice the calories to walk from Baotou's train station to its hospital.

---

[1] According to the author this was a popular song in the late 1950s, sung by inmates of labor reform camps, many of whom had been intellectuals whose background included a Soviet education.

I later realized that food cannot force a man to grow, but hunger can definitely force him to mature. If hunger does not cause a man to doubt his government, then that hungry man was born a slave. Still later, though, when I watched hundreds of millions throw themselves wildly into the Great Cultural Revolution, I gave up hope for man's maturity.

A cold, barren, dust-covered road, earthen houses, leafless trees and bony donkeys, donkeys so still they seemed like carvings in front of a grave . . . only the clouds speeding above had vitality. Set off against this bleak background, the beauty of the morning sky approached the absurd. When the first golden ray of light fell on my body, I felt as though a flame had been lit in my heart. My throat was parched and dry, but my hands were sweaty: in Chinese medicine this phenomenon is known as the 'weak fire rising'. My weakness was so total it could never be conquered by strength.

The dream of the night before floated stubbornly before my eyes. The more I examined it the more confused I became, until in the end I had mixed several dreams together: was I, right now, on the Champs Elysées, or in San Francisco, or on a dusty street in Baotou?

Mixing memory, imagination and reality can cause a violent chemical reaction. My head ached as the bones of my skull seemed to split open. The illusions of starvation danced like stars before my eyes, like golden threads of sunlight which were impossible to catch.

Only the image of B kept me moving forward.

The wind stopped. The yellow greyness of the world before me settled down to earth. All I thought about was the distant sound of music as her small voice sang Russian folksongs:

> *Dear harmonica, sing softly to me,*
> *Let me remember the times of my youth . . .*

Her trembling voice matched the trembling of her fingers as she led me along. I followed carefully, as though the two of us were crossing a single-plank bridge. She took me to a place that was thick with flowers, and again I heard her voice singing to me:

Spring flowers have blossomed in the garden,
Spring girls are even more pretty . . .

It had been spring when we first saw each other, not only in nature but also in the intellectual world, when all the fools in China were celebrating the country's 'early spring weather'.[1] She wore pure white clothes and a pure white doctor's mask, and I thought whiteness in the universe must have been created for her. Only her eyes were so black they shone – when I saw those lustrous eyes I knew that my former life was over.

Premonitions like that had never failed me before.

I saw her eyes rest on my name in the hospital record, then watched them light up. Certain that once she must have noticed those doomed characters at the end of some poem, I did not know whether to be ashamed or proud.[2]

The stethoscope that she placed against my chest took a long time to measure the beat of my heart.

She laughed shyly later when I said I had quite openly bared my heart to her the first time we met. Her laugh was like the sweep of a swallow, one low flash over the water and it was gone.

But her large dark eyes held a hidden bitterness. Her pupils were like clear, cold, deep wells. B once told me in passing that she was an orphan, that she had been raised by her mother's 'friend'. I guessed at the relationship between her mother and the friend. Just as she was graduating from medical school in Shanghai, the Organization, as she called it, judged her protector to be a 'historical counter-revolutionary'.[3] Before she had a chance to see him again, he had hanged himself.

She told me that the last time she saw this man she had not seen his face, only his feet, sticking over the door on which they had stretched his dead body. Her tiny voice seemed to come from a

[1] The 'Hundred Flowers Movement,' of 1956–57, during which intellectuals were urged to voice criticisms of the government.
[2] The author was first sent to the camps for writing poetry. He (or this character) is uncertain about B's reaction to his 'crime'.
[3] A 'historical counter-revolutionary', as opposed to a regular 'counter-revolutionary', is one who operated against the communists before 1949.

disembodied spectre. Each time she said 'the Organization', the words were filled with dread, and this terrible dread had destroyed her life.

Because of her undefined, oblique relationship with the 'criminal', the Organization sent her away from Shanghai to the distant frontier. They assigned her to work where few went voluntarily, to the great northwest of China.

Back then, when I was listening to her story, I never imagined that I too would soon see innumerable pairs of feet sticking straight out of their makeshift wood or reed matting coffins. Such inadequate containers never seemed able to hold a full corpse – it was as though each dead person was unwilling to part completely from the world that had tormented him.

I remember that when I took a walk with her that evening the glow of twilight lit up the fields outside of town. Luxuriant reeds beside the lake hummed with the low-voiced poetry of summer. As we passed through a silent cemetery, hand in hand, she quietly told me her ultimate hope: that I would never be bad to her. I did not realize that with this statement she was entrusting her life to me. I thought she was letting me know that, other than her hand, I wasn't to touch any other part of her body.

Who was it, when and where, that taught me to be so degenerate?

Later I wondered why we always had to meet in a cemetery. Yes, Yinchuan was too small to have a public park, but why not choose some other place? In summer the cemetery's wild flowers were unusually thick, but they were flourishing on top of decomposing bodies.

An evening glow, a local cemetery, broken tombstones . . . branded a rightist, I should have realized that we were doomed from the start to play out this kind of tragic scene. 'Never begin to believe you can change your fate!' This message has played counterpoint to my entire life.

And yet, there were those Russian folk songs:

> A *small, winding road, narrow and long,*
> *Leads out into the vast distances . . .*

Listening to those songs in my head now, moving through Baotou, I walked slowly up an incline at the end of town. Even the glorious morning light could not give a lustre to this place – to a world that was starving and a town that was ugly. Roads criss-crossing the town were like wrinkles on the face of a dying old man. And yet I continued towards my goal. A glance at a street sign was sufficient to tell the way – she was silently guiding me.

I had burned the letter she sent me in the sick-room of the camp. The listless flames as it was consumed in the *kang*'s[1] fire made me painfully aware of my own impotence. I had always thought of her voice in terms of mild southern rain, but in that letter I discovered her passion. She wrote, 'I feel so small, I feel that you can love me up in a moment, whereas you are so very large I could never finish loving you. My love for you can never end.'

But it was all too late. The ashes of the letter were a memorial to our stillborn happiness. Love may come several times in the course of a lifetime, but the happiness in that cemetery could never be regained.

I was coming closer, step by step, and yet I had no idea why I was going to her. With my death, one year earlier, everything about me had died – my idealism, knowledge, work, and of course my love. Now, when I was just crawling from the grave, why should I come to frighten her?

With the Russian folksongs calling me, I could not stop my feet. The weakest thing about me is my body. It could be torn to shreds and the pieces tossed to the wind, but my willpower would still direct those pieces to ride the wind towards her. Death was nothing to me; after all, I had plenty of it, could pay with it just like signing checks. In this one way I can honestly say that I am richer than anyone else.

Her last letter said that the hospital had transferred her from

[1] A brick platform, heated from below, which doubles as a bed in homes in northwest China.

62

Yinchuan to Baotou, since the Organization had discovered that 'the lotus fibers were still joined although the root was severed'. But instead of openly stating that our relationship was the reason, she said, the Organization told her she was being reassigned for a noble cause: 'to support the base area of steel production'.[1]

When she wrote the two words 'the Organization', I could tell that her hand had been shaking. Nonetheless, she said that since Baotou was larger than Yinchuan, at least it had a public park.

She wrote that it had a park: did this mean that we would no longer have to go to the cemetery? Did this mean that she thought our love had taken a turn for the better?

I did not see any park as I climbed the steep slope. As I trudged, I recalled the story of the emperor who supposedly came here to hunt white deer – the deer were said to have died on this very mountain.[2] The legend whetted my appetite and I gulped back saliva, dreaming of the taste of roast venison. In a more modern and realistic version of the legend, she would soon be preparing a sumptuous luncheon for me on this mountain. She would watch in silent approval as I gorged.

Why did I have to send her that letter?

I asked the prisoner who slept next to me to write it on my behalf, telling her that I had died of starvation, which was only half a lie. He was one of China's premier scholars, an expert in degenerative potato disease. He died not long after I did, by secretly eating potatoes that had sprouted. His death was permanent, however, which made me guilty. The letter he wrote was his own obituary, not mine.

'You're right to do this,' he had said. 'Since there's no hope for us, it's wrong to let people on the outside hang onto dreams.'

The End! Since I had already died, why had I come all this way, risked travelling without a ticket, just to see her? I had 'slipped

---

[1] In the 1950s, with Soviet assistance, the small town of Baotou became an industrial center and one of the largest steel-producing areas in China.
[2] The original Mongolian name for Baotou means 'Place of Deer'.

through the net', just as today there are so many 'slipped-through-the-net rightists', 'slipped-through-the-net counter-revolutionaries', and 'slipped-through-the-net bad elements'.[1] I was a 'slipped-through-the-net dead person'!

And yet the songs were irresistible:

> A *small, winding road, narrow and long,*
> *Leads out into the vast distances . . .*

She whispered, that summer day, that she wanted to hear me sing it one last time – but I was hoping that she would leave early so that I could start in on the food she had brought.

I was able to appreciate the full romance of the scene only years later. Summer shade from a thick willow tree sheltered the gurgling canal; a grasshopper jumped lazily beside the two of us. Sunlight was filtered through the transparent wings of a dragonfly that stood, unmoving, on the end of a waving reed. A breeze brushed against the water before gently blowing back her long skirt, as though a white swan on the bank was stretching its wings. She put her tiny hands in the middle of my rough palms, her skin soft and velvety against my callouses. Holding her hands did not lessen the distance between us – I felt, on the contrary, that she was moving away.

She said that she had pretended to be my fiancée, and that the labor reform troop leader had finally agreed to let me out for a short time to see her. The tone of her voice changed as it swelled with new courage.

Her big eyes looked resolutely into mine, searching in them for some sign of hope. In return, I stared at the package she had brought, estimating how much food was packed inside.

Twenty-five years later a critic wrote that I was 'a writer of the school of "realism"'. That hurt. I alone knew how many beautiful things my 'realism' had destroyed, how I had never accurately measured the enormous weight of weightless feelings. When the whiskey wears off and the soybean fragrance is gone, all these past things are again irretrievable.

---

[1] People who have not been 'brought to account', who are at large in society and can be arrested as soon as they are recognized.

Every day that I passed the canal after that, going to or from the fields to work, I glanced up at the patch of earth where the two of us had sat. For a while, that two-rump-sized space was the most cherished spot in the world. But every time I started to climb the canal's slope to the place, I would hear the stern command of the government saying 'Halt!' Immediately after, the Organization would pull back the bolts of its guns.

Then the autumn grasses withered and the dragonflies died, and I had nothing more to hope for than to watch the changing shapes in the clouds. During the second winter a large snowstorm flattened the remaining contours of the place. I decided I would take the memory itself and escape.

In fact, all I could remember by then was the sight of B's back, leaving me.

Pushing her bike, she made her way alone down a rocky road through the wilds. It was the same Vladimir Road, between Petersburg and Siberia, that exiles had so often walked. Before her, fifty kilometers away, was Yinchuan, deprived now of its city walls, submerged under the vapors of a summer's day. Behind her was only the memory of a song, shimmering like the mirage of a streamer in the air, or like the silver track of a falling raindrop. I wanted to run after her as I watched her small, helpless form move away, but the remains of my shame held me back. I tossed two tears to the skies and turned to open the package she had brought.

I gnawed on the bread as I watched her vanish in the distance. My stomach was satisfied but I had lost the steady focus of her gaze. Forever after, I would see her with her back towards me.

> A *small, winding road, narrow and long,*
> *Leads out into the vast distances . . .*

So I had to follow the same road, had to go in search of her. Without the memory of her eyes I was like a dead meteorite that had fallen aimlessly onto the planet. She was my only connection to the world.

Although filthy, the world would still have color if her eyes were there to see it, it would still carry an interest that would allow me to live. Buffeted by wind and sand, I staggered towards her – I had to tell her that, finally, I understood the meaning in her eyes.

MAHJONG GAME

Jing Hui's house,
morning after arriving in San Francisco, 1987

HE COULD NOT remain in San Francisco for another day – he made
the decision before opening his eyes.

Having made it, he sat blankly on the side of the bed, watching
the sunlight steal through a crack in the curtain towards a patch of
fall grass on the yellow rug.

He had forgotten whether it rained the day before or not, but he
vaguely remembered seeing an off-color moon. And at midnight
the sound of water had dripped through the seams which joined his
slumber and his restless dreams. His mouth was bitter and the stupor
of a hangover was all that remained of the night before. A fine veil
had been pulled over his memory, the past was again indistinct.

The bottle of whiskey was empty. The world's amber trans-
parency had been replaced with the wan light of day.

A faint sound of scratching came from the door.

It was Freedom sitting on his haunches, gazing up at him with
reproachful eyes. He removed the letter attached to Freedom's collar
– the lady of the house notified him that she had gone shopping but
would be back by noon. Breakfast was waiting for him on the table:
she hoped he'd slept well.

During dinner the night before, Jing Hui had told him that she
was unable to join Joe in New York because of Freedom. Freedom
could not adjust to the climate on the East Coast. As soon as he
arrived he began to cough and found it hard to breathe.

This unusual reason for husband and wife living separately made
him doubly aware that he had entered a different world.

While taking a bath, he again thought of escape. Should he take advantage of Jing Hui's absence and go straight to the airport? Thinking it over, he carefully lathered every part of his body, almost to the point of caressing himself. Cast off by women he loved or, rather, having cast them off, all that he had left was himself. Involuntarily he thought of his wife, sleeping on the other side of the globe – would her dreams give her any idea that her husband was so dissolute?

Marriage is one of China's greatest social problems: the abnormal development of a society creates abnormal personal lives. His own misfortune was that he had lost the ability to be happy, hers was not understanding a man who had so often been close to death. She failed to use femininity to keep the broken pieces of his soul at home. What he needed was a mother, but the only role she could play was comrade. The best thing she brought to the relationship was her comradely indifference to his extramarital affairs.

As he massaged his skin under the soap, he reflected that in this dissolute world he could still be considered normal. He could not refuse the stimulation offered him by the world. Since fate had manipulated his life up to now, all he could do was give himself over to its whims. If he was faithful, it was because he had no other opportunity, if he was unfaithful, it was because the chance was there.

After the bath he felt as pure as a baby, and he began to hum a tune. The stimulus of having love in his heart was like having the old penis begin to stir again. The next moment he was feeling that the world was beautiful and that he had to love everybody in it.

By the time he lifted his razor he had stopped humming the tune – the sharp blade seemed to sound an alarm. He realized that what he had been humming was an old Russian folksong . . .

He followed Freedom into the dining room. The dog sat courteously by the table, head cocked up at him. Yes, Freedom, you and your name alike deserve to be loved. The hospitable lady of the house had laid out newspaper and breakfast for him. It was as though she had laid herself out and was lying there naked for his pleasure.

'I read in the Chinese papers that you were coming . . .' Who had said those words?

He chewed his toast slowly while using thumb and forefinger to open the paper. It revealed a part of the world that was much like any other. A change in the names and you might think this was a street rag put out in China: murder, armed robbery, pilfering, car accidents, fires, prostitution . . . and everyone was talking about the spread of AIDS.

As his eyes shifted from the paper, he was surprised to see that outside the window the sky of California was a transparent blue.

Several white children and black children were tossing a frisbee in the street – the whites seemed overly white and the blacks were a glossy black. The frisbee carved an arc in the air before falling in front of the garage. He took a large gulp of fresh orange juice.

A sense of comfort began to expand inside him, a sense of well-being which warmed his body like the sun. As he felt the orange juice flow through him, he rejected the idea of flight. Tranquil now, he settled down to wait for Jing Hui, as if she were a wife who had gone shopping.

He imagined himself master of this model, middle-class, American home. His cousin Joe, Jing Hui's husband, had been his childhood playmate in Shanghai. Like the children outside, he and Joe had played in the garden of his home in the French concession of Shanghai. Joe was a slow child with a constantly runny nose who, even with the help of a tutor, rarely had passing grades in school. He remembered treating Joe exactly as the white children outside were treating the blacks.

The slapping of mahjong tiles issued from a small parlor as the two boys ate ice cream under the buzz of a cicada-laden tree. In those days women came to play mahjong riding in their own sedan chairs. As they were trotted by the bus stop where the common people waited in line, they heard the shouts that 'number eight' was coming. When they announced this in the parlor the result was such alarm that tiles were scattered all over the floor. These ladies had been accustomed to shuttling around town in their Chryslers, Austins and Citroëns – they had no idea what a local number eight bus was, nor could they comprehend the absurd difference between that number eight and the Eighth Route Army.[1]

Rather than eat pastries from 'Shaliwen',[2] he preferred steamed cakes peddled by men with their goods suspended from either side of their poles; inside was delicious glutinous rice. The containers gave out huge billows of steam, together with a whistle that sounded like a pigeon. This rustic rice seemed to have a calm solidity amidst the Westernization of bustling Shanghai. Every time he ate it a signal would sound inside him, perhaps a premonition of the future rural life he was to lead.

And then the Eighth Route Army did come, the game was decided, and those days of childhood were swept clattering from the table like mahjong tiles. He and Joe simply became chips that had been put on different stacks.

The world of ice cream melted away but the results of the mahjong game lived on. Many years later, as he wrote his 'self-investigation' in jail, he knew that this one mahjong chip had been forfeited. The gamblers had run away and the chip had got stuck with their crime.

On his last trip to New York, two years ago, Joe had remarked, 'If Uncle and Aunt had brought your whole family out to America then, you'd be doing even better here than I am.' Through his flush of alcohol, he had looked sideways at Joe. 'I'm not doing so badly on the mainland, either!' The wine and his pride rushed together to redden his face.

Yes, if we had brought the whole family to America I would certainly be doing better than you. In America, anyone can be a success, start with bare hands and set up a family, not only commercially minded Chinese. On the mainland of China, on the other hand, sons of certain families were looked down on as the 'enemy

---

[1] This was the major communist army that eventually took over China.
[2] A famous restaurant and patisserie in Shanghai before 1949.

class'. Years later they were belatedly made 'intellectuals with a contribution to make to the Four Modernizations'. But these sons, every one of them, had to have been extraordinarily talented just to stay alive. Do you know that?

Neither he nor Joe spoke during the drive home. Emotions that fate had played with so lightly were set rigidly on their faces, to the point that they didn't dare look at each other. Several days later Joe brought Jenny to see him and, with a woman in between, they were able to talk. Only where sex was concerned could the two men feel equal.

All the rooms in this model American home, dining room, large guest room, small guest room, study, gave an impression of artificial luxury, of being inferior to the solid wealth of the 1940s. Technology seemed to have produced only ersatz objects, artificial hearts, lungs, stomachs, arms, genitals . . . until in the end it was making artificial people. It was easy to pass off fakes as genuine in home decor, down to the antiques and the famous paintings.

He remembered how his mother's qipao[1] had been made to order by the best tailor in Shanghai. The man would come to the house to take measurements and then again to deliver the order. Today clothes were mass-produced, the world seemed to lack depth, the prosperity of the West had made wealth into something vulgar.

Walking through the large house, hands stuffed in pockets, he failed to find the luxury he had known in his youth. The best way to preserve a memory is to seal it with the ashes of history. Then, to remember it, you need only reach inside your mind. This furniture seemed familiar but on second glance it was wrong – it became painful to him to see its falseness.

Time is clearly witnessing a lowering of standards, he thought. He had lived for thirty years in the cavelike innards of an earthen hut; emerging from it, here in America, he found that he was

[1] A tightly fitting style of Chinese dress, with a high collar and a slit up the side.

disappointed. The reality of the outer world could not begin to approach the splendor of what lay buried in his mind.

Jing Hui returned. She came up from the garage in the basement, various sizes of bundles clutched in her arms. Her tanned body smelled of perfume and leather. The brown skirt she was wearing made him think of chocolate cake – or perhaps she was more like a Chinese pastry, since her outside was sweet while her inside was bitter. 'Good morning! Did you sleep well last night?' He became aware that she was also quite pretty.

She put what went in the icebox into the icebox, and what went in the cupboards into the cupboards. Her long legs were as slender as they had always been – as she moved in front of him, he hoped this trip to America would produce some adventure.

Where would it be? Whom would fate allow him to meet, and when? Last night A had failed to meet him, and yet his premonition told him that this trip would make the start of another good play. His shattered fragments must soon attach themselves to some woman's body. He felt that the moment was not far away.

Jing Hui was excitedly telling him about something. She asked if he had turned on the TV when he got up. It seemed the police had caught a murderer, a man who was known for attacking lone walkers at night. Killing had become a form of entertainment to this man, a way to pass the time. She said that the police had been on his trail and had posted his picture everywhere. 'I've been scared silly these days!' and she placed five long fingers over her breast.

People on the mainland might say 'very scared' or 'extremely scared', but they would never say the Taiwanese phrase, 'scared silly'. For this one small difference, he wanted to kiss her. But he held himself back and told her impassively that he had to fly to New York today.

'Today? Why? Didn't you say you were leaving tomorrow? Look, I've just bought all these things to eat that you can't find in China.'

He had indeed said that he would be leaving tomorrow, but to stay another day here would be to waste a day of his life. As she turned around in astonishment, he saw the flash of a nineteenth-century elegance, like the pure lines you can see only on an antique vase. Refinement in China had been blown away by the gales of revolutions until there was hardly any trace of it left. You could only catch a glimpse of it in this or that woman – women are, by nature, living fossils.

He was enjoying the sway of her skirt, the way it moved softly around her, like phoenix-tail grass flowing in a stream. He felt moved by her and so he quickly wove a story about having spoken with an old friend on the phone – the two of them had agreed to leave together today.

As he saw the disappointment on her face, he thought of how Joe was wrecking a good life. Treated coldly, a flower, a view, a cloud, a person, loses its significance. It was strange that the furniture in this house that he had thought cheap and vulgar now seemed to have its own special charm. Wherever there was a woman, there was vitality. Even a thousand-year-old sacrificial corpse dug from the ruins of Gaochang[1] would, if it was female, excite speculation.

It was also strange that here, as well as in Taiwan, there were women who scrupulously maintained the Oriental ways of being a woman. He blew out a smoke ring, unable to decide whether the mainland's 'revolution' should be applauded or pitied, but in a few minutes he was relieved because his thoughts returned to himself.

Jing Hui was making him lunch. Their voices had taken on a comfortable family tone. His eyes passed over the shiny electric stove, the stainless steel cooking utensils and clean white cupboards, and came to rest on a small red flame in the oven. That flame smelled of remote, wild mountains, as it crackled with the wood-spirits of kindling and grasses. The spirits cavorted in the stove, then funnelled out the chimney to return to the open air. The woman working by the stove was not this woman, but another, who used a rough finger to brush back a strand of black hair falling on her forehead, and

---

[1] Gaochang is the site of an ancient ruined city in the desert near Turfan in Xinjiang, northwest China.

73

then a sleeve to wipe her nose. With strong arms, she kneaded dough for noodles on the cutting board, then began to roll it out flat.

A cloud of steam rose from the iron wok like an enveloping mist, an unexpected vision. He felt the capillaries opening throughout his body.

Year after year, month after month, dawn after dawn and dusk after dusk, what he searched for was this ordinariness, this peace, this sense of what was basic. The seductiveness of the commonplace went beyond the lure of refinement. He leaned back in the chair at the table and stretched his legs onto another seat. Tapping the ash from his cigarette, he told her not to forget to add a little salt. 'We have a saying in China,' he said. 'Tasty or not, it's all in a pinch of salt.' She flashed him a warm smile.

Simple, peaceful, commonplace – life here spread itself out comfortably between all the plastic bags, and the paper bags, paper cartons and occasional tin cans. This constituted the happiness of a modern household. He realized that some people spend their whole lives trying to be normal, yet in the face of normality discover that they have become abnormal; he was an example.

Extreme abnormality had been forced on him by the environment, just as a certain environment created a murderer.

'Well come on, then! Here's to a good trip!' The wine in her glass looked as if it were blood recently drawn from her veins.

CHINESE CONSULATE

*In an airplane over the United States,
going from San Francisco to New York, 1987*

*Chinese Consulate in San Francisco,
the day before leaving for New York, 1987*

I ENJOY sitting in the last row of an airplane next to the window, and I hope business on US airlines will always be so bad.[1] A blonde, blue-eyed stewardess and a South Asian stewardess are sitting in the empty seats nearby, discussing a failed marriage in low voices as I view the continent below.

Over Nevada I find familiar terrain – pressing my hand against the plane's window, I want to caress the undulating earth. My mind moves over each of its folds in turn as my eyes measure them out in huge strides. I know that at each stride a puff of dust rises in the air, but unlike the tread of feet my eyes leave no trace behind. No, the earth that holds my footprints is on the other side of the world.

Over there each step taken on it calls forth the curses of buried ancestors. Here the yellow earth is crying out to be developed; there the yellow earth is crying for man not to ravage it any more. Scars of ravines in my ancient earth are the wounds made on my heart when I was young.[2] As I look down on this new land, I feel scorching jealousy.

'Nah, she doesn't know herself what kind of man she wants!' The two stewardesses are giggling.

*

[1] Chinese flights are invariably full.
[2] Land in northwest China has been ruined by overpopulation and unwise agricultural policies. As a convict, the author was forced to participate in its destruction.

I did not leave San Francisco last night, but stayed in a small hotel after saying goodbye to Jing Hui. Her attitude suddenly became cold as I left, and I realized how dangerous it would have been to stay. Traps seem to have been set all around me while I, perhaps not unaware, was also setting them for others. After all, were these traps not also pieces of paradise?

Standing on the edge of one such trap, the two of us said goodbye with exquisite politeness. I knew that a cold wind from a mossy well would return to possess that big house as soon as I left, that an antique vase would be smashed to pieces as I waved my hand in a final salute. Her elegant style would again exist in a vacuum.

But although I might betray others a thousand times, I was not willing to lose Joe, the friend of my youth. The future was uncertain, its battles lay ahead: the one thing that could be depended upon was my memory of the past. I treasure the past the way others treasure the promise of the future.

He told the taxi driver to take him to the Chinese Consulate.

Long experience had taught him that he would soon be floundering in the bureaucratic snares of Beijing. It was hard to believe that the big house he had just left and this Chinese Consulate existed on the same planet, that it took no more than twenty minutes to get from one to the other.

He proudly told the guard that he had not come because he had to, but because he wanted to – he had been asked to deliver a gift to a relative here by a friend in Beijing.

Forget it! Correct procedures had to be observed. The friend in Beijing had apologized profusely for asking him to do this favor, but the minute he walked into the consulate the tables were turned. He was now the one who had to hang his head, lower his voice, and beg. The guards at the entrance saw no reason why he should be treated differently from anyone else. He was nothing more than a document to process, the only thing he lacked was a seal stamped on his face.

Back bowed, he performed all the necessary steps, amazed at his ability to acquiesce. Reverence for authority is a genetic disease in Chinese blood, forcing the Chinese to feed on bureaucratic red tape. As soon as Chinese people enter their own institutions, they begin to shiver as though the air is cold. In this waiting room, for instance, fake antiques flashed the message 'Chinese culture', and he shivered at the thought that what is fake is what endures.

He sat uneasily on the edge of the sofa, not because he had been a labor reform criminal, an escapee, the object of investigation, but because there had been no buffer of elapsed time between emerging from one lifestyle and being forced into another. Rapid passage from one to the other did not allow a person time to rearrange his mind.

At the same time, he found that he could adapt quickly to oppression – this too is an innate Chinese trait. A Tang three-color ceramic guardian-figure standing on the exhibition shelf looked as though it might at any moment charge down and crush him, similarly the nearby Han dynasty *Horse Standing on a Flying Sparrow*. Contemplating the horse, he realized that Chinese people have always wanted to crush what was strong and vigorous. They have needed to, in order to prove their greatness to themselves.

The consular employee who came to greet him was surprisingly warm and receptive. The man's pitiful tie and over-sized collar reminded him of the Service Department for Chinese Employees Going Abroad.[1] This was one of his own kind, but he still had better be careful, even though he had no secrets to conceal.

The young man had not shaved the stubble on his chin, which showed he had not yet cultivated Western habits. He felt apologetic at the sight of this unshaven chin, as though he were intruding on the normality of someone else's life. The young man thanked him for 'bringing me the warmth of my relatives'. This line from a Model

[1] These are stores in China where the best of Chinese-made clothes and articles are bought before or after going abroad – a valid passport has to be presented to gain entry. The author is ridiculing the outmoded style here.

Play[1] disgusted him. It turned him into nothing but a character role, a member of a 'group sent to convey solicitude'.[2]

The new culture of China had sucked all emotions into the orbit of politics. He had no idea how this phenomenon had been accomplished, how human relations had been ground into mere flavorings for political use. Nonetheless, he accepted the role, and coughed slightly to express the proper dignity.

The young man not only knew of him and had read his books, he also knew that an English translation of one was selling well in the States. 'How much are you making in royalties?' this employee of the consulate now asked directly.

'China hasn't signed any international copyright convention,' he explained, intentionally holding out empty hands in front of himself as he spoke. 'Royalties depend entirely on the goodwill of the foreigner.' The young man became indignant on his behalf, and quickly calculated how much he might have made if China were a member. This fellow seemed to be the consulate's accountant.

When he heard the figure the accountant came up with, he felt ashamed of himself. He had 'reformed' to the point that he could only figure up political accounts but not economic ones. For decades in China it has not mattered if a factory loses money, the important thing is that it makes the correct political or ideological decision. Economic loss is less important to our leaders than political gain. He had learned this well.

A price had never been put on his previous occupation of hard labor, nor did he value his current occupation in terms of money. What he did was not a means to a livelihood, or a pleasure, or even a need – he simply did what it was his destiny to do. He began to wonder what he had depended on to keep himself alive for fifty years.

As the young man's arguments flowed into his ears, he stared at a wall-hanging of the Great Wall and examined his soul. He was

---

[1] Eight Model Plays were promoted by Jiang Qing, wife of Mao. They were the only drama allowed in China for several years.

[2] This stock phrase was used frequently in 1989 when China's leaders were televised visiting injured PLA soldiers in hospital after the Tiananmen Incident.

being urged to try to get more royalties. The young man's talk was making his heart begin to pound: oysters, whiskey, candlelight, a small hotel . . . No matter how small, these things needed money.

In going from the big house full of illusions to this consulate full of ideals, somehow or other his mind had changed. Whether it was to nurture the warmth of love, or to enjoy the elegance of an antique vase, one needed the shading of money to bring one's dreams into relief.

'Why doesn't our country join an international copyright convention?' he heard the young man ask.

'China has translated a huge number of Western works without giving authors royalties,' he explained. 'Translations of Western works are far more numerous, now anyway, than translations of Chinese works in the West. If China joined, we would soon face a cultural trade deficit.'

The young accountant quickly saw the light. 'Oh,' he said, without a break in stride, 'then we must at all costs avoid a further reduction in our foreign exchange. We must all sacrifice personal gain for the needs of our motherland.'

Listening to this abrupt change, he found that he had been persuaded by the earlier argument. For the good of the motherland, he thought, I have sacrificed the happiness of half my life, and I am capable of sacrificing on down to the end. There is no need for you to preach noble causes to me.

Then he had to smile to himself – he had known that this visit to a government institution would end in some such encounter. Everyone who worked here would start by telling you what you had lost, and would then proceed to tell you what you were not entitled to in the first place. They would not only give you advice on how to brush your teeth and what to wear, they would tie these things in to the benefit of China.

The stewardess beside him stood up.

Her tightly encased sky-blue rump finally drew his eyes from the window. The airplane was humming along – Nevada's deserts had been left behind. He asked for a glass of orange juice but the stewardess brought him Coke. He forgave her, because of her smile as well as her rump, and offered her a smile in return.

He was yawning when something seemed to strike his chest. Even after a cautious feel, there was no indication of where the jolt had been. Every time he left China he thought he could leave the past behind, but like the skin on his body, past events took to the air with him.

Often as he sat in an airplane he fixed his eyes on distant clouds, dreaming of allowing his soul to float, unencumbered, through the air. No airplane, no passengers, no stewardesses – only a disembodied, wandering soul. Maybe that jolt had been memories of past lives, called back now to his soaring spirit.

Heavenly winds might have been roaring before he emerged, wailing, onto the earth. Clouds might have been shooting by like arrows when, by chance, he dropped onto a piece of land called China. The only major choice to a wandering spirit was between heaven and hell, but a physical body had also to consider such troubling details as nationality. Such details make up what are known as experience, and they will exist forever, after the body itself is gone.

PROOF OF IDENTITY

San Francisco, the night before
leaving for New York, 1987

ALONE AND ADRIFT last night, I looked west from Fisherman's Wharf, toward my home beyond the white-caps of the waves. Tall masts seemed like leafless trees in the fall. As I stood there, I savored their solitude.

A mast with its sail down could warn me of dangers ahead far better than one that was eating its fill of wind. A new continent lay before me, an old one behind – during this voyage I would have to decide where to drop my anchor.

I did not go to have oysters. It was not so much that A did not come to the airport as that the young man at the consulate had destroyed my dream. I had only to walk through the door of that piece of my country to be reminded of poverty: the Chinese have a wealth of illusions, all we lack is a bank account.

I gazed at the restaurants lining the ocean, their lights illuminating the black water. Any one of them could oblige my dream. It need not be a big one – a small booth would be sufficient for courtship. We could easily enjoy eating anything at all there since, unlike in China, everything was arranged to give the customer pleasure. The most complex music had been rewritten as a popular tune, so that a tone-deaf person might find it easy to enjoy. But even the smallest booth required money.

I thought of the cultural differences between East and West, so often analyzed by scholars. It seemed to me that rational and objective study reached the wrong conclusions. The enormity of those differences could only be understood by the subtlety of intuition. Moreover, those intuitive wisps of feeling lost their meaning

81

when they were fixed by words on paper – real wisdom on this subject cannot be articulated. The moist air of this new continent, laden with electronic music, now brushed against my cheeks as I thought of home. I heard the golden crops calling me in a pulsing rhythm of sound, heard the land summoning me to the harvest again . . . How could mere words possibly describe this feeling?

How far back would we have to go to start again? To 1949? 1956? Back to 1911, or even earlier? Perhaps we Chinese should make a clean start and go back to the Reform Movement of 1898. Even in America, I did not find the question irrelevant. My wandering soul might have landed in China by chance but, once the yellow brand of that peculiar country had been stamped on my skin, there was no way to scrub it off.

Bizarre experiences in that country had battered my body and cracked my soul. When my body was gone, the soul would crumble in the slightest breeze. And so it was during this one lifetime that I had to heal its wounds.

> *Baikal, our mother!*
> *We come to your side*
> *Struggling for freedom, for equality.*

In the past, I focussed my eyes on what was then the future, now I cast my eyes back to the past. It may seem a mark of senility, but I still dare to dream dreams. I dare to dream of our strange country starting over again.

But I, personally, can wait no longer. Unlike the country, I cannot forever fix my sights on an unseen future. Only by starting from a past point in time can I feel that I have lived a complete life.

For I know that my dreams for China have already been disproved. If the Chinese people could go back a certain number of years they should be able to know what is coming, and with such foreknowledge should not make mistakes. I experienced a certain period of this country's history, however, and I know that foreknowledge is not enough. My experience makes me shrink back from the opportunities now presenting themselves to China. I also shrink back in horror at my desire to self-destruct.

I turn away from Fisherman's Wharf to go back – until I realize I have nowhere to go. Following my feet, I finally find I am crossing the road. On my right, a string of headlights has had to stop and stare at me, like fools. When I hear the clamor of traffic moving again behind me, I realize that my equivocation has held up the progress of others.

A vagrant sits by the corner, playing his guitar. I pull out the change from the taxi ride and throw it into his hat. My satisfaction is equal to his as I hear the clink of coins. I have enjoyed dispensing these handouts all around the world. The pleasure comes not from my beneficence, however, but from the concrete proof that my luck has turned.

'For art's sake, mister!' the vagrant calls to me. Sure, for art! For art, I too once came down in the world like you. The green of a traffic light illuminates half the young man's bearded face. His chords strum out a sweet-sounding desolation, like the frothy waves of the ocean strumming on the glass of the night. Back then I did not even have a guitar.

Now I find it hard to believe that I actually lived that life.

Walking up the hill, I turn around for a final look. Fisherman's Wharf is lively and I consider returning to join the fun – until I remember that my passport is still held by the Chinese Consulate. Luggage and passports no longer follow people. People now have to pursue their passports.

Proof of identity has become more important than the person being identified.

BLOOD

Airport in New York,
meeting C after flight from San Francisco, 1987

I HAD NO idea when I first saw you that the two of us would become lovers, or perhaps I should say that we would be making love.

You appeared to be a married woman, possessed of gentle virtue, as you tried to help me with my luggage. Your attentiveness was like that of a mother for her child. I thought to myself how lucky your husband and child must be but I also thought, 'The woman I expected on the West Coast didn't come, while here on the East Coast an unexpected woman has appeared!'

Wherever one goes, the world has women.

I followed, pushing the luggage cart, conscious of the self-assurance with which you made your way through the crowds. You had caught me like a mayfly and I was willing to be caught. For a while I could escape the feeling of being in freefall.

I enjoyed the swivel of your hips from the rear, their rhythm like a flow of water bringing life to all around you. Your petite buttocks had a lilt to them that seemed to send out a message, an appeal. I followed quickly, afraid that I would lose you. The knowledge that I could never lose you came later.

I had just got off the airplane and was so tired and dazed that all I wanted was a bath and bed. I had stayed in a small room arranged by the consulate the night before, and had been kept awake by a hollow rhythm coming from the walls. It was hard to believe the sound was water running through pipes, and yet damp stains on the ceiling above made me feel I was immersed in water.

Lying in bed in that room, I thought how in the past I had had to make decisions although I was given no freedom of choice. Now, with plenty of freedom, I found myself strangely unable to choose. Should I live inside or outside China? Should I even live at all . . . ? My energy had been stored up, waiting for freedom. Once I had it, it was whittled away by the demands of too many choices.

I was thinking back a little regretfully to the comfort of Jing Hui's home when I heard an evening flight pass directly over the roof. As I listened to the roar of the motor, I saw the black belly of a wooden craft pass over like a cloud of ink. Immediately after, a human head floated down, weaving and bobbing through the duckweed. Crimson blood spread from it like a great halo, like the rays of a setting sun.

I knew this murder had been performed by my ancestor, up there on the surface of the water. An arm the color of ancient copper flashed and somebody's head and body parted ways. The movement of my ancestor was as neat and dexterous as I felt my own writing to be. The color of blood was as stimulating as the most stirring passage of any book.

The scene changed. My ancestor now wore the yellow mandarin jacket of a high official as he stared at me through a haze of incense. His world was now framed in the shape of a square.[1] I listened to words he spoke from between tightly closed lips.

Silently, he told how he had gone from being a bandit to being a high official. His narrative was clear but when I woke up I found that I had not understood. It was enough to understand that, every time I lost consciousness or began to die, his wild blood would start coursing through my veins, filling my body with a primitive barbarity.

I believe the reason I have been able to stay alive is that I am the descendant of a bandit. China has indeed had many periods of history that do not accommodate the gentle refinements of intellectuals.

The noise in the walls was still reverberating inside me when I landed and met you at the airport – the rhythm of it had turned into my pulse. Instead of water flowing through hot-water pipes, it had

---

[1] Ancestor portraits or photographs were kept in square frames in ancestral halls in China.

been the blood of past generations flowing through my veins.

It was you who changed the phrasing of that pulse, who was able to restrain the wildness in me.

You raised your hand to signal to me and I saw the sun flicker through your fingers. Your rings must have added to my impression that you were married. You later told me that jewelry and clothes were of equal importance, that without jewelry to adorn your body you felt naked. So when we parted, I promised to send you a keepsake and you asked me to buy you a ring. You wanted one of those cloisonné enamel rings made in Beijing – it came from China, it was cheap, and it would be unique.

Listening to these three reasons, I thought that they could just as well apply to your evaluation of our love.

You drove me into the city yourself; you had rented the car from Hertz. 'I'm responsible for taking care of visiting writers,' you said. 'I do the work as an unpaid volunteer.'

I glanced at you as I thought, 'Sure, you can afford it. She already has plenty to eat.' In that glance I saw your long eyelashes rake the green trees beside the road.

As you drove skilfully onto the freeway, you reminded me to fasten my seatbelt. You were always attentive and thorough about all arrangements. I thought of you when, standing in front of my wife back in China, I opened up the suitcase that you had so carefully packed.

The two of us chatted, staring ahead at the highway racing to meet us. I told you I could see immediately that you had come from Taiwan. 'What are the differences between women from the mainland and those from Taiwan?' you asked. 'How can you tell so easily?'

'It's similar to the way you can distinguish a Taiwanese publication,' I answered. 'By differences in the quality of the layout and binding. Also the obvious difference of simplified versus traditional characters.'[1]

[1] Taiwan uses the more complex traditional Chinese characters; the mainland uses a simplified version.

You pressed me to tell you about differences in the contents. 'I find works from the mainland easy to understand,' I said. 'I know their most obscure allusions and can read their most obtuse styles. I have to work hard to comprehend anything from Taiwan.'

You laughed, but I was not sure what the laugh meant. Yes, I would have to study you to comprehend you.

For a long while you did not say a word, as you let the silver Ford run ahead almost as it wished. I caught the faint fragrance of your perfume as I watched the trees flash by. I also saw your wrinkles, and tried to guess your age. Later, when you had no inhibitions in front of me, when there was no need to dissemble, you quite naturally peeled off your artificial eyelashes like taking off earrings, and I knew that you were middle-aged.

Several nights later you told me of your premonition while driving, that you had foreseen all that would and would not be possible for us. 'How thoroughly I've aged,' I thought. 'One symptom of old age is a loss of intuition. I, too, once had a certain sense about meeting someone in the future, but I couldn't have imagined it would be someone as far from me as you.'

At the same time, I wondered whether every man you met aroused the same kind of premonition in you.

ABNORMAL FOETUS

Baotou, Inner Mongolia,
at the hospital where B worked, 1961

YEARS LATER I realized that what destroyed me was not 'injustice', it was not my 'misjudged case'. It was not famine, nor was it being made to go to the execution ground. All those things were mere jokes that politicians played on me.

People have always enjoyed playing tricks like that, and they will keep on playing them as long as there are politics. A political party need only exist for it to begin to make 'mistakes' because political parties are only composed of men. A 'great' political party is one that makes great mistakes, and then carries out great 'corrections' of those mistakes. History is moved forward in these cycles, whereas human beings are born and die in them.

What destroyed me was that I insisted on going to see B.

The bare branches of the elms on the streets of Baotou reached out in anger toward the sky that day, like the hair of Satan writhing up from hell.

It was a cold day. Without leaves to massage it, the winter sky was even more severe. The wind would have blown me away if that Russian folksong had not nailed me down to earth.

As I trudged up the slope I hummed the lines about 'walking the uneven, unending road of the world'. The song did not actually emerge from my mouth – the piercing air and the chill in my own thin juices froze the sound inside my throat. I imagined what her expression would be as she saw me: astonishment, hurt, regret, delight? I was afraid she might faint with the shock of strong emotions.

My desire to see that tender, lovely face was no less strong than my desire to find a lovely steamed bun by the side of the road.

I finally arrived at the hospital.

The white sign at the front gate said 'Number Four People's Hospital at Baotou'. As I read it, I again felt the words, 'The End!' The sign had been painted in a haughty and forbidding style, unlike the delicate strokes of the return address on the letter she had sent. I could hardly believe the two places were the same.

The hospital she had written of had a flower garden outside the front door, like the one in the song she used to sing, *In spring the flowers bloom* . . . Approaching it, I felt an acute sense of foreboding and heard a voice saying I would soon fall from a fairy-tale into the cold, cruel world.

No sunlight or any other light guided the way. I entered and was swallowed up by the dark brick building. A long, dim corridor wavered before me. Along it were hung small, crooked signs, nailed haphazardly at the side of each door. As I looked down the swaying corridor, I had the feeling that the large sign outside had given birth to a monstrous set of bunch-of-grape foetuses.[1]

Although accustomed to stinking smells, I could hardly stand the stench. The few people I saw looked oppressed, like lost souls, who were there to transmit pain and misfortune to one another. This was not a hospital in which the living administered to the dying, but one in which the dying tried to pull down those still alive.

I pressed on, using whatever courage remained. I found her one small sign by intuition rather than actual sight. Among all the others in that cluster of abnormal foetuses, only this one baby seemed created to give happiness. I embraced it with my soul as I sat on the bench opposite the door.

I have forgotten now exactly how it all happened. Did I ask some doctor if she was inside? Did I ask some sick person where she might be? In the many times since that I've recalled the scene, all I can

---

[1] According to the author, a 'bunch-of-grapes foetus' is a kind of abnormal foetus that sometimes occurs in China.

remember is that I did indeed see her. The sight of her face cut off all memory of what went before.

Thinking back, though, I imagine it must have gone something like this: I sat on the bench in a trance not thinking of anything at all. I was sitting exactly at the point defining two parts of a human life. To pass the time, I began cleaning under my fingernails. I was pleased at the harvest, for they held a long trip's worth of dirt. Seated at this crossroads, I looked around in all directions, not quite sure where I had come from or was going or why I was even there.

The sound of a baby crying brought me out of these inchoate thoughts. I looked up to see a baby boy. Above an unusually large nose, there were bloodstains on his forehead, whether his own or his mother's was hard to tell. No, I have mixed up this occasion with something that happened later, waiting outside the delivery room for my son to be born. The reason must be that in jail I often dreamed of having a child with B, a child that was conceived when we sang the duet: A *small, winding road, narrow and long* . . .

Twenty years later I did have a child, only it was borne by someone else. I remember putting my face against that of my son, not knowing if the wetness was blood or tears that had come too late.

It was noon by the time she finally emerged. She appeared punctually before me, as though keeping an appointment. I saw her walk out of the room with the small sign. Yes, it was her, it couldn't be anyone else. And then I did indeed fall from a fairy-tale into the callous world.

Her face was not tender, it was grey and closed. It was like a corner of the building that had grown mould, a dark corner that reflected no light. Her hands, those hands I had held so tightly, had been so scalded by chemicals that the skin had come off. A layer of blackheads surrounded her nose. Her white jacket was so dirty that it physically hurt me to see it. My heart ached as my dream was polluted.

I never again believed in life, or in memory, or in dreams, and I no longer believed in myself. A person can be shot dead without ever hearing the bullet – in a similar way, I can't recall how I lost myself.

And yes, there was also her pregnant belly which would haunt me forever, a swelling that told its own story of what had happened to her after I left. Inside her stomach I saw two tiny hands frantically rejecting the outer world, trying feebly and helplessly not to be born.

She did not see me. I saw from her eyes that she did not want to see anything at all. Even though I had had a long journey, she looked the more tired. Her cloth shoes were spotted with grime, her trousers dragged on the ground. Jacket, trousers, shoes were all too long and too large. She carried a few possessions in a torn paper bag.

I sat there, shaken and horrified by her cold detachment from the world. Yet I knew that if I rose to greet her she would be horrified by my warmth. To call back the past now would be incomparably cruel. We were both cracked, and would be shattered by a further shock.

As she dragged slowly past in front of me, I thought it would be best if the corridor could be laid with mines. We would find our final home in one final explosion. In the sound of singing, we would return to a beautiful time.

Nothing happened. It never did, no matter how many times I hoped it would. While being criticized and 'struggled against', while being investigated, while writing self-criticisms, while accompanying others to the execution ground, even now, while writing this novel, the ground has never exploded under my feet. Instead, I have been worn down by the truth, tormented by the lies. My desire to destroy myself started from that moment.

I remained silent and motionless on the bench. I had lost the desire and the strength to go on. As I watched, the various parts of her body were stuffed into the paper bag, and were dragged out by the line of light at the end of the hall. When she was gone, the two of us completely parted ways.

After being dragged away, she would have a child. And I? What was I going to do? The sound of singing had been shredded, the wind had lifted its pieces and was scattering them like ashes. How could my helpless gaze ever draw them together again?

Having written this novel to this point, I am not sure where to take it: I have begun to equivocate between truth and fabrication. If I were truthful, I would write that after a while I simply left the hospital, like a dog leaving behind a meatless bone.

But no reader would be satisfied with that. Readers like to be stimulated. They like characters that react strongly to trauma. I have thought of it many times, however, and I did not do anything unusual – that I didn't was, in itself, extraordinary.

I sat. I waited until all the doctors had left for their midday break before getting up and walking outside. The earth had not blown up, the streets were still straight and dull. By the look of the sun, it was already early afternoon. The cold wind had paused to rest on the tops of brown roof-lines. I was glad for that, and also for the fact that I still had my five-*yuan* note.

With some difficulty, I found out that there was a stall selling buckwheat noodles on a certain street corner at a certain distance from the hospital. I quickened my pace and set off in search of it.[1]

Neither the world nor a man's life should be looked at head on, but I had to try to do exactly that.

---

[1] The difficulty was due to the scarcity of food, and also to the absence of any private enterprise. Only canteens of organizations served food in those days, and only at prescribed times of day.

BOW TIE

With C in New York,
attending a literary conference, 1987

YOU SEE, having been through these things, how can I still have feelings left for you? You should treat me like an expired credit card and simply throw me away.

My oars have been broken by the waves of the ocean, but still the wind drives me on.

The first thing we did in New York was attend a buffet reception. It preceded the opening session of the international literary conference I had come to attend.

Dozens of people of different nationalities were aggressively discussing literature in the brightly lit hall. That there is anything to discuss about writing is, in itself, odd. If you are a writer, you write, and that is all there is to it.

It was still a sunny day, despite some clouds in the sky, but inside these people were seeking the obscure and so the place was lit with lamps. The attendees poured champagne down their throats in the stark light while their faces gradually flushed with an uncontainable terror. For countenance after countenance began to prove beyond a doubt that people have no idea how to express their thoughts. Amongst the champagne and the titbits ten thousand shapes and forms were searching for their own adequate expression.

I saw you holding up your wine glass, passing easily through the crowds. The oriental *qipao* you were wearing was, just as you said later about that ring, unique. Unlike the Western women with their bared backs and low necklines, you were wrapped up like a lightweight tank, and because of that you were all the more dangerous.

You paused under a portrait of one of the great forefathers of America. I chewed an hors d'oeuvre and watched you laughing as you gossiped. Your every motion, every gesture, had an underlying rhythmic charm, like the almost undetectable perfume you wore. For a moment I was annoyed by the chatter all around and wanted to go to you, grab your hand and find a dark corner.

But in that instant a white-haired British professor walked up to me. I saw from the gravity of his bow tie that I too should assume a serious manner. He courteously inquired about freedom of literary expression in China.

I had heard the question thousands of times before, so I knew exactly how to respond. 'If you ask any writer if he has creative freedom,' I said, 'he will answer that he does – otherwise he would have to admit that his work is so much farting in the wind.'

I thought I would take this opportunity to pull you in as our interpreter, but you had left the American forefather and probably entered the embrace of some Russian philosopher. I looked around for you, my mouth flapping as I answered questions. Fortunately, the British professor soon went away, quite satisfied with my answers and even thanking me. I had just insulted his intelligence, but I felt that you too, with your hide-and-seek, had insulted mine.

Everyone now herded together and began to move into the conference hall – professors, scholars, writers, students – reminding me of the flock of sheep I used to tend in the grasslands. I saw you glancing about and knew that you were looking for me, so I was happy to delay my entry and punish you a little. Who asked you to be responsible for me, anyway?

Putting down my glass, I walked out of the hall. The colors of an autumn evening were creeping over the lawn, birds were singing in the twilight as an old red maple helped to prop up a young night sky. A nearby marble bust of the hall's donator looked melancholy, as though he were distressed to see his money being used on these anti-capitalist writers. I lit a cigarette and let the smoke wander in the fresh air.

Separated by glass doors, your image came into the corner of my eye. Your face was flushed, either from alcohol or displeasure. You said you had been looking everywhere for me. You never dreamed I would come out here to take the breeze. I said I hadn't known you were looking for me, I wanted a smoke, was there anything wrong in that?

'Never mind,' you said, 'there's no time to argue. You have to get up on stage and give your speech.'

I was unaware that you had the authority to assume this imperious tone. Moreover, I was so delighted by your use of the Taiwan word for 'argue' that I felt I simply had to argue. Like 'scared silly', never heard on the mainland, this 'argue' seemed so fresh that it was like a come-on.

'To move my speech up a day without even notifying me,' I dryly observed, 'is clearly an expression of this conference's lack of respect. The organizers of this affair should please not forget that behind me stands a country with millions of writers, more writers than any other in the world.'

Your mouth instantly twitched in a most comical way, as if it couldn't cope with such a big number. But you were, after all, a woman, and one with a certain upbringing, so you used that mouth which had just twitched to beg my pardon. You said that since the speaker from one country had become ill, the man presiding over the conference had moved my speech up to today. You seemed to want to indicate that speaking on the opening day was a great honor. You cleverly and expertly provoked my sense of vanity.

Days later, for one reason or another, we began to argue again. The even, white teeth in your mouth declared how fussy we mainlanders seemed to be about hierarchy. 'Fortunately,' you said, 'the first letter in "China" is a C. If it were a Z, China might have to disrupt international convention.' My argument had already lost its wind by then, since your call from the bed was almost turning me inside out.

Everything between us seems, in retrospect, to have been so well arranged, to look so casual, while leading, implacably, toward the bed.

Standing before you by the sliding glass doors, I replied that I, too, was sorry, but I had not brought the notes for my speech. You instantly conjured up a sheaf of papers. I don't know where you could possibly have had them hidden. Surprised, I took a second look at your tailored *qipao* and, as you turned to go, found that I was mesmerized by your poppy-red buttocks.

I followed those addictive poppies as they swayed along. With my mind thus preoccupied as we entered the hall, I found it hard suddenly to adopt the weighty attitudes of the others, hard to make literature a burden that had to be carried on my back.

You looked meaningfully at me as you settled me into the last row in the hall. Later, after I knew you better, I realized what the look meant – it was my own fault, you were saying, that I had to sit in this remote corner.

I soon made a discovery, however, as I sat back there: before me spread a field of evenly-spaced bald heads. They looked like the glacier-polished stones that covered a mountain slope I used to know. Time rolled back for an instant before dropping into the present.

I gasped in admiration at the intelligence reflecting off those heads.[1] At the same time, I remembered being told that the prevalence of baldness among Westerners is the consequence of years of unrestrained sexual licence. I secretly thanked our Chinese sense of asceticism, and the social circumstances that had made me celibate for so many years. Comforted, I rubbed what could still be considered a flourishing head of hair, and warned myself that it would pay for any over-indulgence.

A burst of applause brought back thoughts that were unmistakably drifting downwards. Thinking over what I had just intermittently heard, I felt that this Latin speaker had not revealed anything new; at least he hadn't used any unfamiliar technical terms. On the contrary, he even went so far as to use an obscenity, a word that could be seen in New York subway stations and in toilets around

---

[1] In popular Chinese belief baldness is a mark of intelligence.

the world. From his talk, I concluded that, East or West, we writers were nothing but a bunch of grown-up children.

We had written ourselves out, thought ourselves out, been through enough in life – now we wanted to let go a little. Being so noble was hard to take. We wanted to break through the barriers that were holding us back, so that we could comprehend the divine while still tasting the earthy, could appear to be lofty while we enjoyed the obscene.

The same human impulse made someone think up this conference, I decided. Nobody had any illusions about getting anything out of it, beyond relaxing, performing, and feeling good. We were all indulging our libidos.

The next person to take the stage was a woman from Western Europe. Her speech on women's rights drew rounds of laughter and enthusiastic applause. I found her seemingly brilliant, amusing speech hard to understand, and I leaned over to ask a Singaporean Chinese sitting next to me what it was all about. Covering his mouth as he continued to snicker, he told me that she had announced that men were wimps, that women might as well not pursue them at all. Women should simply masturbate if they felt horny.

So . . . it was on things like this that I came up against a communication gap.

Her speech had touched a chord in the audience, however, and the hall livened up. From the uncomfortable feeling of having nothing to talk about, everyone now wanted to say a few words. All who mounted the stage basked in the envy of the others – envy not for what they said but for their chance to say it. Then I saw you coming up the aisle to me, floating along like a gaily-colored boat.

It was your sashay that made me change my mind. By the time you reached me and bent down to speak, I told you that my speech would be impromptu, that the lecture notes I had prepared so long ago could be damned! You gripped notes you had painstakingly translated into English and stared at me, reminding me of a cat that has been dumped in a lake.

You made no effort to conceal your disapproval, as though the official nature of our relationship were already ambiguous – the discourteous annoyance in your eyes was the kind that comes only after two people have been in bed. I felt virility course through my body. I love this stage, when two people are becoming but not yet being. Eyes can stir a man's desire more quickly than the stroking of hands – one glance from you was proof.

So I, too, began to give orders. I said I did not want you to interpret, that I would rather find a man.

You glared and said it was a shame to give up my prepared speech. I said it was nothing more than a dry dissertation, which would be badly received by a wooden-faced audience.

'It would be wrong to stop the surging sexuality of these people,' I said. 'Readers know authors by their works, but authors know each other only by hearing each other talk about the opposite sex.'

You finally agreed, but you added that if I wanted a man to interpret for me then I had to find one for myself. While I was enjoying the flash of your dangling earrings and imagining the message they might be sending me, my mouth was saying that I would be glad to oblige. I asked you to deliver a message to a friend.

'Well, all right, but limit your talk to ten minutes,' and you swivelled around and left. The motion was that of a bird banking sharply in a strong wind, and I wondered momentarily if I was pushing things too far – but then, I really did want to catch this bird.

You took the message up to my friend. After reading it, he turned and smiled: men understand the needs of other men.

A VIRGIN BOY

Literary conference in New York,
then later a café with C, 1987

I HEARD the chairman announce my name. After I signalled to my friend, we mounted the stage.

Innumerable eyes looked up from the dimness below, all expecting to be entertained. I said first that before coming on stage one of the organizers of the conference had repeatedly warned me not to exceed ten minutes. I said that I sympathized, knowing what she meant. 'People from China excel in long political reports. All occasions must be preceded by propaganda from the Communist Party.

'However,' I said, 'I intend to do the opposite. I want to tell you an ancient joke.

'Long ago there dwelled in China an accomplished scholar. He worked for three straight days and nights but was still unable to finish writing an article. His wife was concerned, and asked why it seemed harder for him to write the piece than for her to give birth to a child. The scholar replied, "Having a child is easy for you because you have something inside – my problem in writing this piece is that my mind is empty."

'In recent decades,' I continued, 'China'a authors have been through a number of cataclysmic disasters: while our stomachs are empty, our minds are enriched and full.

'Anyone reading my novels, reading one love story after another, would think that in the midst of these disasters I must have been warmed by a considerable amount of love. The reality is quite the opposite. Until I was thirty-nine I was as pure as a virgin boy. I hope that you men sitting in front of me never have to experience that kind of sexual repression. The subject matter of my novels is a product of my imagination.

'Realize that I would wake up every morning in a primitive town, with the frost thick outside when the cocks started crowing. Over me would be a worn sliver of a blanket that was cold as steel. Think how easily I could imagine that next to me lay this or that woman: I caressed her and she caressed me, and in her loneliness she found things to comfort me in mine.

'My solitude was peopled by the company of imagined lovers. By the time I had been given the right to write, and even the right to publish, I simply dropped their images one by one onto a sheet of paper.

'As a result, I feel that I begin to understand what literature is. Literature expresses the dreams of mankind, dreams that in themselves are a revolt against reality.

'After going through twenty years of being criticized, struggled against, "making a clean breast of one's crimes", or repeatedly writing self-examinations, of attending large meetings, small meetings, ad infinitum, of being paraded through the streets as an example to the masses, of ceaseless impromptu debates . . . there is not a single Chinese intellectual who is not an expert in oral eloquence.

'The unending political movements in China have created wave upon wave of masters of the Chinese language. Those who were not articulate all died – who told them, after all, that they had the right to be inarticulate! It was only proper that they die!

'Those who lived were those who could talk and could write self-criticisms, and consequently they are all professionals. All Chinese intellectuals who are alive today know how to cater to the tastes of an audience, how to tailor their speech to the mood and the time available, and how to end when it is time to end.'

I had just touched on the main theme of my speech when I nodded my head in conclusion and left the stage. My friend and I had matched each other well, rising to the occasion like a pair of cross-talk performers.

The sound of thunderous applause followed. The audience had

wanted to be amused and the speaker had wanted to bolster his self-esteem – neither had been disappointed.

When the conference adjourned, the chairman, beaming from ear to ear, came up to praise my speech as both humorous and profound. He clapped me repeatedly on the shoulder, congratulating me. I suddenly felt ashamed for this kind of Western grown-up child: in terms of experience, we Chinese are at least a hundred years old.

At the same time, I thought, 'But our Chinese race hasn't grown up either, despite being around for five thousand years.'

The crowd in the convention hall gradually dispersed. Through the doorway, I could see the darkening night. A water truck or perhaps a fall rain had wet the pavement, cars passed by with the slick sound of wet tires. The jolly mood of the meeting evaporated as I put up the collar of my windbreaker. I saw you standing alone by the side of the silver Ford.

You had a light nylon coat on and it, too, was a silvery color. Against the blackness of the night you radiated an appealing chilliness, as though you were in need of somebody to come warm you with his hands.

You used a starry-eyed look to call me. Your eyes, like your earrings, were a beacon in the night. I walked silently toward them.

Without a word you got into the driver's seat and I silently got in the other side. When the two of us were seated you did not start the car. Your tired face looked as though it was still waiting for something.

Years later, in Paris, when I emerged from a similar conference and got into Natalie's car, she too sat expectantly. That time I did not hesitate to move close to her and kiss her. The gear shaft rammed into my ribs making me think a gun was pointed at my heart. Was someone trying to get me for my sins? Because as I kissed her, I was thinking of you. You had taught me so much.

You had not yet begun your lessons then. Instead of moving to kiss you, I rolled down the window and lit a cigarette. I let you dangle for a while, just as you are now doing to me.

After a moment the car slid smoothly into the traffic and I was given a view of Manhattan at night.

I am not sure who first suggested going for a cup of coffee and a bite to eat – it may have been me, since my excess gastric juices always worry me. As you drove, we spoke a few desultory sentences to each other – lost words, like moths seeking a flame in the night. You finally found a small café that had a parking place in front. We headed for an empty corner with the same silent intent, and our unspoken agreement already seemed significant.

Your coat slipped off on its own accord in my hands, and for a moment I thought that your body under it was completely bare. In that instant I had a premonition of what would happen; when I heard you speak, I knew for sure.

MOTHERS

Coffee shop in New York, with C, 1987

OF COURSE, you know what happened, I need not repeat everything here. Yet I believe you may have forgotten things you said that night. How it started, how I followed it up, and how it ended. Even I who have been 'investigated' for so many years, even I have forgotten.

The kind of investigation I am talking about is something excruciating: we who were investigated had to link our lives together, conversation by conversation, sentence by sentence. And we had to remember each sentence as though it had been given a serial number. Otherwise we would soon be attending our own funerals, or at the very least be viciously beaten.

This training drilled into me the ability to write. The person who is investigating is responsible for drawing out the life story of the person being investigated. The one being investigated must therefore continually try to concoct his own life. He must relate, for example, what his conversation was with such and such a person and at such and such a time . . . The process is like both reading and writing a novel. This strict exercise has given China many modern Shakespeares.

But I do not want, right now, to write about you as a character in a novel – I just want to tell you which of your words affected me.

You spoke of the husband from whom you had been divorced. You said that what men seem to need is woman in her primitive state – that you felt too civilized. You had already been molded by civilization to the point where you could hardly feel you were a real person. You wanted desperately to return to being natural, wild.

'When men get together,' you also said, 'it annoys me that they always discuss women, even though I think they hardly understand us at all. The only ones who really know women are women themselves.'

I said that women could misunderstand women just as men often misunderstood men. 'The only ones who really understand are the few with any intelligence.'

That we have mostly forgotten the words we said then is because they were all for show, they were like lines in a play. We were using language as a walking stick. Leaning on it, we were joining hands to enter the cave.

You coughed lightly and covered your mouth. From the elegant gesture, I guessed at both your refinement and your annoyance with that refinement. I realized that you had been born complete with jewelry and lovely clothes, that you brought all the packaging of civilization along with you at birth. These things had formed your foetal membrane. Only now, in middle age, did you want to break through the membrane and contact the world. When I had been thinking you were naked, you had been wishing you *were*.

'I can smell an animal smell on the bodies of people from the mainland,' you said. 'Your bodies are like those of foxes or wolves who have just run out of the forest.'

I smiled involuntarily, remembering how I am the descendant of wild bandits who, incidentally, belong to the most revolutionary class. By changing their class and becoming aristocrats, my ancestors unfortunately made me a prime target for the Revolution. A later revolution again made me into a thief.[1] Revolutions followed, one after another, turning me into who knows what – perhaps even, as you said, a wolf or a fox.

'You're right about some women,' you finally conceded. 'For instance, I think the European speaker who championed women's rights fundamentally misunderstands the nature of women. Our strength isn't that we don't need men, our strength lies in the fact

[1] The author means the Cultural Revolution, during which he was forced to steal in order to eat.

that we are mothers. Mothers give birth to everything, men included. The great fuss that men make in the world is only so much twisting and turning inside their mother's womb. Mothers watch serenely over everything, encompass everything, forgive everything.'

As I listened to you, I was reminded that Sun Wukong was unable to leap outside the palm of Buddha.[1]

By that time your eyes looked like coffee with warm milk in them – they had become a woman's eyes. I secretly wished that you too could encompass me. I wondered at the same time why your husband had left you.

'Daring to do what you did, throwing away a prepared speech like that and speaking to such an important group off-the-cuff, is something only a wolf who has just run out of the forest could do. The civilized world has its own civilized rules of the game.

'All jokes, high or low, have to be cooked up first at home. Like platters of food, they get carried to the banquet only when they're perfect. The jokes may not be brilliant but that's not a reflection of the speaker's lack of knowledge. It's a result of his inability to adapt instantly to change. You people from the mainland seem quite good at adapting.'

You then said that you had enjoyed what I did, but that you didn't appreciate the contents of my speech. In fact, it upset you: you felt that the whole speech was nothing more than an encouragement to make love.

When you said the word 'upset', I saw in your eyes that you were putting it on. I had placed an advertisement, a request to make love, and you were the first to respond. You were in the process of turning yourself into a woman. Like Western dogs and cats that are over-civilized, you wanted to run back to the forest and learn how to bite people and catch mice. But you already knew too much of the outer world and the knowledge, the living of it, made you more and more exhausted. Knowledge has always been a burden to mankind.

[1] Sun Wukong is the monkey character in the classical Chinese novel, *Journey to the West* by Wu Cheng-en (1500–1582).

I very much wanted to help you lay down that burden, and so I agreed with all you said. 'I know I was trying to please the public with nonsense, but true knowledge can't be verbalized. The most precious things are those learned by experience, learned viscerally. Those things have to stay buried inside. Anything that can be defined absolutely admits a fraction of what's false into itself. So it's better,' I concluded, 'to phrase inner knowledge in the form of jokes than to say with all seriousness things that are half false, half true.'

You applauded my frankness. 'I thought you'd try to defend yourself,' you said. 'Every Chinese from the mainland thinks he knows the truth. Each one of you is also supremely conscious of face.'

I smiled in agreement but noted that writers should be an exception to the rule. Writers are, after all, the least capable of people: only those who can do nothing but dream all day would choose this line of work. If I could make pancakes on a street corner, for instance, I would go out and sell pancakes.

A police siren wailed outside, a stripe of hot light grazed your face. I saw it hit your earring as a reflection of deep red leapt back to my lips. You were calm, though, your movements measured and controlled as you quietly put out your cigarette. 'From your novels I would have thought you'd be an optimist,' you said. 'I never imagined you could be a pessimist to your bones.'

'It's hard to differentiate between pessimism and optimism after one has seen through the world. I can't say which is better or worse. I'm simply myself.'

But you said that you still preferred pessimists – it seemed that you had decided I was one and wanted me to agree. 'Only pessimists have a tolerant attitude. Take Buddha: Buddha accepted that man's life is one great tribulation.'

I disagreed. 'Buddha's pessimism and optimism were equally expressed by his silence. He heard, saw, experienced everything, but didn't speak of it. I don't think there's a writer in the world who would call himself a true pessimist or a true optimist. We're all a bunch of damn cowards who sell emotions for money.'

Damn! Your way of being civilized meant that everything had to proceed in a certain order. Walking through the red light district in Paris, I enjoyed watching prostitutes standing in doorways, opening their coats and flashing bikinis at me. 'Monsieur, voulez-vous entrer?' they would invite me. Their directness made me realize how different you were. You were saying essentially the same thing, but while they said it in a few words, you had to drag in Buddha.

When I lay dying, I realized that I actually preferred their approach. It saved time and it saved thinking. Talking love with you always made me tired.

At the end of our talk in the coffee shop, you smiled and said that my statement 'I'm simply myself' was the purest form of wolf-talk. What I saw you were saying was, 'I need such a wolf.' It was written all over your face.

After all this talk it would have been absurd to part ways just like that. You glanced at your watch and said we might go sit somewhere else for a while. I said, well, either my hotel or your house. You motioned to the waiter and said that the coffee at your house was better than here.

Naturally, I prefer to drink superior coffee.

My fingers stroked your long hair out from under the collar as I helped you with your coat, and as they brushed your white neck I felt a shiver of anticipation.

You went to start the car while I bought a bunch of China Pinks from a young lady at a nearby flower stall. Their red petals were beautifully mixed in with white.

'This isn't something a wolf would do,' you said, as you held up the flowers, and you complimented me on my expertise in courtship.

The sirens wailed again and we were forced to pull over to let the police cars pass. Normally, I dread such animals as soldiers and the police, but that night I found I wasn't afraid.

CHINA PINKS

In Brooklyn with C, 1987

Ningxia, China, 1970

I THINK you probably don't love me. But if you feel at least a kind of sexual love for me, then it must have started that night.

That night you slipped out of your negligee. The silky fabric floated to the green carpet with an earth-shaking roar. As it fell, I watched you emerge from the surface of the water.

You slipped out of your negligee that night and I climbed into your womb. With primitive energy we returned to a primeval state. Together we smelled the wetness of caves and the forest. Together we experienced the joy of savages. To move from civilization to barbarity is as hard as going the other way, but you and I were able to travel back ten thousand years in one night.

I was aware of nothing but a haze of pink, like the flesh-colored light coming through your ear lobe. The haze emcompassed me, as though I had returned to a mother's womb. Later, I heard your cries split the earth as you writhed beneath me, and still later the fragrance of yellow soybean meal floated up, like an even greater mist than the haze, covering the world.

When I awoke to see a thin sliver of light, I thought that the window was the mouth of a cave. We were in Brooklyn, but I felt that I was inside a remote mountain, that if I extended my hand through the mouth of the cave I could pluck a fruit. I scratched an itch as I considered this for a while. It finally came to me that the flashing lights before the cave were headlights of cars, not the eyes of prowling animals.

You were stretched out by my side, sleeping like a barbarian. Your thick hair covered your sweaty face, your lips were slightly open. Your elegance and education had been swept away. With my help, you had reached your goal.

I found I loved you for returning to that original state. When you did, you became completely honest, as honest as a slab of meat set out on a butcher's block. The distance between us grew when you again cloaked yourself in civilization. Right now, for all I cared, you could grind your teeth, fart, growl like a female beast. Indeed, together we could fart and growl and, instead of lying on a rusty metal bed, we would be hugging the great revolving globe as we slept.

I feel a tingle crawl up my back when I think about that night – it was your ring raking up and down my spine. The feeling was as though, once the universe went mad, all the stars left their assigned positions and cavorted through space. Other memories of the evening have paled, only the one of your ring remains strong, since that particular form of contact only happened when we made love.

One of us was wanting to move from a civilized state to a primitive one, while the other wanted to move from savagery to civilization. We found each other at just the right time. Slightly earlier or slightly later and it would not have worked. Our impact drew fiery sparks, brilliant sparks, and nothing else. My collision with you pushed me to the crossroads, but I could not decide which one to choose . . .

. . . because on waking, on seeing the sliver of light from the mouth of the cave, I saw that it shone directly on the China Pinks. Somehow, the flowers were oozing blood. Small rivulets of it were dripping onto the verdant carpet.

I smelled the raw smell of blood and felt a wave of heat slap my face. I touched the wetness, not knowing if it was blood or sweat. It might have been both, since my face was both cold and hot, and at the same time I felt a bullet worming its way to the back of my brain. Instead of plunging straight in, it twisted bit by bit toward the top of my skull. My body was enflamed, tongues of fire leapt from my throat.

This feeling comes over me after every successful love-making. The strange thing is that this feeling and the feeling of being executed are the same.

'Would they really let me die so easily?' I asked myself. I was being shoved up onto a cart. Instead of resisting I felt grateful for their kindness in selecting me, but I also felt a little reluctant to go. There was nobody I felt sorry to part from – my mother had passed away, all the women I had known had turned their backs on me. So I turned to look at the State Farm cadre who was taking me in, the man who had tied me up to take me to the Military Control Commission of the Public Security Bureau. The more I looked at this cadre, the more warmly I felt towards him.

He wore green army fatigues without a badge or insignia of rank – in the midst of a crowd of militiamen, this seemed unusually mild. He had not shaved the hairs on the end of his chin – he'd probably been too busy this morning, getting me off to the city to take part in the magnificent execution of counter-revolutionaries. Since then, I have always felt a twinge of guilt when I see someone who hasn't had time to shave.

As we jolted up and down along the way, he took a small wad of bills out and began counting and recounting them. He said he'd wait until after I was executed, then his old lady had asked him to take advantage of being in town to buy some things at the store. 'It isn't all that easy to get into town!' He was glad to have such a good excuse to make the trip.

This ability to make use of every opportunity won my admiration, together with his demonstrated skill at grasping the tenets of realism.[1] We chatted as the tractor engine pulled us down the road in a small cart. When he saw that we were approaching the city and he no

[1] Realism was one of the isms preached by Chairman Mao and studied by 'the masses'.

longer had to guard me so closely, he slightly loosened the rope on my wrists – he commented that he couldn't abruptly loosen it all the way or I would find that my hands were useless. I had implicit faith in his words, for this man was one who should know – tying up and beating people had been the chief occupation of cadres for the past few years.

But then he chuckled and said that, anyway, it was the end of the line for me. Whether my hands were useless or not was nothing to anyone now – might as well loosen the rope a little more. As this old cadre put it, it went something like, 'Fuck it! A little comfort's better'n none at all!'

After the rope was loosened and I discovered I still had hands, I felt even more warmly toward this man. I said, 'Dammit, you're a good man! A man can't use his ears to get out of a well – what's the use of two hands when you're dead? You and I might as well relax a little. There's some cigarettes in my pocket – help yourself, and could I trouble you to get one out for me as well?'

The tractor began to weave back and forth as he exerted considerable effort to get a cigarette stuck into my mouth. On account of this comedy, the two of us laughed again. After the laugh, his eyes narrowed. He looked at me and asked, 'Why aren't you afraid?'

'What is there to be afraid of?' I said. 'Chairman Mao instructed us long ago, "One, do not fear hardship and, Two, do not fear death." If I were to fear death, I wouldn't be a good soldier for Chairman Mao!' He guffawed at this, and commended me for reforming myself so well. Even here, on the way to the execution ground, I had finally become a fellow comrade of revolutionaries.

Yes, in order to win the approval and forgiveness of the Revolution, all that intellectuals can do to prove their sincerity is to die.

Then he pulled a small pouch out of his breast pocket. He handled it gently, as though it contained a small bird. He opened it up very delicately, and I saw that inside were a clove of garlic, a scallion, a few peppercorns and a pinch of salt. He said that these were the things his old lady wanted him to buy in town.

As he spread them out for me to take a look, I felt tears come to my eyes. It made me remember the old cook my family once had, I remember his name to this day, and like this old cadre he too was illiterate. Every evening he would report the bills of the day to my mother – he'd bring a small bundle of assorted items into the parlor. With great concentration he would arrange them on the side table. A chicken feather meant he had bought a chicken that day, each fish-scale indicated one *jin*[1] of fish, one vegetable leaf would be one *jin* of that particular vegetable, and so on. The wisdom of this man's old lady was like the wisdom of our old cook. In human affairs, you find the same things everywhere.

But this State Farm cadre suddenly frowned. All that would be simple to get – it was just this fabric that was troubling him. He held a small piece of cotton up high as though raising a flag, and said it was the fabric of the cotton jacket his old lady was making. She had been sewing and sewing away and then realized that she was short one foot for the sleeve. She had told him that the fabric had to be identical to this piece. The two of us lowered our heads in dismay, pondering this knotty problem under the wind-tossed flag.

After a moment, perhaps because my circulation had improved when the rope was loosened and I'd grown sharper, I announced, not to worry. After I was shot I would be seeing Yama, King of Hell, and would ask him first off where to buy this particular kind of cloth. It is said that all those things not found in the Yang world can be found in the Yin, which must be why the Yin world is sometimes known as Paradise.[2] I also said I felt sure one wouldn't have to use coupons to buy fabric in the Yin world.

He immediately cheered up, stopped frowning and again praised my superior attitude. He said that with an attitude like that I should have been allowed to be executed long ago – he just couldn't understand why they had dragged it out till now.

Naturally, I wanted my attitude to be as good as possible, right

---

[1] A *jin* is a measure of weight equal to half a kilogram.
[2] The Yang world is the living world, the Yin world is the netherworld after death. Yama, King of Hell, is also known as Yan Wang (see below).

up to the end, and so I begged to differ with his analysis. I said that things decided by our leaders were never, ever wrong. Didn't our China have an old saying, 'If Yan Wang says you'll die at midnight, you won't see the light of the next day?'[1] It was imcomparably fortunate that China had that kind of leader, who was capable of arranging everything, even when one should die.

He slapped his leg in appreciation as he agreed. 'You sure couldn't have said it better!'

I was supremely happy to be praised by this representative of the revolutionary masses. To die without uttering a single counter-revolutionary word would be to die a worthwhile death!

Covered with dust from head to toe, we bounced on into a city that was decked out as though preparing for a major festival. The streets and lanes were already full of people. Fluttering slogans hung down from all the buildings.[2] Dragging our cart, the tractor put-putted under a large banner strung across the street which read, 'We must obliterate all pests which are harmful to men.' As I watched this poem flutter over my head, I felt that the great poet's great ass was sitting on my back,[3] and at the same time that Chairman Mao's large hand was kindly stroking me. The sensation was so strong and so bizarre that for a moment I was dizzy.

The Public Security Bureau was in a large grey building. Later, I discovered that it was the same color as the Cathedral of Notre Dame. We chugged into the front gate and jumped out of the cart, one to the front, one to the back. Two military men immediately approached us, two short soldiers from Sichuan, and they clapped their hands on my old cadre and began shoving him towards the building. All arms and legs, he frantically scrambled backwards, shouting, 'Not me, him! Not me, him!' As he pointed at me and yelled, I saw a great mouthful of teeth.

[1] Chairman Mao is being equated to Yan Wang here: he knows everything, even when one will die.

[2] Since Chinese characters can be written top to bottom, official political slogans are painted on long sheets of fabric and hung from windows when any political message is being broadcast by the government.

[3] The line is by Mao Zedong, who was considered by some to be a great poet. The 'pests' refer to counter-revolutionaries.

I hastened forward, standing erect as I said, 'Young comrades, you are mistaken. I am the one who is to be executed, not him!' I couldn't use my finger to point, since my hands were still tied behind my back, so I turned around and indicated 'him' with a couple of lifts of my rump. In my entire life, I have never dared to correct anyone with such absolute assurance, but in this second of my life I felt the pleasure of saying something that was utterly and undeniably true. It was worth dying just to have this one chance to be so rightly and righteously arrogant.

My pleasure must have expressed itself on my face. The excited faces of the two 'young comrades' darkened as they barked out, 'Who are you calling comrade?' With one great blow, they kicked me into the building.

As I staggered forward, I cast the old cadre a significant look, meaning to say 'get out of here, before these soldiers get it wrong again and haul you in too.' He not only didn't run away, however, he actually brushed off his clothes and tried to follow right behind. The two young comrades blocked his way, saying sternly, 'Beat it! You've brought the prisoner in, now go!' But he said to them in a fawning voice, 'Comrades, let me watch! Comrades, let me watch!'

A large group of men already stood in the room, lined up in rows as though they were praying. I found my own place at the tail-end of the last row, and glanced sideways to try secretly to observe the others. Tall, short, fat, thin, they were each one different, but all similarly hung their heads as if in abject shame. This seemed to be the attitude that people who were going to be executed should display, and so I silently copied their example.

Just as I was wholeheartedly putting on this aspect of going-to-be-executed, an officer of the People's Liberation Army walked over and began berating me for being late. I didn't know how to respond to this, so I decided it would be best to make myself tremble with fear. Fortunately, at this moment the old cadre yelled from outside the window, 'Captain! Captain! That's the one I brought in from the State Farm. The farm's a good fifty *li*[1] outside of town, and we

[1] A *li* is half a kilometer or .3107 of a mile.

got the notice so late we didn't even have time for breakfast . . .'

He wanted to continue, but the Captain stopped him with an abrupt wave of his hand. 'So you even have an excuse for being late!' I saw the saliva fly from his mouth as he screamed this out. 'Do you have any idea what trouble you've caused? Everybody in this city is waiting to see this execution!'

Although the old cadre seemed to shrivel up with the rebuke, his face still beamed with the delight of having narrowly escaped.

I suddenly felt a sense of pride, even of conceit: here was I, with such a huge audience. Thousands of people would be out there, crowding shoulder to sweaty shoulder – this was not an honor that everyone could share. Although the cadre's words reminded me that I hadn't eaten breakfast, I straightened my backbone and stood up tall.

The back of my head immediately received a blow. 'Lower your head!' came the order from behind.[1] So I realized that in order to put on the right show for the audience, it was necessary to assume the appropriate appearance: you could not have a face that was too deadened, nor could you show too much spirit.

This was quite a lot for me to have figured out. There on the wall of the Public Security Bureau was a Quotation from Chairman Mao: 'Arrogance leads to downfall, humility leads to progress.' The blow that I had just received must have been punishment for my arrogance; an appropriate attitude in these circumstances could be figured out only by a humble mind.

With my newfound humility, I gradually assumed the demeanor of my assigned role. The Captain was now reading a list of names – one among them seemed more familiar and I remembered that it was mine. Like a leech, this name had stuck to me for more than thirty years, relying on my own lifeblood to feed it. So I almost cried out when I heard those three words – it was as though the leech had just stung me.

It took the Captain considerable time and effort to finish his

[1] The author notes that students arrested and shown on television after June, 1989 appeared ashamed, with their heads hanging down. It may have looked as though they were free to raise their heads 'but the authorities have their ways of keeping those heads down'. Under such circumstances, he says, it is impossible to try and be a hero.

recitation of the names. Then he drew a long breath and summarized by saying, 'Altogether, forty-one.'

Hearing this number, I was reminded of a weird Russian novel, which I seem to remember was also about executing people.[1] We forty-one names were then pushed out of the room. Each one of us was pinned in by two People's Liberation Army soldiers. This made me think of the sloppy way our State Farm was managing its affairs – sending me in with only one cadre to guard me really showed too little concern for the needs of the audience. It shouldn't have mattered that this was July and the busy harvest season for the farm.

I gave the old cadre one last fond look as I climbed onto the flat-bed truck. With no relatives here, no friends, no women I had loved, the only person in the world worth turning around to look at was him. I saw him in the midst of the crowd, leaping up and down as he tried to see over the heads. The others were leaping too, looking like a great field of dolphins playing in the ocean.

We forty-one convicts were divided among ten large trucks. Just before we set off, a group of soldiers ran up carrying large placards with the inked characters still wet on them. In a great happy frenzy, the soldiers passed these up to the People's Liberation Army soldiers standing with us in the trucks. They had the air of handing out candy before a picnic. The soldiers hurriedly hung these placards about our necks. The weight of them was just right – not too heavy and not too light. We weren't able to lift our heads with them on, but neither were we prevented from moving about. As I watched the excitement, I missed seeing what had been written on my placard, and as soon as it was clapped below my chin I couldn't read it properly. I began to worry that they might have written something like murderer, rapist, arsonist, or thief.

During the parade which followed[2] that was the one thing that

[1] This was actually an anti-Stalinist movie made in the Soviet Union in the 1960s and shown briefly in China before being banned. Most Chinese intellectuals of the author's age would understand the reference. Forty out of forty-one white prisoners in the Civil War are shot, eventually the forty-first is also shot.

[2] Prisoners have historically been paraded through the streets of Chinese towns before being executed, and the practice of public executions continues in China today. In July 1989, for example, public executions were being carried on in Zhoukoudian, to the south of Beijing.

kept bothering me. Although this was truly insisting on having face, even to the point of death, it was hard to change old ways. The sun was brilliant that day, as they always said about Mao, 'shining with radiant resplendence'.[1] I then saw countless sweaty faces looking up at us, enraptured. They had the most adorable looks on them as they tried to read our expressions. From their own reactions, I did my best to figure out what was written on my placard. This proved to be in vain. I soon realized that all they were interested in was the drama, not the crime. It made virtually no difference who was being executed – what mattered to these people was the execution itself.

Some women had brought their children along to watch. Their little hands and feet pointing at me from under their mother's breasts made me almost wild with elation. Since children could not read what was on my sign, the more that came the better. Years later, a political leader criticized my novels for having too much sex in them. He said that this would be a bad influence on the youth of China. My feelings as I heard that criticism were the same ones I had during this parade – I thought how utterly inappropriate it was for children under the age of eighteen to read my books, how much better for them to see as many executions as possible. Not only were executions entertaining, they also had great educational value.

Our ten large trucks circled the city, then drove to the Central Meeting Ground. The Central Meeting Ground was located on the site of a former graveyard at the edge of town. We would be shot to death there as soon as the leaders announced our crimes.

I had been to this graveyard before – in fact a lovely young lady and I once strolled there – but as my thoughts continued I realized that I must have remembered wrongly. Our walk together had certainly been something from a previous lifetime. If it had happened in this lifetime, the cruelty of life would have been too much to bear. I found I was often mixing up things which happened in a previous life with things in this one, like, for example, the cook who

---

[1] The sun, and particularly the rising sun, is a symbol for Mao Zedong.

calculated our bills. The confusion showed that I was already developing symptoms of mental illness.

Perhaps being executed once would help cure me.

Thinking of how I should treat my unstable mind, I failed to listen carefully to what the leader was saying. From time to time, I heard him spouting various numbers. He was saying things like 'one blow against the three,'[1] 'six kinds of people, ten manifestations,' and also making frequent references to Type One, Type Two, Type Three. Our Chinese people really have reached the apex of intelligence when they can use a few precise numbers to sum up the infinity of the world. So few numbers, to pull everything together, and then to split everything up again into 'types'. The most wonderful thing about this kind of world-view is how it can simplify people's brains.

Just as I was marvelling at this, that leech took another bite from me. I heard the leader shouting out my own crimes to the audience: in 1957, I wrote reactionary poetry, recklessly attacking the Party. Later I did labor reform twice but stubbornly refused to repent. During the Cultural Revolution, I tried to reverse the verdict on my case, and so on. Listening to this, I felt that I should be moved to tears of gratitude: here I had committed a crime back in 1957, yet they had delayed my execution by almost fifteen years. In the history of the world it would be hard to find a case of such leniency.

A ferocious shout from the masses in the audience now interrupted my penitence. By swivelling my eyes toward my forehead, I saw a forest of arms spring up before us. The assembled crowds were sitting cross-legged on the field; and as a result I thought for an instant that all these arms were crawling out of the ground. For a moment, I felt my body shake with fear, not from the people's anger, or the slogans they were now shouting, demanding our immediate

[1] The 'one blow against three' political movement was against the three evils of corruption, waste, and bureaucracy within the Party, government, and army and mass organizations. The phrase was used first for a movement in 1951–52, but the author says that it refers here to a movement in 1970. The 'six kinds of people, ten manifestations' refers to a political movement organized in 1970, also during the Cultural Revolution.

execution, but from the shock of thinking that all these people had been buried alive.

After the shouting of slogans, instead of returning to silence the Meeting Ground came alive with the hiss of angry whispers. And as it did, I became deeply aware of the meaning of that phrase, 'Arousing the indignant feeling of the masses.' Two gallant and heroic soldiers of the People's Liberation Army now grabbed me by the back of my collar. With a practiced gesture, they shoved me to the right and then to the left, and I knew by this that it was time for us to march forward. Each of us followed the heels of the person in front, as we moved in single file to the edge of the Meeting Ground. Oddly enough, the convict in front of me was wearing two different kinds of shoes. Fortunately both moved forward in the same direction, or I wouldn't have known which way to go. Since I was saved the trouble of wondering which shoe to follow, I had time to look around for the old cadre.

I had to find him. In the moment when I had been jerked to the right, I had clearly seen his patch of fabric in front of me. The pattern was identical to the one his old lady wanted him to buy, and it was worn by a young girl of around ten years old. It had a blue background and tiny white polka dots. It was strange that over this fabric was also hung a large placard, so large that it came all the way down to the little girl's knees. I thought that perhaps her placard was an ad for the cloth – perhaps the cloth was newly-arrived goods at the department store. I had to tell him so that, even before I died and saw Yama, he would know where it could be found.

We were pushed down to a lower part of the field. The sun was already hanging in the west. From the shadows it cast I could tell that all around me on the higher ground were rows upon rows of people. Openly now, I began to look to the right and the left, searching for him and also keeping an eye on the girl. I thought to myself that before I died I absolutely had to point out her dress to him. By now, the gallant and heroic soldiers were quite obliging – although my head swung this way and that, they refrained from hitting me again. Because of this, I looked gratefully at the soldier on my left. I saw that his front teeth were pressed tightly to the outside of his lower lip.

Ping! The sound of a bullet rang out.

I heard it ring in my ears, but could not tell where it began. It sounded as though the crust of the earth had split open – but I cared less about that than about knowing where the sound originated. Was it from the left? From the right? In front of me, or behind me?

As that vast sound echoed in a circle around the fields, I saw it rise up like a mushroom cloud and I realized that the sound of the shot had come from inside my own mind.

Another shot rang out like the first. Then they came faster and faster and louder and louder like a string of firecrackers working up to a staccato explosion in front of me. Finally, I saw their results.

I saw a field of China Pinks.

GROWN-UPS

Night in Brooklyn, with C, 1987

Execution ground in Ningxia, 1970

I STARED at the China Pinks until they no longer dripped blood.

They stood on a carved chest by the glass doors leading to the sun deck, looking as tranquil as a still-life painting. I found I began to like the vase they were in – its simple, fluid lines made me feel calm. It was like fine white jade, and also like that old cadre without any fussy badges. I felt more relaxed after swallowing several gulps of saliva.

I watched you sleeping, and wondered if it was better for you to have changed me or for me to have changed you. I noticed your exquisite ear lobe and the tiny curve of the top of your ear. They were like a drop of paint that an artist has allowed to flow of its own accord to achieve a round, liquid tenderness. Civilization definitely could not improve upon this ear.

From deep within me came the urge to ravage you. The sensation of this lust was supremely natural, just as when the stomach churns with too much acid.

Please forgive me. I want to make love with you simply to prove to myself that I exist. Right now, women who can most thoroughly prove that I am alive are the ones that I must love most.

When I saw the China Pinks at the execution ground, a sheet of wetness covered my face. Since my hands were still tied behind my back, I could not touch my face to find out what the wetness was.

The whole point of the gunfire seemed to have been to let me see those China Pinks – once I had seen them, the gunfire stopped.

China Pinks have white streaks mixed in with the red. The two colors are very like the thick liquid I saw on the grounds of the graveyard. After the sound of gunfire ceased, one of the soldiers carrying a gun stepped backward until he almost bumped into me. I heard a slurping sound under his feet as though he were wading through a marsh. When he turned around, I saw his eyes. Absolute horror filled those eye sockets.

The crying of a little girl erupted not far from my side. It was a wail that could only have been produced by a ghost. I have always known that man must cry as soon as he is born: can it be that man also cries as soon as he dies? When can all this crying be expected to end?

When I turned to look, I found the patch of fabric on the body of the little girl now violently shaking. Red spots had been added to the pattern, something like the China Pinks. I felt sorry that the cloth was so spoiled, since it might have been used to make the old lady's sleeves.

A man came running down from his higher vantage point, so excited that his entire body was trembling. He bent down to embrace the little girl, saying over and over, 'Lan-lan, don't cry! Lan-lan, don't cry! The grown-ups were just playing a little game on you . . .'

Amazed, I felt that this man said it rather well. Right now we certainly did need to play a little.

The lower field now burst into noisy activity. People's Liberation Army soldiers prodded the two or three among us who could still use legs to walk, and we all clambered up the side of the slope. Although the little girl was still sniffling in the arms of the man, she seemed to have accepted his explanation about playing and was quieter. When I reached the higher ground I saw the rays of the setting sun.

Laughing and smiling, two soldiers took off my large placard. I quickly looked at it and was so astonished I almost fainted: written on this placard was not my name but the large characters for 'The counter-revolutionary, Lan-lan'!

I felt that I must certainly be dead. Could it be that after death I had entered another womb? Was some new father now calling me Lan-lan?

The old cadre came wriggling up, full of high spirits, even jubilant. He grabbed the rope hanging from my wrists and danced around in front of me. He then dragged me along, leading me out through the ranks of people, spitting out huge quantities of phlegm in his excitement. It was undeniably my own name that I heard issuing from his mouth – I was again awakened by the bites of that leech.

So it seems that I am still I.

After a string of exclamations describing his appreciation, such as how fabulous the execution had been, he said he had no idea I was being brought along merely to accompany the others. He thought all along that I was really going to be executed. He told me that in the future I must truly rectify previous errors, and never try to overturn my case.[1] Otherwise next time I too would be left back there, lying on the ground.

Whatever else they did, his words clarified my position and helped to stuff my soul back into the shell of my head. I had to answer him in some way or other, and so I quickly pointed out the fabric.

The fabric had not yet gone, it was still shaking in the man's arms. The strange thing was that when I opened my mouth to speak, no sound came out, not even an 'Ah'. I think this was probably because my mental illness had been cured.

The clever man saw what it was I wanted to say, and he began to tell me about this little girl. It seemed her crime was to have yelled reactionary slogans – that is, when she should have yelled 'Long Live Chairman Mao!' it came out 'Long Live some-other-name.'

'Teach the little whore a lesson!' he said. 'Give her a trip to the execution ground and leave it at that. But if she'd been a grown-up, she definitely would've been shot.'

---

[1] To appeal for a new trial, in order to prove innocence.

A People's Liberation Army soldier started collecting ropes from the few who were still living, yelling out, 'The ropes have to be kept, we'll need 'em again next time. Don't let the bastards get away with them!' So I was not able to find out who else was alive. It did not make a great deal of difference to me. I felt it was sufficient to know my own name.

Just then I saw that my name was written on the large placard being taken off the little girl. It had not, after all, been an advertisement for a store, since after the name was written the words 'Counter-revolutionary'. It was then that I heard not me but some ghost inside me yell through my own throat:

'She's me!'

'I'm her!'

'And neither of us is anyone!'

SONS

Paris, 1988

IT TOOK no more time to tell you this story than it took to smoke a
cigarette. Now that I've written such a pile of words, you must think
my writing lacks the vigor of my speech. I feel the same. When I
take up my pen to write, I find that the letters begin to go crooked.
Where I should write 1, I find I've written 0, and I put the
punctuation marks in all the wrong places. Please don't think I'm
trying to do a Joyce or a Faulkner, writing damnably long sentences
that no-one can understand. I am simply becoming less and less
able to write novels. These days, I often take the truth to be
imagination and what I have imagined to be the truth.

'The End!' I write, and my heart begins to tremble.

I have just realized that 'I' did not experience those things. I
took them from my last life and wrote them into the account of this
one. This, again, is a symptom of mental illness. I will probably
have to be executed again to be cured.

I do not blame you for not coming to Paris. I can treat our time
in New York as something in a previous life.

I walked alone through the mists to Notre Dame. Generally
Natalie and I arranged to meet there, but today I didn't want to see
anyone – I wanted to come see this grey building by myself.

In the Place de Notre Dame I encountered a group of brightly-
dressed American tourists, and thought how only Americans and
Chinese would venture to sightsee in this kind of weather. Americans
had to work off some of their excess energy, while the Chinese had
to get rid of a surplus of dreary gloom. The Americans smiled as
they greeted me, and I smiled and nodded my head. I pulled open

the heavy door and walked gravely into the solemn hall. The Holy Mother with her Divine Son in her arms was soaring over my head.

Tossing down ten francs, I selected a candle that was not yet broken by tourists. The candle's waxiness was long and white, like a naked you. I lit the candle in the still solitude of soft light.

I felt that I should pray for someone on this occasion, so I thought of you, or her, or her . . . but all of them were women from previous lives. Gazing at the Holy Mother, I suddenly thought of the little girl who had gone with me to the execution ground. I had carried her name and she had carried mine, as we paid a visit on death. Even now I do not know if we avoided execution because our names were mixed up, or if the militia had all along wanted to 'play a little game on us'. If I still had a shred of love left in me, she would be the one I should love. She would be approaching thirty by now. Perhaps if the two of us made love, it would be proof that life still clung to the husks of our bodies.

Then I laughed, realizing that I had remembered wrongly again. I had hauled something from the life before last into the life that I am leading today. A person can be buried by the past if his memory is too strong.

It appeared that I had not had a woman at all in this current life. I had only a child. Last year when I was criticized again,[1] that poor ignorant six-year-old son of mine locked himself into the house and violently flung his arms and legs about. He was trying to practice martial arts to learn to be a Huo Yuanjia.[2]

He said, 'Papa, you tell whoever hurts you that I'm going to come and beat him up!'

I smiled at him, and thought, 'The sins of this world can be forgiven so long as they don't take you to the execution ground.'

I placed my lit candle that was so like all of you in front of the Holy Mother, and then moved backward several steps. When I

---

[1] The author was criticized in 1987 during the Anti-Bourgeois Liberalization Movement in China.

[2] Huo Yuanjia was a famous general in the Ming Dynasty (1369–1644).

looked again, the candle had dissolved into the general pool of light and I could not tell which candle was you or her or her . . . But I did see the haunting eyes of a young girl, staring at me through the snow-cold light.

RED FLAG

Paris, 1988

I EMERGED from a friend's house in a fine rain and walked over to the subway station at La Motte – Picquet Grenelle. Lowering my dripping umbrella, I thought of going to see the Eiffel Tower at night, then realized that because of the weather I would see only the boiling darkness of the sky.

So I stood undecided at the station entrance, amidst the wind and trash blown out from the subway's bowels. The ground was littered with discarded yellow tickets. As I looked at them, they turned into the wings of dead dragonflies. B had not died, it was the summer sunshine that had gone, together with the dragonflies and the reeds and the canal's flowing water. I no longer had the strength to go and look for any 'her' of the past. When I reached inside a breast pocket for my monthly pass, I secretly felt for the beating of my heart. It was still there, although I knew it had died long ago.

A group of Chinese and French people had just been talking heatedly about the Great Cultural Revolution in the brightly lit living room of a friend. The Great Cultural Revolution is probably like wine: the more years you keep it, the more you find to say about it. These people drank Bordeaux and ate cheese as they talked, and nobody but me felt the bizarreness of it, the absurdity. Before leaving, someone suggested singing a song together, one that both Chinese and French knew how to sing. In the end, everyone settled on 'The East is Red'. All sang in unison of how China had produced the great Mao Zedong.[1]

[1] The opening lines of the song are, *The East is red, the sun has risen, China has produced Mao Zedong* . . .

I stood in the lift after the party, feeling that all of this was unreal. As the lift descended I felt that I must be in a trance. If my head were set down on a railroad track right now, I would stay there, immobile, believing the coming train was a mirage.

One thing moved me during the evening, a story told by a Chinese student in Paris studying for his doctorate. The story was about Mao Zedong in his later years. During the Cultural Revolution, the student's father served for a short time as a very high-ranking official, so the story was likely to be true.

For several years before his death, Mao apparently sank into a deep, inner loneliness. He would spend the evening before every Spring Festival[1] alone. There were no relatives around him and naturally he could not go out to visit anyone. He would stay in his huge residence in Zhongnanhai, and call a guard to bring him firecrackers. Then he would sit there and listen as the guard set them off, one by one. He would sit alone, listening to firecrackers, from sunset until the early dawn.

Sitting by myself in the subway car, I felt a taste of Mao's loneliness. This single revealed flash of human nature was much the same as whatever humanity remained in me. Mao lost all happiness through grinding down other people, whereas I lost all happiness by being ground down. Suffering from an aspect of the same disease, I could finally feel a measure of pity for him.

I should go somewhere and set off firecrackers too, I thought, to try and ring in a future.

Two pretty French girls playing guitars came into the subway car. Again, it was 'for art's sake', and 'to entertain everyone', but I was pleasantly surprised to hear them play a sweet Neapolitan folksong. The red hair of one of them was like a red flag from May 1968 which had floated down to this subway car from the Latin Quarter.

An empty Coca-Cola can beat out the rhythm of waves as, red hair leading, the ship of our subway car headed for the rising sun.

[1] The Spring Festival is China's New Year celebration, when the family gets together to eat and to rest. It is the biggest holiday of the year.

I was so absorbed in their song, their music, their beauty, that I realized I had missed my stop. I had to hear more while I could. I knew that under the relentless commands of any red flag, the beauty of the song would eventually be gone. Passionate lovers of art would eventually use hands that had created art to tear it to pieces. This was not a premonition – it was my own cold experience.

I finally followed the flow of passengers moving up to the air, not knowing or caring which stop it was. The weather and the women in Paris are the same anywhere you go. To my surprise, I found that there were stars above.

JOKES

Paris, 1988

Atlantic City with C, 1987

YOU DIDN'T COME to Paris and so, fortuitously, you can serve as an imaginary lover to whom I pour out my heart.

It is all the same whether you are here with me or not and, anyway, you used to say that seeing each other only increased the hurt. When you said that, your face was again over-civilized, while I had lost a sense of the meaning of the word. To me, hurt differs from happiness only in the number of strokes necessary to write the character on a piece of paper.

I often feel that neither you nor I nor even the world exists, that all things in the past and the future are illusory. I have searched for the appeal of another country and found only the prevailing presence of the Chinese and the past. I cannot walk out from under this enormous shadow. Watching the ballet *Giselle* recently, I heard the calls of my comrades from the graveyard, as our most respected Troop Leader disported with slender actresses on the stage. So I quietly left, putting up my collar, and walked out into the drizzle and dense fog.

I realize I have been so reformed that I am no longer tolerant of pleasure. I have spent a lifetime learning how to withstand hardship – asking me to enjoy myself now is asking too much. Ultimately, it is easier for me to suffer.

Yesterday, in the library of a Sinologist, I saw for the first time a Chinese *Encyclopaedia of Jokes*. It was published by a Chinese publisher specifically at the request of Mao Zedong. The blue eyes of the Sinologist matched the lovely blue of the binding, as he described to me how difficult this work had been to obtain. He had to spend a large amount of money to get it. In order to make it easier for the elderly Mao Zedong to read, the whole book was printed in thumbnail-sized pseudo-Song typeface characters. Comfortable on his rice-colored sofa, the Sinologist thumbed lovingly through the *Jokes* as though he were stroking a beloved dog.

I sat across from him, looking at the book in his hands – I knew that its contents couldn't be more elevating than the illustrations of *Playboy* or *Penthouse*.[1] I was thinking that when Lan-lan and I were taken to the execution ground, Mao was probably sitting on the pot, reading and laughing at these *Jokes*.

I excused myself abruptly and ran into the bathroom, and got rid of a certain amount of whiskey in the toilet bowl. Strange that jet lag should affect me now, after several months in Europe.

When I lay dying I began to understand that everything in life can be seen as a joke. It's just a shame that the realization came so late.

I don't speak English, nor do I understand French, so in conversations with foreigners I have lost my own tongue. In conversing with the Chinese, however, I have begun to sense that we Chinese also do not understand each other's words. In the end, I can only tell myself what I want to say.

You once said that the words of mainland writers have a latent or even an obvious strain of violence, no matter what age the writer might be. You said that they lack the tranquillity of things written by overseas Chinese. You said that as we walked along the boardwalk in Atlantic City.

I am sure you remember how your high heels kept getting caught in the cracks, and how I kept having to bend down to get them out. I complained that you knew perfectly well that we were coming to Atlantic City – why did you have to wear those uncooperative shoes?

[1] English in original.

135

'My shoes have to match this marten coat,' you said. 'Also, I like to see you kneeling down to me. When you kneel like that, you're no longer a wolf.'

The hell with that! So you only want a wolf in bed!

You pointed out an elderly couple sitting on a wooden bench beside the ocean, and said that they had been watching us and laughing. They must have thought we were a middle-aged couple and found it amusing.

In fact, when I hugged you in that marten coat I felt that my arms held nothing but a wild animal with a thick coat of fur. It's a mistake to think that I am now a gentleman. All I want to do is drag you into the forest, escape from other people, strip off our clothes and bay together with you at the sky. I will never be able to wrap myself in the trappings of an easy, carefree life.

I watched you packing the bags when we left Atlantic City, and discovered that you had brought along several pairs of flat and wedged shoes. You had been determined to wear those high heels just to annoy me – to make me extract them, and to create a spectacle.

Spray tossed up by the ocean's waves carried the chill of mid-autumn as undulating swells broke against the embankment. Sea-gulls swooped and dived over us, their voices shrill with loneliness. We stopped beside a statue of Kennedy, who stood facing west, with his back to the ocean. He faced his country and his lover, Marilyn Monroe. I told you that when news of his death arrived in the labor reform camp, we all held a great celebration. The disciplinary cadre in charge of us said that, 'The head of American imperialism has died! Imperialism has been dealt a mortal blow!'

You did not comment on this, just laughed. From the look on your face, I saw how history degenerates.

A few days ago you lay on a sofa reading to me from an American newspaper. It seemed there had been a drought on my loess plateau.[1] I reached out to grab a breath of wind, trying to smell in it the odor

[1] Yellow earth, or loess, is fertile windblown soil that covers wide areas of northwest China.

of my native yellow earth. I tried to calculate how many days it had been since that earth had felt the rain. But then you brought me a whiskey with ice, and after knocking it back I was unsure of where I was anyway.

When later I returned to my beloved yellow earth, I found it decrepit, old, feeble. It had been plundered for too many years by too many people. Forests had been wiped out by indiscriminate felling. Silently I gazed at a bare ridge of hills, and similarly tried to catch their air. The wind in my hand scorched my palm, which still held traces of the scent of your marten coat. That evening I drank half a bottle of *Baigan*[1] by myself and again was able to forget where I was.

As we stood in front of Kennedy's statue, you asked me which way I wanted my statue to face when I died. I knew you were hoping I might say facing you, but instead I said, 'Any direction. It doesn't matter where I am or which way I face, since the world is round and everything is connected.'

With so few tourists around in the autumn chill of Atlantic City, the two of us enjoyed an empty stretch of beach. We leaned against a railing, shoulder to shoulder, facing a northern wind. Only when your hair whipped against my face was I reminded that beside me there was a you.

You were like a silk doll made in Japan, adorable, but with a wooden expression. I saw that your thoughts were far away, that your spirit had fled your body. Gazing out over the ocean, I saw nothing but its reflection in the crystalline sky. Not a single boat moved across those thin, watery wastes. Although we stood next to each other, each of us was lost in solitude.

I could not help thinking that an ocean without a boat is lonely, but an ocean with a boat is just as lonely.

[1] This is a strong, cheap Chinese liquor.

LITERATURE'S WHORE

Writing in Paris, 1988

About Atlantic City with C, 1987

HERE IN the Bois de Boulogne, I have found your soul. I am lying on the grass, embracing you, making love with you up in the branches. Last year's pine cones still hang on those branches, and now they are cracking open, one by one. The ring you used to scrape against my spine is making such a noise that the pine cones feel moved to join in. They are chiming like the bells outside your window.

After a while, I realize that the rare spring sun in Paris has seduced me.

I awoke abruptly under the pine trees, and could see the lime daylight still exuding its mint-green smell, but I could not see which way the sun had moved. All I knew for certain was that your hands had slipped out of mine, leaving my palms suddenly cold.

Those slender white hands of yours always made me think of piano keys – hands like yours were born for a piano.

You once lifted the lid to the keyboard in your flat in Brooklyn and said you wanted to play me a piece. I covered my ears, begging you not to torment me, telling you that I had no ear for music. The little musical training I ever received had been washed away by the *Quotations of Chairman Mao.* My eardrums had been hardened by the screaming of slogans.

You asked me, 'Well then, what do you like?'

'I don't like anything, except having sex. Other than that what I most enjoy is watching a dog fight.'

You only went to Atlantic City to humor me. The whole way down you described the philistine lowness of the place, as well as my own vulgarity. Watching you talk was like watching a tropical fish in an aquarium. I could see your mouth opening and closing but could not hear your voice.

A Greyhound bus carried us toward New Jersey. We were passing through the birthplace of a new country. The scenery flowed past: factories without smokestacks, fields without people, houses without chimneys. I wondered what the people in this bus would think if, over the sound system, they suddenly heard one of our labor reform camp songs:

> Little sister, I'd like to take it
> And poke it all the way in,
> Poke it in,
> Yes, poke it in,
> Poke it all the way in!

I should thank you for trying to soothe my mind. There are good reasons for my country's being in a mess and you know that the reasons upset me. If you were not here comforting me, I might begin to shout out the window, 'Don't look down on us! Don't despise us! We cannot reform the world, but we can certainly reform human beings!' You put fingers that should have been on a piano onto my chest, knowing that when I see the wealth of another country my mental illness erupts again.

It was dusk by the time we reached Atlantic City. The Greyhound glided silently into the bus station and slowed to a halt. The door sighed open. Neon lights were shining from casinos onto cold, empty streets. But you were not interested in gambling – you wanted to watch the ocean darken under the shades of the evening.

'The ocean is just an ocean,' I said. 'It can't change into anything else. People have written altogether too much about it, it no longer knows what pose to strike. Seeing the ocean isn't half as good as seeing the desert.

'The desert is the virgin of literature,' I added, 'whereas the ocean has become literature's whore. She lets any poet play over her as he wishes.' You scolded me for being as dry and unromantic as a desert.

So I had to accompany you in a walk along the boardwalk. Somehow the normal click of your high heels disappeared, as though we were walking on insubstantial billows.

When we leaned against the rail, it was some time between morning and night. There was neither a moon nor a sun in the sky. I could see only your ivory face. I hugged you, afraid that you would fly away. I was moved not by you, however, but by the thought of my own solitude. I always found it strange that you did not ask about past loves, or whether I had other lovers now. Women on the mainland feel they have to root out every detail, probably because they bring years of political training to their search. As we say in China, with them it is all or nothing. They are appallingly dictatorial in love, possessive, exclusive. I found your utilitarian attitude much more relaxing. The great thing about your love was that it would not become a burden to me.

I knew, even as I hugged you, that you had flown away again, but I did not know where you had gone. And so I decided to annoy you. I said, 'You people in the West seem obliged to emphasize the bad in order to try to be creative. Your bellies are full to the point of bursting, yet you complain just to pass the time.'

You immediately came back at me, saying, 'On the contrary. The art of the West is at a stage of trying to express truth in the most beautiful and most individual ways. You on the mainland are still at a stage of trying to express truth in any way at all.'

You were not far wrong. For over thirty years, we were not permitted to speak the truth. Now, when we are given the chance to say even a little, we toady to the outside.[1]

It was then that you made certain remarks about mainland writers and I found that I might have a violent streak in me after all.

[1] Outside of China, meaning the West.

STEAK

Atlantic City with C, 1987

WE LOOKED at several hotels but none suited your taste. Either the cheap rooms were no good, or the supposedly cheap rooms were too expensive. You would lift your little nose as you emerged from each place. Your sense of pride was as admirable as that of Lan-lan, although she, of course, was going to her death, while you were going to a place to make love.

Because of the similarity, I couldn't help but kiss you right there in the street. You said it was fine to kiss, 'But please don't be so unrestrained. I don't want to get my lipstick messed up.' You wanted happiness, but you also wanted to avoid redoing your make-up – to put on the right face for others you sacrificed your own pleasure. In this, you were a lesser person than Lan-lan, who was natural and graceful even in the face of a gun. Lan-lan was generous about letting all those young friends who loved to watch executions see as much as they wanted to see.

Your requirements for a place to stay had become so fastidious that I began to think you, too, were a little crazy. This pickiness of yours was never cured, even till the day I died. You came running from America to see me on my deathbed, but the minute you entered the hospital, instead of asking how I was, you complained that the lights in the room hurt your eyes.

As we followed the idling tourists of Atlantic City in a stroll through the streets, we came upon a group of people clustered around a luxury hotel. I saw with amazement that each one had a large sign hung around his neck. These people were clearly not waiting for their execution – with hands in pockets, they seemed to be busy doing nothing. We Chinese have others put placards on us, whereas this group of Yankees had made up some placards and put them on themselves.

I pointed out the expressions on the faces of these people, who did not really seem to be wearing the placards voluntarily. You pulled me along until we were some distance away, then told me that these people were all on strike. They were fired employees of the hotel, who were demonstrating to get their jobs back. I pushed you aside and said, 'Great! If you want to spend less money and still stay in a five-star hotel, follow me. We'll go into that hotel and register, and then you'll see.'

We did, and we paid only a quarter of the normal price. We were even given a suite. When you registered, you asked the young white female receptionist why it was so cheap, and she said it was off-season so all the rooms cost less right now. Standing to the side, I laughed when I heard this.

The room was beyond our expectations. We pulled the curtains aside, and the ocean you loved so much roared toward us in its night attire.

You still had your nose slightly in the air, though, when you said that the shade of grey in the rooms did not quite suit your taste. I wasn't sure what shades you did like, since your home in Brooklyn was a cacophony of colors; it was so like a modern painting that it gave me a headache. Now I feel that grey suited you in every way: you emerged from the mists and ultimately you dissolved back into them.

After you combed your hair, we went downstairs to the dining room together. As we waited for the menu to arrive, you said, 'It takes a communist to know how to use class struggle in order to get something on the cheap!'

Of all the ways in which you made fun of me, this was the only one that also made me ridicule myself. I saw through the one-way tinted glass windows that the unemployed with their placards were still demonstrating under the streetlights. Nobody bothered to read their placards except the bleak fall wind off the Atlantic. It occasionally flapped at the corners of the signs to have a look. The group stopped every tourist coming into the hotel to plead with them. They had pleaded with us too before we came in.

I should have embraced these people as my comrades, should have struggled shoulder to shoulder with them. I should have taken on a placard and stood in solidarity in that bitter wind . . . Instead, I was sitting in a five-star hotel preparing to eat steak.

The Russian folksong had been blown away by the sound of gunfire. Impregnable fortresses stood in every corner of the world. How could I remain in America? How could I return to China? Where was I to find my home?

CORPSE SHED I

Atlantic City with C, 1987

Corpse-shed of Ningxia labor reform camp, 1960

YOU HAD already left the room when I woke up in the morning. The light from the sea was shining off the nightgown you had thrown on the dresser – it seemed about to ignite.

You must have stood by the window for some time, since the tasseled curtain still held your warmth.

You had wanted to see the evening colors and now you wanted to see the dawn – from dawn to dusk your eyes followed the sun. We have a similar phenomenon on the mainland in the 'Red Sea' of China, where sunflowers are so numerous they're like mold on walls and wherever they are they always face 'the sun'.[1] No wonder I suddenly ached to annihilate you last night when we were making love.

I stood at the window without a shirt on, relaxing and smoking a cigarette as I watched you below. Your relaxed approach to life had begun to rub off on me.

You were wearing a black swimsuit and sitting on the beach, on the white sand amidst white mist from the waves. From the height of a twelve-story building, you looked like a small pebble – what a beautiful height this was! It occurred to me that I could hurl myself down, through the whole sequence of our beginning to end, and in the eternity of the moment savour the seduction of bare wind . . . before landing on you and smashing you.

Smashed into pulp and bones, there would be no telling us apart.

[1] Mao.

The thought occurred to me since I knew you were sitting there enjoying the sensation of being alone and lonely. Rather than reject loneliness as I did, you actively sought it. I knew that the two of us had not been able to comfort one another, that after intercourse we again parted ways. I knew that the only way for us to be united was for us to be smashed together . . .

. . . I knew because of what happened last night. It was either last night or early this morning. Whether dawn or midnight, I awoke to the most superb moonlight.

Nothing existed except for that light, nothing except for the sound of waves. It was hard to tell if I had died or if the world had died.

The moon expanded, its markings coalesced in a terrifying way. Its rays struck my chest like spurs of ice, while the waves pounded ever more loudly in my ears. Finally, with no place to hide, I screamed in terror, 'The End!'

I am not afraid of dying, but I am afraid of terror. I fear it more than anything. I don't know why.

After a moment, everything calmed down. I wanted to look at you but the moon's rays kept me from turning my head. I could only rivet my eyes on the moon. In its embrace I lost my body, lost my penis, lost everything but a pair of eyes. My eyes and the moon had become glued together.

I became aware of my terror because of our love-making several hours earlier. Making love with you or with any other woman always brings back dying that time – particularly if the love-making is on an unusually moonlit night.

The moon is what I saw, when I finally opened my eyes. It was motionless, framed by a square window, the archaic kind with the feel of a scene in a classical Chinese play. I thought at first that I had returned to the Middle Ages, and then that I had arrived in the halls of Yama, King of Hell.

The remains of a tattered newspaper placed over the window gently fanned the round face of the moon. With the infinite slowness of a louse, the moon's rays climbed over its Chinese characters. One crimson character they crawled over, ironically read 'Leap'.[1]

Gradually the wind died down and the newspaper shreds dangled in exhaustion. Shaken free of the words now, the rays appeared brighter, cleansed, but tragic as they moved slowly toward me. The four rotten boards of the windowframe were dissolved in the brilliant light.

I stared for a long time at the light's source, unable to decide where I was. All was quiet. I heard nothing but the steady breathing of the moon.

With infinite care, my eyes moved the moon's rays downward. Under the moonlight was a wall, and in the dark shadow of this wall were several men, crouching. On further reflection, I realized my mistake – I often link together walls, dark shadows and crouching men, since one often sees them in jail. After a moment, I noticed that a spider's web on the wall was made of countless whips: whips to fan up the waves of the tide under the moon.

Immediately after that, I saw a foot. Thrust into a pool of light, it was rigid and straight. Its five thin toes were splayed out, as though preparing to trample on the moon. The moon's rays traversed five cracked toenails under which hid the mud of the world. He might have just crawled out of a paddy field, and been in such a hurry to reach the moon that he hadn't wiped his feet.

A voice told me, then, that rigid feet signify death. Whose voice was this? Never mind about death – I wanted to touch that voice.

I raised my hand and, as I moved, stalks of rice rustled under my body. I realized that I was lying on the ground, that someone had taken away my warm *kang*. Only when I knew that I lay on a muddy floor did I feel cold, and then I began to tremble. I lost interest in who might have told me about rigid feet – now I wanted to know where I was.

My fingers touched something and the feeling brought back a compelling memory: icy, rough, and oily as wet moss growing on a stone . . . What I touched was a naked corpse.

[1] According to the author, this refers to the Great Leap Forward, the disastrous economic movement begun in 1958.

I was not afraid. My most recent memory was that of handling the dead. On my left were an art teacher in middle school and a horse trainer in a KMT[1] regiment, on my right were a store manager and the chief of a regional fire station. They had probably died around the middle of the night. When the work bell sounds and a roomful of labor reform convicts scrambles from bed, yet certain men flagrantly dare to stay under the covers, then undoubtedly these are men who are dead. Only the dead can defy the orders of that bell. One after another I shook the four men – none awoke. I wondered if something malicious, like a demon, might be adhering to my unlucky hand. While I was living I often examined that hand, thinking that it did not seem mine, did not look at all like my original hand. The claws of some long extinct creature had grown out of my wrist.

Beloved, I am using this very hand to stroke your body. You are quite good, you are not afraid. You know that from that night onward this hand has sought only tenderness and warmth.

I once lay down on the bank of a field when I had a fever. The troop leader yelled at me, said I was pretending to be sick. He said that labor could cure a hundred ills, that the root cause of my problem was that I was born lazy. He hauled me off the ground and dragged me along, and in the struggle I pulled out those life-grabbing claws and gave him a swipe. As I struck out, I thought, 'This time, troop leader, you are going to die.' He dragged me for two hundred meters, as I jumped and bucked, and then with the strength of a dragon-tiger he shoved me back into the field. Beloved, don't think that we did not resist – our hands were turned into claws for good reason.

I can only vaguely remember what follows, and only vaguely remember the setting: an early morning sun was suffused with oyster-shell

---

[1] Kuomintang – the political party of Chiang Kai-shek, which lost the civil war to the communists in 1949.

clouds, the stars had not yet gone, a hundred-soul bird[1] began to sing. It was the hour of day for the troop to go to work.

A light breeze blew gently as the sun stretched over the land, and a line of skeletons began moving over ancient earth. If you listened carefully, you could hear their bones clacking in the wind. Those who were upright were still breathing – they were still alive. Those they carried had already died.

As I walked in this line, this cruel joke of a funeral procession, not a single thought passed through my head. For a period of time I did not have the energy to think. I did not have sufficient calories to support that activity. There is a blank spot in my memory now and this, among other reasons, may be why I have never grown up.

Life relies on nothing so much as habit as it rolls along. This scene was repeated over and over again, day after day. Every morning I would walk in the funeral procession, bury the dead, then do hard labor. But gradually I developed an unusual trait – that of not being able to sleep with the dead.

There was no good reason why the living could not sleep with the dead, particularly since I was often uncertain which category I belonged to. But I had done it too many times, and I knew that I could no longer sleep beside what were known as 'the dead'.

It was this new trait that now made me raise my head from the cold ground, and begin to pant as I looked around. If I knew nothing else, I knew I wouldn't be able to carry the men sleeping beside me. I knew it would be best to try to move to some other place.

The moonlight was exceptionally bright, like the sunlight on the execution day. Now I could see a number of men, as the light slowly found every face. They lay jumbled together on the dirt floor, their eyes open and unseeing. Their sleep was both twisted and serene.

I saw them, watched them, and yet I failed to see what the line was between life and death. I became afraid as I watched, not of

[1] The author notes that this is a solitary bird that lives in the deserts of northwest China. In English it is known as a Mongolian lark.

their being dead or that I too might be dead, but of now being somehow different from them.

I have always tried to be the same as others. I was frightened when I was first marked as a rightist, but later there were so many rightists that I recovered. I was glad to enter the labor reform camp, since most of the people there were like me. Now, seeing them motionless while I was still able to move, I felt ashamed. If they were gone, I would rather be dead myself.

Instead, the light of the moon brought me to life. I began to realize that I was being resurrected after having passed away. For me it is harder to die when I have already died once and been brought back to life. So I decided that since it appeared I could move, I might as well try to crawl toward the door. I knew which way the door was – it was the area without any light.

When I thought I had just about made it to the door, I discovered that I was still lying in the same place. The moonlight had nailed me to the ground by pressing her rays against my chest. I now doubted my resurrection and thought that I might have entered a dream after death.

I felt, nonetheless, that the dream was beautiful. Any kind of dream is better than no consciousness at all. I decided it would be best not to move, to avoid interrupting this dream. In it I had cast off the burden of hard labor, and there was no-one cursing me any more, no-one berating me. If I had not in fact died while others thought I had, then in this slim crack I had achieved a certain kind of freedom.

When I realized this, I began to feel quite comfortable. Sleeping beside dead men was a rare opportunity to get a little rest.

As my body relaxed with this realization, I gradually went to sleep or perhaps died again. And now, in the grips of that death-slumber dream, I saw the donkey cart that hauled me here. I watched again as I was deposited with such nonchalance in this corpse-shed.

I am no longer able to prevent the dream from taking over, from controlling me, as it demands that I repeat once more the experience of dying:

I saw the moon's rays, but took the moonlight to be sunlight. Warm sunshine washed over my body as we jostled along. Two bedraggled convicts chatted as they drove the cart, about whether or not to strip my body . . . like the others.

The older one said, 'My sentence will be up in another two months, and when I get out of this hellhole, I'll have to dress like a human being! I could wear this guy's jacket if I mended it – his jacket belongs to me!' The younger one, walking beside the cart, glanced at my underpants and said, 'So if we strip him, let's take it all. After he's buried nobody's going to be admiring this one anyway.'

Then the two of them struck up a local folk song. The opening line went, 'Heaven, ah heaven! When are you going to stop ruining us?' They sang only that one line, over and over. I wanted badly to hear what the next sentence might be but it never came. From time to time I ran out in front of them to try to catch it, but I grabbed only emptiness. Forever travelling the same old territory in the song alarmed me.

I swayed from side to side as I lay in the back of the donkey cart. The donkey's tail swished at flies, conveniently brushing my forehead and eyelids. Intermittent sighs came from above my head, after which I would smell a rich compost mixture of crushed grass. The donkey's farts took me back to the wide open plains, and for a moment I thought I was already buried beneath them.

After some time we seemed to arrive at our destination. I recognized the place, which was about a mile from the labor reform State Farm's clinic. It was set off by itself on the edge of the open prairie, and was said to have been a storm shelter for sheep herders for the past hundred years. The two raggedy convicts whoaed the donkey to a stop, then the older one turned to examine a corner of the padded blanket that was still stuffed under me.

'This thing is worth using,' he said, 'never mind the holes. The covering could still withstand a few washes, and if you shook that cotton padding, it would be good as new. Damn it all, by the looks of this cotton, this guy must have been a cadre from the city. That's Number One grade, isn't it?'

After they had critiqued my cotton bedding, one took my head and the other my feet, and together they hoisted me off the cart. I have always been mortally afraid of being tickled, but when the younger one stuck his hand under my armpit I was able not to laugh. They tossed me like a wooden log onto the ground, and I thought of yelling at them to put me down in a softer place. In the end, though, I was disinclined to say anything. Then they set to, removing my clothes.

Fortunately, they started with my underpants. They had just got them past the thigh when the older of the two began to laugh. He let out a string of obscenities, and then said, 'Forget it! You see this guy's little prick? It's only as big as a damn silkworm! If we let him go bare-assed to see old Yama, even the ghosts would start joking when they saw it. Let's leave him alone and build up some merit for ourselves on this one.'

The younger convict said that he didn't care one way or the other, and added, 'So if we leave him alone, let's leave him intact. That jacket you were wanting is about to fall apart. Besides, this guy's so thin all he's got left are a few bones to prop each other up. Who's to say, we might meet him again on the road to the Yellow Springs.[1] Forget it, let him take the jacket with him.'

I felt that my face should be turning red with all this but it did not. I thought I should cover that silkworm-sized penis with my hands, but I did not. Might as well wait till I saw those ghosts to cover it up, I thought. To tell the truth, there were reasons for the troop leader's saying I was born lazy.

But the words of these two convicts affected the rest of my life. Every time I made love with a woman I would be aware of that little thing that even ghosts would joke about, and I would feel horribly ashamed.

As I was reflecting on all this, they picked me up, threw me into the corpse-shed, and left. In the end, all they took was my cotton bedding.

[1] Tradition has it that when you die in China you walk along the road to the Yellow Springs. On the way, you meet an old lady selling tea.

I heard the creaks of the donkey cart grow weaker and fainter. It was my only connection with this world but I did not regret its going. Wherever I happen to be is all right with me. The sound became thinner and had stopped by the time I awoke to see the moon. After the moon appeared, all the sounds in the world melted away.

THE PURE AND THE HOLY

Atlantic City with C, 1987

WHEN YOU said what you did, I felt that you might actually love me. You said that that little thing of mine, which even ghosts would joke about if they saw it, was not that small – that if all the pleasures of your love-making with other men were added together, they wouldn't equal a single moment with me. Why otherwise would you cry out so much!

I smiled as my head lay on your breast, and I would have laughed out loud except that your breast was so soft. My greatest asset is that I know myself. All that criticism of me for all those years made me habitually criticize myself. I knew that you were trying to comfort and encourage me, because at the same time you kept caressing my back. If it hadn't been for the hot chill of your ring, like steaming blood and also like cold mud, I think I might have believed you.

Instead, I was thinking, 'Out of everything I have told you, all you remember is that others think my little thing is small.' I was sorry I had talked so much.

Despite my regrets I felt moved by you, and so I penetrated you fiercely to show you that your efforts had not been in vain. I thought that I should make you even happier than you said you were.

I visited a number of cathedrals in France, ancient and modern, some magnificent and some in ruins. I slapped the stones of their massive walls, but heard no echo in return. You had sunk deeply into the river of forgetfulness in my mind. Hymns played by pipe organs reverberated through colored light. I smelled the wet compost of crushed grass, smelled the ocean air, smelled the atmosphere of a grey room and the fragrance of yellow soybean meal, and everything that had ever happened in the past seemed a trick of memory, seemed like the vapors of my mind.

I raised my hands toward the statue of Jesus, but could not catch the slightest trace of past time.

All I saw amidst the hymns was a carved statue expressing pity and pain. I dared not look at Jesus too long, for in the holes of that stone or bronze I might see the eyes of my co-inhabitor. The moment I saw those eyes, I would want to squeeze my finger on the trigger.

The reason I am telling you all this is that I often think of what you said that day, the day we floated together on the Atlantic, and you told me that my sexuality was like that of Christ.

That day, after successful love-making, the sun leapt irreverently out of the ocean. It passed through the room, turning the two of us a crimson red. For a moment I remembered a time when an arc light turned my body and that of another woman a crystalline blue, so glassily blue that we seemed to have been fused together. This memory inflamed the red features of my face and incited me to further passion. In that instant I might already have pulled the trigger, as my body flowed with sweat. The sweat lifted me up and carried me across the room to the sofa on which you lay waiting. When I fell upon your body, I felt I had plunged into a vast ocean.

You said that you saw blood oozing from my body that time.

Years later, when you hastened to China to see me, I had already been cleaned up by the doctor. I was lying under white sheets and smiling at you. I was thinking how all my life I had been searching for a place to die – now, at last, I could be congratulated on having found it. I looked at you, looked at the white room around me, thought of your flat in Brooklyn so like an art gallery, thought of the grey room by the Atlantic and of all our other rooms, and my eyes begged yours for an answer as though I wanted to have my fortune told. Instead, I was hoping that you, or fate, could tell me why I was dying here, not back then in the corpse-shed.

Who took my body and flung it around the world, making me commit so many pointless sins?

I watched you and thought it strange that you should cry – there was nothing to cry about. Could you not see that I was smiling? Perhaps you were crying because I could no longer make love with you. Yes, even at your age you were well-preserved. Your soft, full breasts were showing through your blouse. Please excuse me, however, 'I'm sorry,'[1] as you so often said: that small thing ghosts would joke about has already been pulverized.

An aura of sex pervades the world, even in a respectable cathedral. With his pained face and bloody body so arousing to women, even Jesus with his naked torso is the epitome of sex. You once said that blood triggers a woman's desire. It was when you saw my blood that day that you fully opened yourself to me.

Yes, this world is truly terrible, which is why the pure and the holy come bravely forward: they have decided to eradicate the sins of the world. They want to standardize people, keep them in order, keep them in place under their own rear-ends. They are the reason I have had to die a hundred times.

The day you embraced me, the me that was oozing blood, you knelt by the sofa to caress my body. You played on me as though your hands were stroking a piano, as though you were playing on the sounds of the life within my body. I know that each of my bones has its own distinctive sound, and together we listened to the symphony. The rattle of bones does not make a melody, however – the sound was mild and crisp, like wind through Japanese chimes.

The sun had already leapt away from the surface of the sea. The red had faded and pale rose now suffused the room. Your hair had become incomparably soft – if I had realized earlier, I wouldn't have spent such futile time on the rest of your body. I still hoped, however, to find something of substance within that cloudlike hair: perhaps there might be a gun hidden inside?

You told me that the scars on my body were like those on an excavated sculpture, and I thought how every time you saw a statue in a museum you would be seized with the impulse to caress it. Its rough surface would no doubt lead you into a quiet trance – with one touch you would step back a millenium into the past. The sense of touch can be that powerful.

You said that when you caressed me, you felt time was something physical, hard and coarse. But instead of wanting me to tell you how this or that scar had been formed, you said that you would rather imagine it by yourself.

I smiled at that. You had turned the historical record written so literally on my body into idle musings.

I am sorry to have to admit that Mao Zedong was right. The two of us basically lacked a common language. I'm sorry! Even though I was murdered by that old man a hundred times, it is because of that that I am accustomed to using his words to judge everything in life. Including the love between you and me – that is, if there was any love between us.

I raised my weathered arms and wanted to cast you away, together with the sunshine, the moonlight, and time. I asked you not to do that, said that when your scorching fingers touched me, it felt as though a hot thunderstorm were pelting down on my skin, a thunderstorm like those we have out on the desert. Like the desert wind, though, you threw yourself irresistibly against my chest.

I soon smell the grit of earth through the rose tint, and the acrid sharpness of brambles, of camel thistles. I smell yellow soybean meal, wafting in all directions . . .

And then I tell you not to move, not to speak. I hear death passing through the cracks in my bones. I tell you that although the feeling is ghastly, its coldness allows me to relax. I return to the edge of death after each vivid episode of sex, since the smell of death and that of an orgasm are the same. I say to you, 'Please do not make a sound. I seem to have found a long-forgotten feeling . . .'

CABBAGE ROOTS

Labor reform camp, 1960

I DISCOVERED that my thinking was childish and absurd, and that it generated further childishness. But this discovery came later.

In the corpse-shed I stared at a stem of rice that was being set in motion by the breath from my nose. Under the moonlight this stem of rice was as greenish-white as the face of a dead man, but at the same time it was strong, and proudly upright. It alternately left me and then came back to my nose.

I was amazed when I discovered that its swaying was the result of my breath: I could actually change the position of something in the world. So I deliberately breathed in again, then out, then in, immersed in the happiness of changing the world. A voice seemed to speak inside me, saying that in a lifetime of being manipulated by others, I had never consciously acted on my own. Yet here, in this rudimentary morgue, was something that I was controlling.

Wanting to crawl towards the door had nothing to do with any dog-fart desire to live. I simply wanted to prove that I was different from the others lying there. I tried several times to prove my independence by reaching the door, failed, and finally decided to give up. Giving up trying was like giving up a great burden – I now felt reconciled to dying.

The stalk of rice was still in front of my nose, indomitably, unceasingly swaying back and forth. I gradually noticed the beautiful tracery on its epidermis and, through those lines, the reflected colors of the cold moon. A single stalk of rice can take a ray of moonlight and sliver it into an infinity of colors, changing a deathly greenish-white into the warmth of living flesh.

Many years later, I saw this transformation in reverse on the delicate skin of a woman. That night was moonlit too, although there was no moon. Nor was there a sun, nor even the blue rays of an arc light. There was only moonlight, shining upon the two of us. I saw the light wrap around her and kiss her, madly, wildly, while she, like you, moaned in ecstasy. I told her that instead of kissing her snow-white skin, what I also was so passionately kissing was the curling embrace of death.

My mind was empty in the comfort of death, but at the same time I felt extremely alert. This kind of mindlessness in the midst of alertness is probably the greatest good fortune to have in life. I was exhausted and exhilarated. At that time I had never had intercourse with a woman – it was not until years later, perhaps centuries, that the same feeling occurred when I first made love completely. I will always remember the good woman who taught me how to make love. Her body smelled of firewood and of noodle dough. I also smelled yellow soybean meal for the first time with her, as it spread over the earth in its all-encompassing mist.

Something floated out of my awareness then and slowly grew, like spring bamboo shoots breaking through the tranquil earth.

I was conscious at the time that whatever it was deserved my complete attention during the time I had left among the living. What grew slowly until it shone clearly in my mind was a handful of cabbage roots.[1] Try as I might to think of other people or other things, everything was overwhelmed by their radiance. My mind was unable to concentrate on anything except the image of those pure-white roots.

They were immersed in water in a rusty tin box. Behind the box was a yellow earthen wall. I remember that, at the last minute, in order to keep people from stealing it, I made a check on its exact position. As I gave it a parting glance, I thought that if it was stolen,

[1] Usually the leaves of this common vegetable, Chinese baicai, are eaten, but since there was so little to eat at that time, the roots had become precious food.

it was stolen, but if when I returned it was still there, then I would have received one of life's great benedictions. Where I was staying, in the clinic of the labor reform camp, what was not stolen could be counted as a bonus, something above and beyond the normal quota. Piling up a little extra income, bit by bit, would allow a man to keep on living.

I had nailed two wooden pegs into the earthen wall, and set on them a small wooden plank from the sluice gate of the canal. 'I lifted it, I didn't steal it!' I remember saying, when I came through the main gate holding this plank under my arm. Bowing slightly as I passed by the 'little government' guarding the gate, I nodded repeatedly at him as I defended myself. The little government actually laughed at me and waved me through. His laugh made the bayonet on the end of his rifle soften till it looked as limp as a noodle.

In those days I could still run, and I dashed back to my prison room with that precious plank. In my distant past, unfortunately as it turned out, I once lived extremely well. A sense of orderliness I developed back then had given me the bad habit of keeping my few possessions in neat and tidy rows. With this plank I would be able to organize my things – put the taller bottles I had picked up in the back, the shorter ones in front.

After a day of reform,[1] I would come through the door and see my bottles standing there, and this would persuade me that in some small way I was still living those old days.

I put finely powdered salt in the smaller bottles, and thicker grains of salt in the larger ones. I put crushed hot pepper seeds in the more transparent glass bottles. Between the red and the white my shelf looked like Snow White surrounded by her fat and thin seven dwarfs.

The stomachs of labor reform criminals often swelled up, perhaps because with little else to add to our noodles, we ate too much salt and hot pepper. Being fat and being swollen looked about the same,

---

[1] The author explains that in the labor camp men did not say they had 'worked for a day', they said they had 'reformed for a day'.

so we rubbed our extended bellies and felt satisfied. After all, it is better to die when you are satisfied than to die when you are not.

The tin box with its cargo of cabbage roots was shining before my eyes right now, glowing faintly with the lustre of moonlight. The rust on the box was the same color as chocolate, so that even the rust could make a man's mouth water with greed. I thought how dying did not matter much, but it would be a real shame to waste those cabbage roots.

The roots had not been easy to get. Unlike some of the other convicts, I lacked the strength to dig in the garbage heap outside the kitchen. Those who had the energy to do so would come to the clinic to trade whatever they had found. The man who brought me the roots was a big fellow from the central Shaanxi plain. I was reminded of him years later when I first saw the horses and warriors of the Emperor Qin Shihuang. His skin was like the rough, baked stoneware of a potter, especially in contrast to the fresh tenderness of the roots in his hands.

This man had once been a performer in an acrobatic troupe. Now his thick lower lip was always full of a reservoir of saliva. Drooling a little, he had told me he regretted not learning magic when he was young, so that he could be materializing cakes and cookies for us now. Instead, he had studied the masterful skill of rotating large ceramic jars on his head, and also the art of bicycling on a circular incline. He was called on to perform when the labor reform State Farm had its celebration for the Spring Festival, but by then his thin old skull could no longer support the heavy jars. All he could manage was a bamboo basket, which he balanced on his head as he circled the stage.

He was then asked by the labor reform cadres to make a report to us convicts, and he stood on the stage, still breathing but clearly exhausted. He said that his reform had garnered such a harvest that he had the following success to report: as all performers know, the lighter a jar is, the harder it becomes to balance, but he was now able to balance the lightest of all, bamboo baskets. This proved beyond a doubt that, through reform, he had surpassed the art of his former master.

The cabbage roots that he brought me had been scrubbed clean and sat fat and luscious in the palms of his swarthy hands. He said, 'Little brother, damn it all, I knew you couldn't move around too much, so I took the trouble of washing 'em for you. To eat 'em, all you have to do is put 'em in water and boil 'em.' As he said this, his two eyeballs roved around, carefully taking in my bunk and every inch of my body. I quickly pulled out a pen, to show him that I still had something to trade.

'Fine,' I said. 'I'll take all of those roots! And in exchange you can have this pen.'

He twisted the pen around in thick, calloused fingers, and moved towards the light to give it a closer look. Then, with obvious discontent, he muttered that this joke of a thing was useless. I, too, had the feeling that a pen and a piece of stoneware did not quite harmonize, but I persevered, saying that with this exceptionally fine pen he could write letters to his family.

Grimacing, he said that his old lady had divorced him, but that even if she hadn't, she was illiterate.

I then said that he could pass it on to his son, and I smiled ingratiatingly as I asked if his son had already begun to go to school.

He cursed and said that the old bag had taken the son with her – what's more she had gone and married a village cadre who was at least eighty years old, if not a hundred. He added, though, that in the old man's home at least they had something to eat. He was comforted by the thought that the two of them were looked after.

So then I flattered his broad-mindedness and his unselfish attitude about the desertion of his family. I said that with an attitude like that, he was bound to live much longer than the old man – even if he didn't have enough to eat.

He said, 'What the hell – when you pull out a radish, the hole's still there. Why should I worry? As soon as I get back I'm going to take that radish[1] and plant it straight back in my old lady. Women

---

[1] The Chinese variety of radish is long and thick.

are like that, you know, anybody can drill 'em. If you don't exercise 'em every few days, they dry out.'

With that pronouncement he crossed his arms over his chest and squatted down at the end of my *kang* to wait. His mouth was still full of spit but his thick lower lip declined to say any more. It was clear that this sexually liberated fellow had decided I had to come up with something better.

If I had known earlier that I was going to die that day, I would have traded him the bedding that was taken by the convict on the donkey cart. But so long as people have a breath of life in them, they are convinced that they are not going to die; it's hard to believe, but people can be that foolish.

All I could do was keep praising my pen. 'Don't you realize that this is a Schaeffer brand pen?' I said. 'It's the most famous brand in America! If you were to sell it on the outside you'd get dozens of *yuan.*'

He stayed where he was, muttering, 'Schaeffer, Schaeffer . . . sounds like a damn knife brand to me. Now if it were a knife, a really good one, I'd trade it with you any old dog's day.'

With sudden inspiration, I shouted, 'Knife, knife, you want a knife? There's an engineer down in sickroom number three who has a damn fine knife, sharp enough to shave with. This man's wife is always sending him things to eat; she brings stuff so often that her old legs have been worn thin. He wouldn't want your cabbage roots. But I guarantee that if you were to take this pen and offer to trade it for his knife, he'd do it. That guy knows a good thing when he sees it. And he knows that when he gets out he'll never be able to buy one like this on the outside.'

I could see that he was wavering, so I continued, 'How's this – you go ahead and take the pen, and if you can't trade it off, you can bring it back. If it doesn't work, then it wasn't meant to be.'

This convinced him, and he was on the point of leaving the roots with me when he gave them one last look and began to change his mind. I summoned all my energy and put on a show of being well fed: 'Don't worry,' I said, 'I won't eat them first. If you're not back by noon today, that will mean you've made the deal. After that, I'll take them and have them for dinner.'

Who would have expected it to be that afternoon that I so unfortunately died!

CORPSE-SHED II

Labor reform camp corpse-shed, 1960

I FELT vitality returning as I thought about those cabbage roots.

Years later, I realized that being near starvation had saved my life, by preventing me from sinking into useless reflection. If it had not been for extreme hunger when I returned to consciousness in the corpse-shed, I would have begun to wonder, 'Who am I?' or similar stinking dog-fart thoughts. Although my stomach was often empty of food, from an early age it has been stuffed with philosophy. If I had thought of hollow words instead of food, I would certainly have died yet again.

Fortunately, all I thought about were white cabbage roots. They signified life to me more than my own life did. As my body began to sweat, I determined again to crawl out of that place. I had to prevent some other convict from putting those ten fat roots to good use.

Once again I tried to move my hands and feet. I wanted to turn over so that my eyes would face the door, but the air still stubbornly pressed down on my body. When I thought I was sitting up, I turned to look and saw that my moonstruck eyes were still staring at the ground. The only thing to do was to put myself back together again. One of the dead men heaved a long sigh; when the sound stopped, I was terrified to realize that the dead man was me.

All this difficulty seemed to be a result of the excessive brilliance of the moon. Under its rays the spirits of the dead and the living had congealed there on the ground. I wanted to move my hand and wave away the moonlight covering me, but could not even raise my arm. Half my face was pressed against the icy earth, allowing me to watch myself seep into its cracks along with the moonlight.

The earth and I were united as one, and my eyes became the eyes of the soil. I could not think about my parents or loved ones or friends, or the fact that after playing in it for twenty-odd years I would be saying goodbye to this world. I had no energy to think of where I was going back to, or of those who had been kind to me or who had trampled on me. There was no energy left to repay gratitude or take revenge.

So I thought perhaps I should simply close my eyes and wait for death. It felt so comfortable to have my face pressed against the soil. It must be even more splendid to turn into earth itself, much more wonderful than running around on top of it. If I had known earlier how unscary dying was, I would not have tried to entertain myself with scholarship and ideals. I had wasted my energy, and also the energy and quite a lot of the spittle of those who had tormented me for so long. When we are born, we enter a realm where our certain death is predetermined – how much better to come from the womb a stillborn child.

And yet, from down in the cracks of the earth, from the stillness of the vacuum and absolute zero, I could not help longing for my white cabbage roots. Who but me deserves those roots? I thought. The few friends who had gone through everything with me had died: one who returned from England with a Master's degree in the thirties, who stopped his research in his own field of mechanical engineering to devote himself to learning how to 'democratize' a government; another who was the expert in degenerative potato disease, the man who had written the obituary for me; another who was the secretary of a high official in the KMT – although he later turned traitor to his old master, he had a good heart. He promised that when he got out he would give me his daughter in marriage. More important, he once gave me a piece of flatbread. I plan to write a story about him, since anyone willing to marry his daughter to me deserves commemorating. All these people passed through this corpse-shed at one time or another, first carried in by others and then carried out again. With landlords and the wealthy classes all 'eliminated', it was a rare luxury to have people ferry you about.

I am sure that these people had never been so comfortable in their lives.

Now I gradually became aware of the blaring of a brass horn, as a line of sedan chairs was carried through the moonlight. The reedy whistles and rhythmic clanging of other instruments accompanied them. Revealed through cracks in the earth I saw the bald and balding heads of the man with the Master's degree, the expert and the secretary. Because of the moonlight, I was able to see them smile. And then the roomful of dead people began to stir as they all sat up, then stood. Shaking out their clacking bones, a roomful of dead men began to dance.

They waved their hands and stamped their feet, stirring up a gentle breeze against my chest.

I don't know what they were dancing, but I later mixed it up with disco. As you know, when I went on the dance floor with you, I felt dizzy and had to grab you in order not to fall.

HAMLET

Atlantic City with C, 1987

YOU HELPED me off the dance floor in your Parisian designer dress last night, and we walked out together under the stars. We stood to watch leisurely waves pulse against the dark beach.

I embraced you and felt my hand move slowly from your waist toward your breast, like my morning-glory at home climbing its railing toward the sun.

You used your soft warmth to make me a silent promise, as your supple body aroused me.

I had thought I was tired of the tedious process of moving from strangeness to intimacy, but you were the one who taught me there is no such process. Either a man and a woman are familiar as soon as they meet, or they are destined to remain strangers.

Nonetheless, travelling with you wore me out. It was a good thing you did not come to Paris or you would have dragged me all over the place. Yesterday evening, for example, you made me take you to the casino. I only felt qualified to pull the slot machine, but you insisted on playing roulette and poker. You dropped two hundred American dollars for nothing, just to buy a little attention.

I began to want to peel you naked. Despite your years of American citizenship, you were not as free and easy as an American. And you also lacked the serious, introverted nature of a Chinese, although you were Chinese by birth and, according to you, even from my own hometown. You said that you were you, in the same way that I had commented 'I'm simply myself'.

I once told you that we were both the dragon's descendants,[1] and you said the statement gave you goosebumps. 'Dragons are a kind of caterpillar! Scares me silly!' The only way to make a person of you was to strip off the trappings and let you step into the world. Only without the markings could you reach your desire to be you.

In Nice, I saw a group of nudists in the distance sporting on the beach, men and women who were completely naked. I suddenly thought of your 'caterpillar', and felt a strange itching sensation all over my body. I wanted to pluck those long caterpillar hairs off my body, together with the scales or shells or whatever they are of a dragon, and take you by the hand and join the nudists. I would take with me only the scars on my body which life had given me. You would leave behind the camouflage that the past had laid on you. Together, the two of us would stroll, naked, along the white sand.

After you had seen enough of the ocean that morning, sitting alone on the beach, you came back upstairs and told me you had been thinking of the night before. You'd been thinking it over all morning.

A cool ocean wind had reddened your cheeks, as though the natural color finally dared to peek through the pores of your skin. I wanted to kiss you, just for that, and if you had let me, we might have become closer. But you were too proud, you wanted to be upset.

'I had nightmares all night,' you said, 'because of the things you told me. I dreamed of dead men dancing on the ocean. I've seen only one dead person in my life – I saw my mother's mother in a funeral home run by overseas Chinese in San Francisco.

'The funeral parlor still did things in the traditional way. She was dressed in a long embroidered Qing dynasty robe with a high collar and wide sleeves, and she wore a collection of fancy ornaments

[1] The phrase is the name of a popular song in Taiwan and Hong Kong, according to the author, and it expresses a kind of national pride, incorporating the folk belief that Chinese are originally descended from a dragon. The sacred nature of the dragon to China can be seen even today – it is forbidden to export antique dragon rugs from that communist country, for example, in the same way that Buddhas are not to be taken out of Thailand.

on her head and breast. When I saw her I felt she hadn't really died, she'd just dressed up to wait for her sedan.

'As a result, I fantasized her death. Until yesterday, I thought she was living well, just in some other place. As I watched the sunrise this morning, for the first time I saw the color of blood in the sun's rays. I saw streams of fresh crimson trickling from the clouds into the black ocean. And then I saw my grandmother floating toward me on the light. Her face had no expression; it wasn't happy or sad. The dance she danced was the same as the one you saw in the corpse-shed.

'I was scared silly! If that's the horrible dance that was in your head when we were on the dance floor, I'm never going to dance with you again.'

You covered your mouth and began to sob. I was sorry to see the natural color fade from your cheeks, and sorry also that my lips were denied their natural resting place for a while.

Seeing ghosts is the result of having seen too few corpses. To tell the truth, I feel nothing but contempt for the limited exposure of you people in the West.

I admit I wasn't really angry at you right then, but I felt I should be and so I began to work myself up. The few times I've been angry in my life have all been directed at you. Anger that I never dared direct against my wife or other women in China, I now unleashed on you.

I remember screaming, 'Who wanted me to tell you all those things in the first place? You asked for all those damn stories even though I can't tell fucking stories at all. I had a much better education than you – it's just that I've been forced to forget all those farting books. Have you ever read *Whither the Nanjing Government* ten thousand times?' I shouted. 'You haven't?!'

I pounded on my stomach and said, 'I've had a bellyful of "statecraft", but these aren't things you want to hear. I can also tell quite a few low jokes that we convicts used to enjoy, but then of course you dislike obscenity. If I so much as started, you'd cover your ears and say it was like Forty-second Street. I want to tell you, though, that those convicts were more aristocratic than any fucking peddler of dildos. Most people in the camps then were distinguished men from the top ranks of society.

'You're blaming me for making you see a bloody sunrise, for ruining your precious aesthetic mood. But yesterday, when I was telling you those things, you were actually crying. When I didn't want to go on, you made me. Why did you forget that the minute you woke up?

'You say you had a nightmare last night, but it certainly didn't look that way to me. All I know is that after howling with pleasure you sure looked as though you went straight to sleep. While I was so wide awake I must have smoked at least a hundred cigarettes . . .'

And so on. I lost my temper. I worked myself up so well that in the end I really did get mad. I felt like laughing too, at seeing myself get angry.

But then I saw you were frightened, lying stretched across the bed. Your big eyes had tears in them again. I found it strange that you cried so often, while I could scarcely squeeze out a tear. Your tear ducts really lack discipline – you should have cried your eyes dry before the time you were thirty. Then, on any battlefield of love or war, you'd never have the burden of tears. Like me, you'd never cry, no matter what happened.

When you fell across the bed, you said that I looked like Hamlet, had exactly his expression as I stood before you. What the devil Hamlet looked like I don't know – all I know is he kept saying that 'going off to die or staying alive' was a 'tough question'. I don't think this was a question at all. If, every time I died, I had to think about those things, my head would have exploded long ago with too much thinking. As it was, I died without their even executing me. Living, let alone dying, was not up to me. So when you said that nonsense about Hamlet, I wanted to burst out laughing again.

Since you had described his expression, though, I did my best to put one on for you. I have long been accustomed to performing to the dictates of others.

You chose this moment to slide from the bed down onto the

grey carpet. In a silvery mist, I saw the gloss of your body transform itself into a tender white cabbage root. You slid on over to me and said you were looking for that little thing that even ghosts would joke about if they saw it.

FIVE HALF-MOONS

Atlantic City with C, 1987

Beijing with C, at age of 65, 2001

ONLY NOW, while I write this book, do I realize that I treated you unfairly.

I find the photograph taken of the two of us, in front of Kennedy's statue in Atlantic City. A seagull is cawing as he passes behind, but the sounds of his cries have faded away. As I gaze at that photograph, I wonder what meaning I should put into the smile I will give you when I die.

I can promise to give it to you but, on second thoughts, you would be better off not taking it. It would only add to the troubles you bear – I remember saying something similar to you that day.

That day as we lay on the bed in the hotel, one of my hands covering your breast, I told you I couldn't leave you anything at death beyond a smile. 'Tell me,' I said, 'what kind of smile would you like?' My deathbed smile is like a rubber pouch – no matter what I pack inside, it fits.

You nodded your head as it lay on me, and I heard your hair brush against my chest – like a breeze passing through a forest, or like small cracks breaking through my lies. I felt a bitter smile crawl up the corners of my mouth, as I became aware that my heart was rotting away.

Separated only by the flesh of my chest, I was afraid you could tell that the heartbeats were wearing out, that my heart was like a ball that has been overused by countless children.

I was amazed that I could call on my political education to deal with you in the arena of love. It was as though, in studying communist ideology, I had been attending a life-long school that taught a man how to cheat a woman. For instance, here I was saying that I would leave you nothing tangible, not even one page from a manuscript, yet you seemed content with my future gift of a non-existent significance.[1]

I felt that I had to match your innocence with my hypocrisy. At least both have the effect of adding to the pleasure of love. But I never actually believed what I said. Like a stagnant pond, my heart has been so still for so long that neither execution, starvation nor love-making can stir up a ripple. While you were so very credulous, so ready to believe my lies, tall tales, wild plans – as credulous as I myself used to be.

Do you remember? We woke up together one night and you screamed in terror – it was either in Brooklyn or Atlantic City. You screamed at me not to use eyes like that to look at you, while I wondered what kind of eyes 'eyes like that' might be. My eyes were the same as they had always been. But you were afraid of them, you said, especially in the dark. Then you hugged me tightly. Wanting to escape my eyes, you came even closer.

Afterwards, I sat cross-legged on the bed like a Buddha, using the approved posture of an old monk to counter the clamour of this Western world. My battered heart is, by nature, suited to practising Zen in an ancient mountain temple, while fate decreed that my Buddhism should be practiced in your womb. Your womb is my Boddhi tree. I could write a book about the enlightenment I received there.

While I sat cross-legged on the bed, in silence, I returned to the past, to the prison, to that earthen room in the State Farm. Even one finger of a woman would have been lovable to me then. If you and I had been able to meet back then, we could have spun out a real heart-throb of a love story. But by now my eyes have faced death many times – how can you ask them to glow with a soft and gentle

[1] The author is indicating that the communist ideology promises 'significance' or 'meaning' in the future, while giving people nothing tangible in the present.

warmth? From now on I can only take the play halfway – it is up to the woman to imagine the other half.

Later that night, one of my arms held your naked body, while the fingers of the other hand stroked you from your hair on down your spine, finally sliding down to the bottom of your coccyx. I used three light fingers to give full play to the massage. Those three fingers were like three falling tears, three wriggling snakes. I did not want to seduce you. On the contrary, I wanted to awaken you. You should not have begun to love me from the start – it is a bad mistake to try to love a wolf. The body of a person who has been through great misfortune carries with it a magnetic force-field of trouble, and this trouble is transmitted to all he meets.

When my fingers neared your anus, I hugged you tightly and buried my head in your long hair. My nose sniffed through it trying to find the white hairs that I knew must be there. You guessed that I smelled my mother on your body, and you promised that whenever we met you would never use perfume.

Your discovery surprised me and, for the first time in many years, I was covered with a childish embarrassment. You had guessed a secret that could make that worn-out old ball of mine still bounce. Yes, I wanted badly to use your body to return to that of my mother. I did not want to be reborn again simply to prolong my years. In going through another life cycle, I wanted to keep my heart from being as trampled on as it is.

Do you know that I actually cried at that moment? Unlike you, however, my tears didn't flow out of my eyes – they went from my nose down my throat and into my stomach to mix with my gastric juices. All you felt as your head lay on my shoulder was that I had to swallow hard several times.

In the second half of my life I've been stingy with life, stingy to the point where I've been unwilling to give up anything to do with my body. Except for the necessary urine and excrement, I have held on to every bit that I could. If a tooth falls out, I swallow it.

We hugged each other and I rocked you back and forth. At one point I thought it was not you in my arms but the me of the past. A me that was so soft, so gullible and so self-confident – I wanted to awaken that old me as well as you by the rocking.

At the same time, I knew full well that innocence, credulity and softness make living easier to bear. I knew it from experience. In the midst of starving and dying they allowed me to feel that both living and dying still held extraordinary interest. I never asked who might be responsible for our hunger, for the deaths of so many Chinese. It was as though hunger and death were just a regular part of life.

Life became heavy and oppressive when I lost that innocence. Do you remember the time we ran along the beach, and I followed behind you as in some love scene in a movie? We should have been happy then, should have been playing, but I felt I was no more than a kite being pulled along, a kite that was so heavy you could never manage to pull it aloft.

That evening, as I rocked you, I really did not know what it would be best to do. We were hemmed in on all sides by walls – as you once said, if this world was not too big, then it was too small. It couldn't accommodate you and me.

And so I went insane.

I am certain that I frightened you. From the loneliness of a thin rain in Paris, I beg your forgiveness.

You once said that you were destined to spend the rest of your life worrying about me, that before we met you had been a carefree soul, but after you met me the worry in the second half of your life would more than make up for the lack of it in the first. This was like the current saying in China, about taking make-up classes in capitalism.[1]

You generously told me, nonetheless, that I should do whatever

[1] In Marxist history, society progresses in the following steps: primitive to slave to feudal to capitalist to socialist to the end goal of communist society. The Chinese government's excuse for introducing a partial market economy has been that the Chinese have to go *back* a step and learn capitalism before being able to proceed to the goal of communism. The end goal is still communism. China is not 'going capitalist', it is just doing 'make-up classes in capitalism' as a means to get to communism.

I wanted. Such blanket approval was something I had never heard before.

And so I got even more than what I wanted. I tried desperately to open the window, below which stretched the pure white sand. Each strand of my hair stood on end, while those eyes which you so feared were on fire.

The people who built those gambling hotels must have known that certain of their guests would want to kill themselves: the windows of the building were tightly sealed shut. I did not want to commit suicide – I believe you will be able to understand that. If I was going to die, I wanted to die on my native soil, on the soil of the country that had tormented me. I saw tolerance and approval in your eyes – you knew that only by erupting could I cure my madness.

Not able to open the window, I turned to the icebox, and brought out all the bottles of hard liquor it contained. I had wanted to pour it out of the window, to let the winds of the Atlantic waft it away. Since I could not cry myself, I would let alcohol cry for me.

All this had been staged in my mind. It had the undeniable flavor of acting, but who among us has not become adept at that? We have been pushed onto the stage too many times, to be criticised and struggled against, not to know that acting has become the most important part of a political movement. Lowering the head, trembling with fear, curving the back as you bow down, demeaning yourself, pretending to be stupid, pretending to be absolutely blank – I had had more than enough experience with all of that. I wanted now to act the role of unrestrained lunacy. Otherwise, my training on this stage of life would seem rather too incomplete.

I opened the bottles of liquor, one after another. Since I couldn't cast them out of the window in a heroic gesture, the next best thing I could do would be to cast their contents into myself. But I couldn't get drunk. It would have taken twice the number of those small bottles, each not much bigger than a penis, to knock me over. I was determined to arrive at my artist's conception of what it meant to be drunk. In the miasma of drunkenness I might find a heart in me that was able to love.

You sat on the bed, watching me in my drunken rage. At one moment, I saw in you the calm eyes of my mother.

I really should love you.

Please forgive me for using the word 'should'. All my life I have been reading and hearing should. Should this, should that . . . Only if I did what I should would I be doing what was right and proper. Even love, irrational love, has its clear stipulations. We have a maxim in China, 'There is no love without its reasons', so that even before getting sexually aroused everyone has to analyze it sociologically.

I followed my lessons to the letter, doing everything that the books and the newspapers told me to do. I truly loved what the regulations said I should love. But the final thing I should love[1] wore me down till there was nothing left, and from then on I no longer dared to love.

In the past, I remember once loving my mother. But then my teacher[2] warned me about her, told me not to love her any more. According to the laws of class analysis, she belonged to the bureau-cratic class – she should not take any pleasure in bearing such vile, evil spawn as me. All the crimes that later came down on my head were the direct result of her happiness in giving birth to me. So my teacher split me off from the mother I loved. Then I fell in love with the first woman I encountered, but the Great Teacher warned her that she should 'draw a clear line' between the two of us, that according to class analysis, I belonged to the capitalist class, and so he split me off from a woman who loved me. With no-one else to love, he said I should love him, that he alone was the saving star of all under heaven. Without him, I would immediately go to hell. And the way to love him best was to fill my breast full of hatred: hate became the ethical standard of the new world.

[1] Not specified in the Chinese, but the author says it would be obvious to Chinese readers that this refers to Mao Zedong.

[2] Again, the 'teacher' here is Mao Zedong.

He had used the slightest tap of a single finger to destroy my primitive sense of love, like flicking over the first of a set of dominoes. From then on my ability to love was maimed. The most adorable creatures in the world could not stir it: it became impotent. When I later began my ceaseless quest for women, it was actually a quest for feelings inside me that would enable me to love.

Yes, you are adorable, and I really 'should' love you. You are acceptable even by class analysis for, at the worst, you belong to the middle class. I 'should not' destroy you, cheat you, frighten you or hurt you. But I have scraped every corner of my heart and I still have not been able to find love. I am like an Oriental *qigong* master who has been wounded and can no longer muster his *qi*.

You say that you have a habit of scratching your sex partner when making love. For the first time in your life, in order not to hurt me in your passion, you have made the sacrifice of cutting your fingernails.

I remember lifting each of the half-moons on those nails and putting them, one by one, to my lips. Please forgive me, it is a gesture I have repeated with other women in my life. Each time I have tried to retrieve the emotions of that first time, a time that is now as distant as though it had happened in another century.

Now, kissing nothing but the ends of your fingers carries another kind of 'significance' – again, please forgive me, you see I have been suckled on that word.

You sit serenely on a square stool by my bed, no longer complaining about the bright lights in the sickroom. In Atlantic City you had seen how I went crazy, now you have come to Beijing to see how I die. I am glad to be able to put on a show for you, to perform the complete and final act. This performance will prove that I have mastered all the tricks of the acting trade. At last I can enter the role of the character I am playing. You always wanted me to tell you of the various ways I died. I have a supremely gifted tongue, drilled in the school of Chinese politics, but I can still act out death more vividly than I can verbalize it.

I see tolerance and approval in your eyes, the same as I saw in

Atlantic City. You have spoiled me rotten. When I went crazy you said it was good to be crazy, and now that I am dying you say it is good to die. It's like when I made love to you, you told me you were satisfied every time. My God!

And so, for one final time, I motion to you to bend forward. I want to smell the odor of my mother on your body. Thank you, you have kept your promise. Busy as you are, you have remembered to wash the lotions and powders away, and you haven't used a drop of perfume. Your unadorned face and hair are now slowly drunk in by the eyes that you so fear.

You spread your hands before my eyes but I lack the energy to kiss those ten half-moons. I can only smile, although this final smile has its own significance. For I see by your hands that you have been waiting, all this time, to make love with me again. Since we last parted ways, in Hamburg, you have been keeping your fingernails trimmed. As I predicted, the second half of our story has been woven by your own imagination.

All you can do now is cover my lips with five of those half-moons. 'Don't talk,' I hear you say.

Yes, do not talk: I have already said too much. Spoken too many empty words and lies. Asking me to say less is asking that I commit fewer sins.

Finally, I see five half-moons rise again. Those fingers which once clawed me now ever so gently close my eyes.

If not you, then whom should I have loved? I had been flapping broken wings, searching for a place to land, when you caught me, and taught me to come home to roost in the fulfilment of satisfied lust. How simple and yet how fruitful love turned out to be. And yet I still pulverized that little thing that even ghosts would joke about if they saw it.

Please forgive me for not leaving you anything.

You still, however, have your imagination: up to my very end you have seen significance in everything.

THE DEAF DOCTOR

Labor reform camp:
corpse-shed to clinic, 1960

I WILL NEVER forget being carried from the corpse-shed to the clinic. It's said that without forgetting there can be no happiness: my misfortunes must not have been brought on by circumstance – they must have been self-inflicted, the result of my superb memory. It's no wonder that we Chinese writers are instructed not to write about the anti-rightist campaign or the Cultural Revolution. If literature did not relive the past by continuing to describe it, if it limited itself to describing the prospect of a glorious future, we could all live much less troubled lives.

When I was carried out, I did not open my eyes. I didn't know the season and I was unaware of the weather. I had spent a long period of time when it was necessary to know the season or weather.

But even as they carried me out I was able to see through eyelids that you stroked down many years later. I was able to see through them and see the sky.

So it surprised me that when you finally stroked down my eyelids, I could no longer see the world. I once used three fingers to massage and awaken you, but my fingers had none of the force of your crescent moons: I've come to realize that it is much easier to infatuate people with promises, or even to lead them to their own deaths, than it is to awaken them to use their minds.

I saw the sky and I vaguely remember clouds. The clouds changed shape as I bade them to, until they came together to form the image of my ancestor.

'Hey,' he said, 'he's still living – I hear his heart beating.' Something cold poked me in the chest several times, and I began to realize it was not my ancestor but the deaf doctor saying these words.

This man was the only convict doctor in the labor reform troop. He was not the man who had encouraged me to cut off my leg. He was a 'rightist'. Although convicted of this crime, his only real fault was to have treated and cured 'rightists'. If one were to follow this particular line of logic, the cooks and other non-convicts working in our troop should also have been labelled rightists. Fortunately, the troop leaders were not schooled in logic: they attached the label only to this intellectual, this doctor.

He was deaf, but he could hear my heartbeat, so my heart must not yet have run down.

Someone else was now saying, 'When we came back to pick up the bodies, we just couldn't open the door, no matter how hard we tried. We had to take it off its hinges. We found this guy lying right behind!'

I had the feeling that a distant finger was pointing at my body. This finger stirred my memory, and I seemed to remember crawling a huge distance in that small morgue.

'So I thought to myself, how can a dead person block a door? And I turned him over and felt that he was still breathing, and then I decided to call you over. Well, what do you say, Doctor, shall we bury him or not?' A person who could ask a question like that must really be a genius.

'Of course we can't bury him!' the deaf doctor barked back. 'I know this man. In fact, he used to be a poet. Get him back to the clinic.'

So I, and my floating world soon began to sway again.

The sky lightened – I do not know if it actually lightened or if the clouds simply went away. It had probably been dawn when they came to the corpse-shed to get the bodies, for the daily burial trip to the fields. The morning air filled me as though I were a great balloon, so that all my internal organs seemed dissolved into nothingness.

Drifting along, I imagined that a short and skinny deaf doctor was walking along beside a donkey cart I was in. His head hung down and I heard the soft slaps of his broken shoes as they came down tiredly against the yellow earth. Four listless hooves kept the slaps company as we plodded along. Not long ago, there seemed to have been someone else singing near me on this same road – the words were so sad and the song so plaintive that it could hardly be called a tune. Yes, that had clearly been a scene on my way to the corpse-shed. If I had been saved, why were they sending me this way again? I did not feel in need of this funeral march. I could not figure out if I was moving towards life or death.

For years to come, this confusion made me unable to keep the Yang world straight from the Yin.

Whether I was on my way to the Yin world or the Yang, it was naturally more comfortable to ride in a cart than to have to walk. The sun was in the place it normally occupied, and a warm breeze brushed over my skin. Now and then ripples of shadow played over my closed eyelids, and sometimes the trickling sound of water flowed into my ears. These sounds brought an awareness of time's eternity.

The awareness suddenly sparked my inspiration. Set between two worlds, I felt I had been given extrasensory powers to see the future.

From the pit of my stomach came an overpowering need to talk, just as when you have too much gas in your intestines you simply have to fart. I had to tell the deaf doctor of the inspired images in my brain.

One day, several years later, when the entire country was in the grips of armed struggle,[1] I fled to the town in which he then lived to try and see him.

A hard rain was pouring down that day, bringing torrents of dirty streams from the highlands and softening the cinder road. I jumped over bank after bank of mud, and finally found his place. It was comforting to see that it was even more primitive than our labor reform camp barracks. If they took him in again as a result of my

---

[1] This was at the start of the Cultural Revolution in 1966.

visit, it would be all the same to him. Short people, just to play safe, should always get used to living in little houses.

Swaying back and forth as I lay in the donkey cart, I foresaw that day in my mind when I stood below the low rafters of his house, while water poured from his roof straight down my collar. A white-haired middle-aged woman opened the door for me and I immediately recognized her from pictures I had seen. Together with two children, she had always been stuck in the doctor's dilapidated wallet, next to his copy of the court's verdict on his case. I remember his happiness on the occasion of yet another anniversary of his long sentence. He had wanted to show me this picture of his family, from which he derived the strength to carry on. Today I saw this woman rise from that torn picture and stand before me . . . and stare at me with eyes that were colder than the rain. Whether it was the rain or that look in her eyes, I felt my body begin to shake. Behind her, resting on a black table, was a photograph of the doctor. It had a black sash tied over its frame.

You and I took many photographs together, in Central Park, by the East River, on the island of the Goddess of Freedom,[1] and when they were developed you watched me carefully examine every one. You asked if I was afraid of their falling into the wrong hands. 'If a comrade finds them, do you think they could be used as a handle against you?'

'The hell with that,' I answered, 'if they get me, then they get me. I'm looking for something different. It's said that a person's picture changes after he's dead: I want to know what changes there are in my photographs now that I have died.'

You said that I was crazy, that I never seemed to think like everyone else. Now you realize that I have seen a photograph of the dead and, at the same time, seen the person alive. I have compared the two, just as the government compares photos on wanted circulars with an escapee. You should realize now that I am not crazy – it is the world outside that is crazy.

[1] The Statue of Liberty is known in China as the Goddess of Freedom. This was written before students erected a similar statue in Tiananmen in late May 1989.

Back in the donkey cart, I wanted to laugh. I wanted to tell the deaf doctor what I had seen on his black table. He had never looked so well-groomed in his entire life, his hair parted in the middle and slicked down on either side. A small smile still played around his lips.

But his wife said that this was a photograph from his college days. She told me he had recently died in an 'armed struggle' between one factory and another. As he was trying to rescue the wounded, an unbiased stray bullet hit him in the head.

I stared at the photograph as though demented, trying to see whether or not the bullet had gone cleanly through the part in his hair.

I found I could not laugh, though, as I lay in the cart. I couldn't even open my mouth. In the cracks between this world and the other, all that I could see of the future made me sad.

The deaf doctor was still driving the donkey cart, and the road seemed very long. Without knowing that his own end was near, he was hastening to save other lives.

I wanted to tell him, 'Look, after you're let out, whatever you do, don't go trying to save anyone else. Let me be the last one on your list.' This was not because I was selfish or even concerned about his life, it was because his death would deprive the world of some of its color. If one is to be concerned for the world at large, then some people should never die, while others should try not to live too long.

His wife blocked the door, and refused to let me in. Many regular citizens on the outside have this misconception. They think that their own relative is the only one who has been wrongly accused – all the others are in the camps for some good reason. They're all undoubtedly no-good scoundrels who deserve whatever punishment they get.

Only their own relatives are entitled to feel wronged by the countless wrongly decided cases in China. Except for one's own case, the skies are blue and the world is just.

This is, by and large, the traditional Chinese way – we take care of ourselves and our relatives, and let the rest of the world be damned. This wife was a good example: as soon as she opened the door her attitude was cool and apprehensive. All I could do was stand in the rain, looking through the doorway at the deaf doctor's eternal smile.

I told her that her husband had saved my life, told her this and that, went through all that was happening today. The rain was making me so wet that my words became increasingly precise. The thought crossed my mind that all writers should be obliged to do their writing in the rain. Nevertheless, perhaps because the doctor had saved too many people, she was not inclined to feel moved.

I hastily raised a bag of sweets and asked her to put them as an offering before his picture. This changed things, and made her somewhat more willing to talk.

She said that the one thing that was bothering her considerably was whether or not the factory would make him a 'martyr'. If they bestowed this posthumous title on him, it would substantially affect her bereavement pension. It would also change the future opportunities of her children. Getting them schooling and a job might depend on it.

This took me by surprise as I stood in the cold rain – it seemed to blaspheme the idea of mourning. She sensed my coolness and, misinterpreting it, thought I must be an official sent from the factory. So she stiffened her back and began to argue. She claimed that although the doctor had not been on the actual battlefield, he had been only a few feet away from the 'East is Red' guard building – it was perfectly accurate to say that he had fallen on the front line.

'East is Red' . . . What is that? I had always thought it was a song. I had just come out of labor reform again and must have grown stupid in my captivity, but I did not understand what this 'East is Red' really meant. Many years later when I heard the song in Paris and was even asked to join in and sing, I again felt myself turn into an idiot.

My doubtful look confused her. It made her think I blamed the doctor for not being sufficiently careful. In her frustration and her rage, she shouted, 'Do you mean to say none of you knew he was deaf?'

The distant sound of her voice, coming to me there on the donkey cart, made me realize that the deaf doctor truly was deaf.

'Yes, and better off deaf!' I shouted back.

LIZARD TRACKS

Paris, addressing C, 1988

Labor reform camp, 1960

ALTHOUGH I lack the ability to make you understand, I must try to explain one thing to you: it is not entirely because we lack a common language. I am lying quietly on the lawn in the Bois de Boulogne, lying beside Natalie, thinking about you.

Natalie is playing with a blade of grass – she says this thin green sliver can predict the outcome of our love. She lifts the grass to the sun, observing it carefully, as her hair spreads a golden net over the spring trees. I have looked the whole world over, and the more I see the more confused I become, whereas she can look at one blade of grass and see in it our future. With this kind of woman by my side, I am forced to recognize that I must be some strange kind of demon. The language of demons and humans is mutually unintelligible.

I fear people will say I am copying Faulkner, or Joyce, by intentionally making my writing incoherent. Those writers turned conversations into a similar sort of demonic language. I beg you, please remember that what I write has its own internal logic. It may sound crazy to the West, but it is fully consistent with the logic of the world in which I live. If you and Natalie were to die several times, then perhaps you too would see the consistency of my words.

Since the deaf doctor was deaf, I couldn't tell him about what I saw. I lay in the back of the donkey cart, allowing him to take me where he thought I should go.

The sun that day was very like the sun now, here under the trees in the Bois de Boulogne. I have always savored the fact that by closing my eyes I can make the whole world into the same place. Because of my training in that exercise, I can believe right now I am in a donkey cart meant for hauling corpses. I quickly wrap my fingers around Natalie's hand, to prevent a sudden slide to another world.

With eyes closed, I caress each of her fingers with my thumb. Unlike you, she does not clip her beloved nails, and their sharp edges make my pulse quicken in fear. I climb each in turn, carefully, like negotiating protruding rocks on the face of a cliff.

Unlike you, Natalie does not have the habit of clawing her unfortunate sex partner. After we make love, her delicate fingers lightly touch my back, daintily playing from my jade pillow meridian down to my anus. Although she must consider it a form of massage, it sometimes makes me think I am already lying in the grave with five active ants crawling down my spine. It has its effect, though, and generally brings me to life, teasing out my virility for another round of love-making.

For a moment, let us say that I am lying quietly in that donkey cart, lying just as I am lying here. Natalie has become the deaf doctor who silently follows the cart, immersed in thought. He does not know he will soon die in a nationwide 'armed struggle', and so he still has plenty of things to think about.

I have decided that we must have discussed something, or else I would feel that I had wasted that stretch of my life. Even though most of my life has been wasted, I am not willing to lose that particular time.

The deaf doctor could not hear, but I was determined to speak. I had to tell him about that extraordinary experience. To be dead and then resurrected is not something every dead person has the good fortune to experience. This was more worth boasting about than even the glorious title of being an Ardent Student of the Works of Mao.

While I foresaw that he would soon be sacrificed, I also foresaw that in a few years' time I myself would be returning to the labor reform State Farm.

I saw that I would have become arrogant, for I had been designated captain of a team of convicts. I foresaw receiving an order one day to take my team to collect human bones from the graveyard.

In the fields some five or six kilometers from the corpse-shed, we searched among the many small mounds of earth and among the myriad garlands of lizard tracks that braided the mounds together in the dust. In those mounds I found the bones of my corpse-shed companions.

Somebody – perhaps that same genius who was willing to bury me – had been clever enough to stand a brick up in front of their common grave. No names were written there, only a date: the year, the month, and the day. The brick had weathered and the traces of carving were faint. Ephemeral, and yet still there, Arabic numerals passed on news from another world. I could still make out that this was today, the date on which the deaf doctor came to the corpse-shed to bring me back.

I shook the dirt from their skeletons, one after another, regretting that from now on they would no longer dance. Then, one by one, I packed them into plastic bags, like those you use in the supermarket. It seemed slightly odd that I did not find my own skeleton.

I listed a handful of sandy soil and let the wind slowly blow it away. And then, in the grey sunlight, I stuck my hand deep into the earth.

I wanted to experience the feeling of being buried, for I knew that among my companions there must have been some who were buried alive. Shock and death can resemble each other. Imagine, if the genius had not called the deaf doctor over, and if the deaf doctor had been noncommittal during his examination, then today I would be finding my old bones among these tombs. I felt the guilt of not having been buried with the others.

If I had been buried alive, the first thing that would have rotted would have been that little thing – that little thing that even ghosts would make a joke of if they saw it. Without that organ of love, even if I had crawled from the grave, I could not have made you love me.

ANCESTORS

*Labor reform camp,
on the way to the clinic, 1960*

AND SO I became garrulous, there in the back of the donkey cart. A man's body has two organs that are alike in being both the busiest and the most powerful. One is his tongue, and the other is his penis. He uses the tongue to conquer other men and to win their approval – either to rally men behind him or to show off as he follows someone else. He uses the penis to conquer women. He begins by giving the sweetest of names to what is basically nothing but sheer possession. And he ends by saying that love-making is the necessary consequence of 'love'. Since the deaf doctor was a man, I pulled together what vitality remained, and stirred up my tongue to conquer him and to please him.

The donkey cart jolted along, creaking as it went. Over its creaking I shouted, 'Hey, Deaf One, do you know what I saw in the morgue?'

Without the slightest sound he answered that he had no idea, that he only knew he had a wife at home and two children, and that if they let him out this time he might be able to have a third.

I mocked his desire for descendants before telling him that I had seen my ancestors.

They stood before me in swirls of incense, lined up on the altar of the family temple. I had taken a boat out to see them, and passed through endless shrouds of white mist.[1] In my death dream I clearly remembered that it was shortly after the War Against the Japanese[2] that my parents and I went to make this obeisance at the ancestral hall. Since I had already died, what harm could come from making this into a voyage of my soul after death?

Although I had my eyes closed in the corpse-shed, I was still able to see the golden ripples of the river under the boat. One of my elders told me that this was the very place where my ancestors had plundered and murdered. At any time a powerful arm might be thrust out of the quiet surface of the water, to demand your life or your money or both. I had just learned the new term 'entrepreneurs' from the newspaper. In those watery wilds, the entrepreneurialism of my ancestors made me shudder.

The elder went on to say that these entrepreneurs were forever turning traitor and going over to the other side. When the Taiping Rebellion came they joined the Taiping Army, when Zeng Guofan came they went over to Zeng Guofan. By going back and forth, my first ancestor advanced from being a bandit to being a Taiping prince and then an ambassador to Xinjiang, emissary for the Manchurian court of the Qing dynasty. Later the descendants of this man turned again and joined the anti-Qing revolutionary army in Tokyo. All these ancestors descended in a straight line to me.

My oldest ancestor now tugged on his white whiskers as he spoke from the altar table, and his wise old smile gazed out at the world with respect and approval. Switching sides so often no doubt implied a certain freedom, but this I learned to envy only later when I was in jail. For by then I, too, wanted to change sides, but the righteous camp of the opposition would not take me in.[3]

[1] The author's ancestors came from the misty, watery region of Jiangsu in southern China, where transportation has traditionally been by boat through a network of small rivers and canals. The ancestral hall outside the house that he mentions was common throughout China before 1949, and is nonexistent now.

[2] The Chinese call the Second World War the 'War Against the Japanese' which for them began on July 7, 1937.

[3] The righteous camp of Deng Xiaoping. This relates to a period in the author's own life, before the downfall of the Gang of Four, when Deng and others were forming an organized opposition.

All the other ancestors on the table had an air of great solemnity. Each wore the ceremonial attire of his own period of history. Official solemnity and a proud, erect carriage are necessary props for those who are either bandits or the descendants of bandits.[1]

All these ancestors glared at me as they asked, 'Did you or did you not betray your family? Did you not, indeed, betray the entire class into which you were born? You were foolish, you tried to surrender to a Western ancestor,[2] and because of that you are writing a self-confession that is over one hundred pages long.'

I thought that my ancestors' voices would have a thick back-country twang, but I discovered that their accents carried the same mix of north and south as mine.

'Yes.' I did not deny it. 'I have written a self-confession, and it will not be limited to this one hundred pages. It may be two hundred or even more – moreover, I plan to keep writing. You don't understand,' I said. 'Things are not as they were in your time. It isn't easy to rebel now, and it's even harder to surrender. At times, people simply don't know what to do.'

One ancestor let out a huge belly laugh which made me angry. He had no conception of how difficult it is to live in these complex times.

'Forget it! Just forget it!' I yelled. 'In the beginning I was nothing more than a wandering soul, which by some fluke happened to land in this particular family, in a country called China. I've been knocking around in this lifetime for twenty-odd years, and although it may not sound like much to you, I've had enough. This planet has so many holes to fall in, it's like a torn fishnet. From now on, I'd like to have done with it all. I take my leave: not only from this world but also from you!'

'Well then,' an old one said kindly, 'you seemed to be wandering aimlessly around, but why did you just happen to wander in here?' I couldn't tell if this man was the second or third generation, as he continued, 'It is clear to me that you are still a filial son. Remember-

---

[1] Although not all of this book is autobiographical, the author says that this part is. The bandit who later became a famous official was his great-great-great grandfather, or six generations back.
[2] Marx.

ing one's ancestors constitutes the true moral excellence of us Chinese.'

His words almost scared me back to life. Yes, it was true. Why had I wandered back to my origins? There were fluffy white clouds out there and a fresh spanking wind – why had I come floating straight to this gloomy ancestral hall? Except for strange portraits of past centuries of ancestors, there was nothing here but a few fat mice. In a flash, I realized how difficult our habits are to change. We Chinese have always looked back to our ancestors – when living and also, it seemed, when dead. No wonder we call it 'going to see Marx' when revolutionaries pass away.

So I said, 'Who wanted to come see you, anyway! It was Marx I wanted to see. It's just that they wouldn't let me in.'

With murder in his voice now, the bandit ancestor growled, 'Don't give me any of your Marx, but who is this "they" who wouldn't let you in?'

I hastily answered, 'They are a group of real revolutionaries – much more revolutionary than anyone who opposed the Manchu government. And the reason they wouldn't admit me is because of all of you. They have tracked the vine back to the melon, following my genealogy generation by generation, and it turns out none of you has ever done anything good. On the contrary, the many sins you've committed now have to be self-confessed by me! Yes! The blood debt you left behind is being paid by me! The things that are happening on this planet are beyond belief. So I came to see what sort of men you are.'

One ancestor in the hall was wearing Western clothes – according to my parents he had studied overseas in England. He had been in the same class as the great translator Yan Fu. In a voice that expressed his contempt for heaven and his pity for man, he now said that he had long expected the world's affairs to come to this. 'Those who take their ancestors to be their glory will also take their ancestors to be their shame. A race of men that puts too much emphasis on them will dig them up and whip their corpses when they want to change their names. If bad times come, these men run to blame the graves – they don't take any responsibility on themselves. These people are not really human, they're merely the tails of ancestors.'

He paused for a moment before concluding, 'And so it was that I wanted no descendants, and wanted to die not in China but in India – when people die in India, they simply put a torch to them . . .'

'Pah! What demoniacal nonsense is this? How can you speak like that before the younger generation!' The old bandit sneered sideways at the Western clothes. Then his voice became soft and benign as he turned towards me again.

'I'll tell you, my good child, ancestors are nothing more than a front. You shouldn't really look on them as anything but a show. Remember that in the beginning, when I was a rebel, I hadn't the slightest idea who my ancestors were. Our family was so poor that the empty pot clanged against the wall of the kitchen. Where were we supposed to find any genealogies?[1] Only people like us can rise in rebellion – sons of pedigreed families are tied down by their past. After I became an official, I had my pick of pedigrees: I could choose one at random from a great pile of them. It was easy to find a famous man with the same name and from the same county.

'So you see, my child, at the beginning you needn't worry about ancestors. Think about finding the right one only after you've become an official.'

'Ha, ha, ha!' The cold laugh of the Westernized ancestor rang out in the dark hall. This man must have been close to the bandit in seniority – he was probably a direct son in the line. 'That trick of yours has been around forever, but you've mixed up cause and effect. Take the old lady in the Stuart dynasty – genealogy was no use to her. Her generation had already retrogressed – they had to go out and find ancestors before they even rebelled. I bet they would have had to find a precedent in some classic before they even dared to fart. No matter what else one might do wrong, you can't afford to get your ancestors wrong! Whereas

[1] A genealogy in China is called a *jia-pu* or a family register. These are books made of one long sheet of accordion-folded paper and before 1949, every son's name was recorded in such a book. Many *jia-pu* were sold in the streets of Hong Kong in the following decades as antiques. They have now virtually gone in China.

look at you there, living so free and easy. Finished! Finished!

'And so it was,' he droned on, 'that I wanted no descendants, and wanted to die not in China, but in India – when people die in India they simply put a torch to them . . .'

'Idiot!' the bandit screamed, interrupting this incoherent speech. 'A child like you brings disgrace on us all. You've never deserved to receive offerings in the ancestral hall – you've used the one lousy book you wrote to cheat people and to steal fame . . .'

'I have long been unhappy about standing here among you,' the man intoned, and he began stripping off his Western clothes. The jacket he had worn remained standing in the frame, looking like the window display in an antique clothes store in Manhattan. 'He who serves as the slave of ancestors must be a slave to his own descendants. He lives not only for the ancestors but for thousands of future generations of sons and grandsons. The only one he never lives for is himself. I go! I go! I do not want ancestors, and I want no grandsons to pay obeisance to me.'

'Ho there! Stand!' Despite his yellow court clothes the bandit still behaved like a bandit. Pushing back the broad sleeves of his official's gown, he pointed into thin air as he gave the order. I thought that an ancestor without clothes on would be a naked ancestor, but to my surprise this one had already turned into a puff of smoke. It paid no attention to the demands of the bandit as it happily and freely floated out of the main gate.

Among my rows of ancestors, some were so angry they were shaking, while others were obviously bent over in laughter. They all began to shake so much that the wall became a mirage of colors, and I discovered that I, too, had become a puff of smoke.

I fear that I am the generation that has truly retrogressed, for I dared neither to push back my sleeves in indignation like the bandit, nor to float out the gate like my learned great-uncle. I lay flat on my back, gazing up at the kaleidoscope . . .

YELLOW SOYBEAN MEAL

Clinic of labor reform camp, 1960

THE DEAF doctor was the first thing I saw when I opened my eyes. His face and his hair were yellowish, as though the world and I had come down with a case of jaundice. I blinked, afraid that he might be a portrait painted on fading silk.

Fortunately, he opened his mouth just them, to smile a queer and tragic smile. He said, 'You lousy bum, you're going to live!'

I blinked again in response and as a token of my appreciation. By concentrating, I realized that I had seen these rows of ancestors on the way to this clinic.

The kaleidoscope was still revolving, and I was dizzy and weak. Once Natalie and I rode the ferris wheel at the carnival park in Paris, and I had a similar feeling as I staggered off the ride. I said to her, 'Now I understand the Chinese saying about being "so happy I could die",' but Natalie only smiled and handed me an ice cream cone. You see, in Paris, in spring, nobody can even conceive of death.

I gradually became convinced that the deaf doctor was not a portrait but a living person, yellowed by a nearby kerosene lamp. He smiled as he bent towards me, his eyes fixed on the end of my nose.

'Well,' he said, 'how do you feel?'

Yellow rafters and yellow walls, a yellow magician with a yellow beard. I saw all this behind a screen of snowflakes and golden stars. It was odd that in the brief time I had been dead the world had managed to make itself so richly golden.

'Well,' he asked again, 'how do you feel?'

He never looked anyone straight in the eye – he had become accustomed to treating the sick, and was mortally afraid of other human beings. His eyes were devoid of any expression as he stared at my nose, which made them all the more mysterious, like the Arabic numerals on the brick tombstone.

I wanted to tell him that I felt terrible, that I felt everything about my life had gone wrong, and that this feeling was more frightening than any illness might have been. First I had crawled into the wrong womb. I should have checked first to make sure I was entering the family of a poor man. Then I became mesmerized by a search for the truth, looking for it in Feuerbach, Hegel and Marx. I tried, that is, to follow the thought of Marx back to its source. In order to do this, several of us formed a small study group which, in 1957, was accused of being rightist. None of us escaped the net.

By the time I realized that all interpretations of Marxism had to come from our leaders (had, that is, to be limited to the level of understanding of our leaders and that surpassing that level would be considered a crime), it was already much too late. Many years later I wrote a piece about this episode, but things had already changed so much that its readers only yawned. They said my prose was superb when I was describing the beauties of nature, but why did I feel compelled to write about all those isms? To put all that theory into a novel turned their stomachs.

They didn't know it was theory that had ground us down to the point that we no longer knew if we were dead or alive. It was theory that made me realize that my life had been lived for nothing, and that I might as well simply die.

I tried, haltingly, to tell him all this, but the deaf doctor seemed unwilling to listen. 'If you've no strength to talk, then just be quiet.' He looked at my nose as he patted my arm.

I did, frankly, think of committing suicide then. You doubted me when I told you about it. After trying so hard to stay alive, why should I want to return to the land of the dead? In truth, I had been so close so many times that I was getting tired of it all. The principal theme in my life had been death, so what point was there in living?

I had not yet begun to think of using a gun, or of where to aim it, I simply thought of dying as though I were longing for home. As I thought of this I began to cry.

'Wonderful! If you can cry you can live!'

I heard the happiness in his voice as the deaf doctor said this. He could not hear my words but he could see my tears.

'If you can cry you can live.' How richly philosophical, how true. His inadvertent words have passed like a thread through all that I have written since.

He understood. I believe I should write for this man alone.

'Do you know what the medicine was that I used to save you?'

My resurrection had made him unusually excited. He leaned close to my face as he asked me this and from his mouth came the smell of fermented soybean meal. I felt as though I had been buried beneath mounds of soybean leaves as a dense greenish sky spread out above me.

The smell of yellow soybean meal makes me hungry – the very thought of it makes me want to eat. The fact is that the labor reform clinic had no medicine at all. What it had were coffee-colored tablets known as restorative pills. Each sick person was administered three tablets, and each tablet weighed ten milligrams.

Five years later, when I was doing labor reform a second time, I happened to get hold of the formula for these pills. I will write it down here exactly as I saw it: 'Seven *jin* of bran or chaff, two *jin* of yellow soybean meal, one *jin* of brown sugar = ten *jin*, from which can be made five hundred restorative pills.'

Sudden enlightenment came upon me as I understood why our medicine always tasted of yellow soybean meal.

When you and I finished making love and I smelled that fragrance around the bed, you made fun of me and insisted that it came from some kind of flower. You had a long string of Latin names for it, together with the information that it grows in Latin America. You should know now why your Latin made me so upset: my love for that smell has nothing to do with Latin or any other language. It is because of the many times yellow soybean meal kept me alive.

To be honest, everywhere I make love with a woman I search for that smell – on the bed, the sofa, the lawn, the rug, in the woods, in the shower. Without it, I can't feel completely satisfied. Some women claim that it smells like shrimp, others say fish or fermented milk, while Natalie compares it to the smells of the pipes in a cathedral's pipe organ. Whether the comparison is secular or saintly, common or divine, I disagree with them all. Pigheadedly I protect my yellow soybean meal in the same way that I would a patent.

It is certain that the doctor was eating restorative pills on the sly. Despite my delirious state, I was still capable of that surmise. The slightest mention of food in those days, or how to get it, could penetrate the brain of someone who was completely unconscious. If you were to run across a man who had fainted on the ground, it was pointless to pour cold water on him or to massage his chest. The thing to do was whisper in his ear, 'Let's eat!' or even 'Let's go steal something to eat!' He would be standing up like a shot. The smell of yellow soybean meal issuing from the deaf doctor's mouth was so strong that I could have derived nourishment from it. Yes, this man was definitely eating on the sly.

Jealousy incited me, the smell of yellow soybean meal aroused me. I opened my eyes a crack to see if I would be getting another two of those restorative pills.

Instead, I saw him take down a small box from the earthen bricks that formed his table.

'Look,' he said in a mischievous, laughing voice, 'Black Chicken White Phoenix Pills! This is the medicine which brought you back to life!' I could not understand his humor – this medicine seemed to suit my condition just fine.

'It's a special Chinese medicine,' he continued, 'made for treating women.' He giggled as he added, 'But there aren't too many of those around here. When the leaders up there allocate medicine, though, they have to allocate some for women too. We must have stored up a good half-cupboard of it. No women about, so I've been giving it to you. You must have had damn near a hundred pills by now. I grind it into powder for you. See,' and he pointed to the fly-like Chinese words on the back of the box, 'it has ginseng, deer's antlers, nutgrass, the root of membranous milk vetch, Chinese angelica, all damn good stuff![1] To be effective you have to mix all that with a white-feathered, black-boned chicken. This medicine is for treating anaemia in women whose periods aren't regular. You were a dead horse, sure enough, but I treated you like a live horse and brought you through. Who would have thought that this medicine could do it!'

---

[1] The author notes that all medicines used in camps were made of local weeds and plants. These are the names of plants used in Ningxia – the more wholesome ingredients such as chicken were missing.

✳ IV ✳

CRITICISM

Joe's home in New York, 1987

HE HAD dreamed a million dreams, but never before one about a tiger. So the first thing he did when he woke up was light a cigarette and think about the dream.

It had been a tiger, yet not a real tiger, more like an oversized toy one might buy in a store. It had leapt towards him as though real, however, and the fear he felt was real. He had dodged swiftly and was not actually hurt, but several drops of blood stayed behind on the ground.

Like the tiger, the drops of blood were real . . . and yet they were not quite real. Definitely not China Pinks, they were more like tomato juice stains.

Everything that follows seems to have begun with that dream.

When he got out of bed, he found that Joe had already left for work. He checked outside and saw that the black Ford was gone. A white railing bordered the front lawn, running along the leaf-covered driveway. Several yellow leaves were fluttering to earth, like little birds falling out of their nests.

He sauntered into the kitchen, calculating that he had another two weeks in America. C had left New York for Latin America and the city seemed empty. Before leaving she had explained that she had to make a living. She had a career and for that she could not complain. The two of them were intertwined on the bed as she said this, which immediately brought her string of Latin names to mind.

They had been hard to pronounce and even harder to remember. The flower they described must be beautiful, he thought – any flower with the acrid fragrance of love-making must have luscious colors. She had gone to Latin America where they used that intractable language . . . Could it be that she had smelled the fragrance again, down there, last night? Why else would she have thought of that country and its flowers when the two of them were lying together in bed?

He had had a number of women, but not one had belonged completely to him. Feeling the distraction of having lost something, he broke an egg into the frying pan.

Joe's black maid opened the door and came into the room. One hand held a black garbage bag while the other pulled a vacuum cleaner behind her like a dog.

'Good morning!'

'Good morning.'

Her white teeth gleamed as she spoke. Even on a hazy day like this, her skin made him think of the sun. She hummed a song as he leaned back and sipped his coffee. When he visited Joe two years ago he had given her a pair of clay dolls from Wuxi and she had told him frankly that she would have preferred a Mao badge.

'Round, like that,' she had said, 'and the bigger the better.'

He remembered he tried to ask her in English what she wanted it for. Instead of saying 'What use?' however, it had come out as 'What's up?' This had brought a guffaw of laughter from Joe.

The black girl said that her friends liked to use Mao badges as earrings. It was fashionable, she told him.

Joe later explained to him the innocence of her request. 'What's up in New York? Well, when nothing's up, people think of a little something to have some fun. Don't worry,' he said, 'she's not asking you for a Mao badge in order to start some kind of American Cultural Revolution.'

She did not bring up Mao badges today – perhaps the fashion had changed. While her rump rotated round the room, she half-hummed, half-sang a lively song. The song he heard as he ate his American-style breakfast that morning was *I Love New York at Night*.

While she was singing and he was eating, the telephone rang.

He thought that it might be C calling from Latin America, and he almost asked, 'Did you arrive safely?' as he picked up the phone.

Fortunately, the person on the other end did not give him a chance, as she immediately said, 'Why didn't you telephone me again after that one call? Can you talk now?'

'Of course I can,' he answered, amazed.

'Is there a woman beside you?' After she said it, he heard a little chuckle.

He finally knew it was A, and thought of saying pointedly, 'Because I didn't want to disturb the two of you.' He thought better of it, however, and merely told her that he had been busy.

Luckily, she let it go at that – after all, she had another person on her mind as well. He now heard her say loudly into the receiver, 'Did you see they've been criticizing you inside the country?'[1]

When he wrote about the experience of criticism later, he thought back to that morning. In retrospect, the sun had not been the same as on ordinary days. The beginning of a notable event always seems obvious in the writing of it, but such clear delineation is only another symptom of man's flawed understanding. Nothing, in fact, can be given a single precise start. In recording what happened, a person can only follow the normal convention and say it was on the darkest day, or the brightest day, that it began. Otherwise, not one of the myriad events in human history could be plucked out and made to stand on its own. Without incidents and events the drama of history recedes – it becomes something no-one would want to read.

He was being criticized again because before coming to America he had written a novel: to tell the story properly he should begin with the immediate cause, the story of that novel. But the cause of writing it was contained in his years in labor reform camps, so that

[1] As the author explains, the Chinese use the phrase 'inside-the-country' to stand for the word 'China', and 'outside-the-country' to stand for everywhere else. The world is split distinctly into these two categories in Chinese minds: 'inside-the-country' represents a kind of 'we', as set apart from 'them', and is both a result of and the continuation of historical attitudes of xenophobia.

to record the event of this new criticism properly he would have to record the day he was first sent to do hard labor.

To do that properly he would have to cover the reason he was sent to the camps, which was that he had been criticized during the anti-rightist campaign. Events would have to be pushed back in this way until it became clear that the cause of this event of being criticized was that in the past he had been criticized. He was sucked into a strange circularity.

Naturally, it would be possible to go back even further. Strictly speaking, this new criticism was a result of his gurgling emergence into the world. Even then, the story would not be complete. He was being criticized but there were, after all, also those who were criticizing. If the event was to be recorded in its entirety, one could not neglect mention of them. Criticism, moreover, has its own strands of logic, its own arguments, its various positions. If one intended to clarify the whole thing, one would have to take the history of thought[1] into account and so any tiny event had to be explained by a full description of the world. Only by starting at the beginnings of history could it all be understood.

Faced with this enormity, he was uncertain why this new criticism had begun, especially since he had already been rehabilitated.[2]

The important thing to him, however, was not to research layers of cause and effect. The important thing was that he immediately thought of the dream he had had that morning.

It was clear that this dream was a portent of his declining powers of imagination – it didn't take a psychologist to figure out the

[1] The word 'thought' encompasses more in Chinese than in English, for example, 'The Thought of Mao Zedong' has ramifications that include 'The Ten Commandments of Mao', 'The Law of Mao', etc. To say of somebody that 'his thought is questionable' is to say that the person is politically suspect and a potential criminal. 'Thought', psychology, especially mass psychology, and politics are fluid and related concepts in China: one's 'thought' is a public, not a private, event.

[2] 'Rehabilitation' or *ping-fan* in Chinese means smoothing away the charge of being 'counter' (*fan*). The crime of being *counter*-revolutionary is punishable by death in China. In the late 1970s and early 1980s, hundreds of thousands of people who had been declared counter-revolutionaries in the preceding decades were told they had now been *ping-fan*'d. As in the case of the author and many others, however, the *ping-fan* may not have lasted long.

connection between a tiger and criticism. This dream could be said to have no imagination at all.

'Where are you now?'

His fingers gripped the receiver and his voice rose involuntarily as he asked the question. Powerless to stop it, he felt his heartbeat quicken.

It seemed that the hardships he had encountered in the first half of his life had not, after all, instilled in him the quality of quiet endurance. They had not, after all, hardened him to the point where he could face each new encounter with a calm demeanor.

Each risk, like each political movement, had its own particularity. The reason political movements in China could follow one on the next, without stopping, was that each had its inevitability, its own urgent and essential nature. In each, the masses could believe that a new song of hope was being sung this time. The seduction lay in the fact that the song had to be sung to the end before the masses would know it was the same old tune.

Right now, he wished that there was someone by his side. His conditioned response to those words 'being criticized' was to feel a cold solitude soak into his body. Joe was no use, nor was C. She and he lacked a common language. China is a country which has lifted the art of 'criticism and self-criticism' to the status of an ethical principle: she would never understand how the same country that exalts criticism can quake with fear at the mere sound of the words 'being criticized'. No, he needed someone with the same cultural background as his own. Only two people who were leaning against a familiar stage setting could enter the spirit of the play, come up with the right lines.

In America, this person could only be A.

'Where are you now?' He felt it was his very heart asking the question.

'I'm in San Francisco . . .'

So he left San Francisco just as she was hurrying towards it! He let out a snort of anger and frustration. 'But I'm just getting ready to go to New York on business. I plan to arrive tomorrow. Once I get in, I'll telephone you.'

'I'll be there at the airport to meet you,' he said quickly. 'Are you coming into La Guardia?'

'No, don't bother, really don't. I still haven't decided which flight I'll be on. I'll tell you everything when I see you. So I'll call you – so long!'

She had forbidden him to meet her at the airport. How was it possible not to know the flight if you were travelling the next day? There must be someone else going to meet her . . . Thinking about this, he uncovered a latent jealousy. In fact, he had entirely forgotten about her since their last meeting – that the third section of this book makes no mention of her is evidence. This telephone call not only recalled her to mind, however, it made him realize that he still loved her. He had long known that when he loved any one woman he was absolutely sincere, starting with the very first one. It was because he had lost the first one that he now kept eternally and unsuccessfully trying to find her.

But in the midst of eternal defeat, he also savoured the feeling that he had briefly found her on each and every woman's body. Love is not something that is constantly kept in mind – it is more like occasional sparks tossed out by hammered steel.

He put down the telephone and continued to sit stupidly beside it. At any time or place a man is vulnerable to two lines of attack: one from politics and the other from women. These two things provide him with the meaning of life, with its pleasures and also its calamities.

Should he consider the woman first, or the calamitous nature of the political news?

He lit a cigarette and waited for the intuitive answer, and seemed on the verge of finding it when it slipped away. The young black woman was in a self-made oblivion, still humming her *I Love New York at Night*.

CHINA'S SHADOW

New York,
in a Chinatown restaurant with A, 1987

WE ARE sitting in a Hong Kong-owned dimsum restaurant in Chinatown.

A fall drizzle is coming down outside the window. An amazing great white cloud is swirling up from an underground venthole. Everything in America strikes me as 'amazing' – if the reader is attentive, he will find the word used often in this book. The glittering pavement shifts under the assault of pair after pair of headlights; cold cross-hatching at the intersection is traversed by hurrying legs. A long skirt flashes past, the sway of its lines cutting a stark silhouette. Two more legs, long and slender come into my line of sight, but I am no longer interested in the outside world.

She was eating a Cantonese dimsum with gusto. She still seemed to be hungry at all hours of the day. It was no wonder that even her handwriting was curvaceous. 'Other people have a Chinese heart, but I have only a Chinese stomach.' She looked at him and laughed, 'What can you do? Eh?'

This suffix 'eh' seemed to curve upward, its note soft and lingering as it cut through all other sounds in the world. He knew that note well, so well that he felt his heart contract.

One night in Beijing, in the space of time after love-making, she had asked him 'What about it, eh?' At that time he could see no correct solution, or was unwilling to accept the solution that presented itself. She had not received a definite answer that evening, and as a result she had kept her face pressed against his chest.

It was after that 'eh?' that she left for America.

He stubbed out his cigarette in the ashtray on the restaurant table, then slowly reached across and took her hand in his. A century seemed to have passed since they had last seen each other, but he was as familiar with every joint on her hand as he was with the bumps of his lane at home. He was familiar with her 'eh', and also with the warmth of her skin.

Her other hand now put down the dimsum and moved to cover his own. The motion was standard for a low-grade movie but it was sincere, it was part of the right play. She knew what he needed and, through her hands, she gave it to him.

For a moment he felt ashamed. Each time he was in danger there would be a woman around to take pity on him and, in all of them, he would see his mother's eyes. He would be happy to die in the arms of a woman. Literary critics had accused him of 'worshipping the female sex', but he was as willing to accept that charge as the one that hatted him with the title 'counter-revolutionary'.

She had just said something to him about herself – it seemed she was planning to marry the American, the one who was 'so innocent he's like a little foreign baby'.

Her willingness to marry an older American man was not due entirely to her need for right of permanent residence. She also wanted a change of lifestyle, a change in her outlook on life. 'Without marrying an American, you can't completely adapt to the life here. You can't beat your way into American circles.'

Moreover, she confessed, 'I actually like him a little.'

A small smile came immediately after. 'Don't be jealous. He may be a white man, but that thing of his isn't any bigger than yours. And in bed, he's not up to you.'

He understood her. He had watched her emerge from the subway station and seen her hand brush her raincoat aside. The curve of a full thigh was enticing but, when their lips touched, hers held no passion. He had been moved by this: nothing could have said more clearly that her coming to see him had been out of unselfish concern. He had immediately rearranged his emotions and, with a brotherly gesture, put his arm around her to cross the street.

The two of them continued to hold each other's hands in the

restaurant. Neither fully apprehended the absurdity of the scene. Not far away was the World Trade Center, that icon of Western capitalism. The imposing buildings were, to the Chinese, the epitome of a Western style of life. Yet as they sat in the shadow of these buildings, with a stack of Chinese newspapers piled before them, they worried about a shadow that was reaching much farther.

An observer might have thought they were middle-aged lovers trying to decide what to do that night. They might have been looking through the entertainment pages, to see if it would be a Mandarin movie, or a cab ride to a play on Broadway.

Instead, each of the Chinese papers carried news of his being criticized. The news item had come from Beijing via an American wire service. In it, an article in the mainland papers that criticized his novel was summarized.

The mainland article said that the novel 'exposes the dark side of socialism', and that therefore the 'social consequences of this novel are evil'. It called for a 'deeper and better consciousness among writers'. According to each of these major Chinese newspapers in America and Hong Kong, criticism of his novel was linked to recent ideological moves within the country. The significance of this was that they felt the article prefigured another political storm in China.

They say that if a butterfly flutters its wings in Beijing, the weather in New York is affected. How much more, then, is it affected by such an implicating article?

If a new political movement really does come to China, even the World Trade Center will find it is suddenly under its shadow.

All he could do was smile and be stoical.

'What would it be best to do?' he said in response to her question. 'I haven't thought it out.'

'I think you should go into hiding,' she quickly responded. 'If you get to be mentioned in the news, there are going to be too many reporters wanting to interview you. No matter what you say, you won't say the right things, and if you say nothing at all you'll be in trouble. Best to hide.'

'Where?' He smiled at her. 'Inside the embassy?'

'That's one place you have to stay away from! No telling, they might send you right back to China. It's things like this that make foreigners wonder what our country is up to.'

'Look at you – you just said the only thing Chinese about you is your stomach, but in fact your Chinese heart is showing through.' He smiled as he said it, and felt how ugly his smile was. 'You're really much better at thinking things through than our own embassy. If they sent me back early, you see, it would look very bad for our country.'

'So – what to do?' She lifted one hand and used a finger to dab at the corners of her mouth. In the second that she lifted her hand, he felt the emptiness above his own, until she brought hers down on his again.

'When I came to America,' she said, 'I realized that we Chinese are always saying "we" and "our". This confused a lot of Americans. They thought that in China everyone was a responsible cadre, responsible for whatever happened. Isn't that funny? "We have made mistakes in the past", "We have walked a twisted road", "We have accepted the lessons", "We are better now". Finally, that Western baby asked me, "Was it *you* who made government policy together with your country's past leadership? Was it you who were responsible for the mistakes of the past, the twisted road that China took? Is it you who think you're so much better off now? If so, why is it they still haven't given you a place to live?" You see, I had told him frankly that the thing I needed most was a place to live, that back in China I didn't even have my own assigned home.'

'You're right,' he agreed. 'Do you know what my first reaction was when I read these papers? It was not that the article criticizing me had done me wrong, but simply that *our* newspapers are no good at timing. Couldn't they have waited until I returned to China to criticize me? How could our papers do this kind of thing when I'm outside the country! How am I supposed to deal with this from the outside!'

'Poor thing!' She patted the back of his hand. 'You are one of the "we's" too. Who is this "we?" Eh?' She rolled the word around on her tongue, tasting it. '"We". Just who is it? Which group of people does the word "we" stand for? And for that matter, who am I?'

A beam of headlights swept over her eyes at this moment, and he failed to see the fishtail wrinkles that he knew so well. He realized that she had become younger, that she was thinner and her face was less lined. The oblique line of her cheekbones made a handsome demarcation above her cheeks. He felt himself becoming aroused.

Her question reminded him of talking politics on the night they became acquainted. That night, however, they talked only after they made love.

A MESSED-OVER
GENERATION

China, first meeting with A in Canton, 1979

THE EVENING they met she radiated a quality that made her stand out from all the others. He quietly leaned over and told her so.

It was at a raucous party in Canton, attended by the cream of the Chinese movie world. Every writer who had ever written a script was there, including those who were just getting hot and those who were past their prime. Scores of similar national gatherings are held every day in China, but this one had a special, romantic tinge. He noticed her as soon as the evening began, sitting alone in the last row of a tail-end section of folding chairs.

The lights in front of the stage hardly reached her corner. Her face was closed, solemn, mysterious. A novel could be written about that face alone. She had been a political symbol, a model for all women in the country to follow, but ultimately, it was not the heroism of her characters but the sensual face that her audience remembered. That this face was chosen to represent heroic battles against the enemy was due less to a director's shortcomings than to his ulterior motives.

Later, as an era faded, this face, too, faded from the screen. She had once turned political slogans into the flesh and blood of living people – now it was those unreal slogans which came alive to accuse her. Times and politics had changed. Directors and the public wanted to forget about her.

So meeting them tonight, here at this function, she was seated in the last row and in a folding chair at that.

She smiled and asked gracefully, 'Why do you think that?'

True enough, the phrase he had used was something thought, not seen. Her beauty was more in the mind's eye now than physically visible. 'Because,' he told her honestly, 'you're the only actress I know. I stopped going to domestic productions these last few years. Before then, when there weren't any foreign movies, you were the only star I ever saw.'

'And did you watch movies so much in the past?' she asked him, curious.

'Not because I wanted to,' he said, 'but because I was made to. In the labor reform camp movies were one of the political means of reforming people.'

'You poor thing!' And like many years later, she patted his hand.

There was a sense of intimacy in the gesture. He summoned his courage and asked if she was really interested in staying for the rest of the show. She smiled a silent answer, agreeing to let him take her wherever he wanted to go. He said they might as well return to the hotel to talk, and she immediately and decisively stood up. Before leaving, she cast a long look back at the folding chair, as though checking to see if there was anything she had forgotten.

A well-known comedian, doing a one-man crosstalk routine, was drawing loud laughter as he took her elbow and guided her out of the hall.

As they stood waiting for the bus, she said that she had read his novels and enjoyed them, that she felt he understood women. As a result, she said, she was predisposed to like him: 'Unlike other women who've read your books, I'm not disgusted by you.'

'But I don't feel I understand women at all. I only know that in some situations some women act in a certain way. So I write them in that way. I've received many letters from women who say they want to pour their hearts out to me, who even say they'd like to "be friends". I'm afraid this is a total misunderstanding.

'I hope to write a novel one day that bares my soul, that shows women just how nasty an animal a man can be.'

'If you really write that book,' she said, 'It would be of inestimable value to women.'

As they stood in the crowded bus in a southern Chinese city, he held her steady with one hand and gripped the bar above with the other. He felt that she had already allowed him to take control. To save electricity, the lights of the bus went out as soon as it started, and in the darkness she leaned her head against his shoulder. Her breathing moved at the same pace as his, and at a moment when each took a deep breath he pressed against her.

She was staying on the eighth floor of the hotel, he was staying on the eleventh. Best to go to her room, she observed, since her roommate had not come. The person assigned to her room was an old star from the 1930s, but since she was a resident of the city and also unwell, she had not even signed up for the conference. The result was the good fortune of staying in a single room. She added a sentence, as though talking to herself, 'In any event, it's unlikely a reporter would be looking me up these days.'

The heating system in her room was more than adequate – as they walked in they both automatically took off their coats. She had just removed hers when she lost her voice and began to cry.

Only later, after comparing it to others, did he appreciate her ability to enjoy the comfort of love-making. In his experience, her approach to sex was unique. Many years later, on the beach in Nice, he realized she was like a sun worshipper.

She stretched out all four limbs and let the man caress her, allowing the warmth to penetrate her body. It was not the sun that was enjoying her – she was the one enjoying the sun. Her satisfaction, her oblivion, had nothing to do with the sun, they had to do with her own half of the affair only. When approaching orgasm, she would suddenly open her eyes and those eyes would be filled with terror, as though a bomber had suddenly flown over the beach. This expression of hers made him lose all desire at first – he was flustered as he jokingly said, 'It looks as though I'll have to get used to you before I can get the feeling.'

She laughed and said, 'I'll make you get used to me.'

When she laughed, the tracks of tears still lined her face. But this sentence was equivalent to signing an eternal contract with him. Later, after he did indeed get used to her, he found that her expression only added to his pleasure. When he saw it, he felt immeasurably powerful, like a fighter bomber.

She told him he had appeared when she was approaching a nervous breakdown. She had begun to feel she could no longer go on. As she was listening to the popular songs on stage earlier that evening, she was considering committing suicide. 'But perhaps,' she added, 'it's just that my period's coming.' She also told him she hadn't been with a man in four years.

'Thank you!' She gave him a long, deep kiss. This kiss of thanks made him feel demeaned, made him feel he had become her tool. It helped to think that he might have prevented a tragedy that evening.

'The reason my husband and I were divorced,' she went on, 'was, on the face of it, sexual incompatibility. My husband was a government official during the ultra-leftist period.[1] He wouldn't allow me to go to Tiananmen when I wanted to mourn Premier Zhou,[2] and the crack in our relationship began ostensibly at that time. After the leftist era ended, I used this as a pretext for divorce.

'In fact, I simply felt that my husband was less and less like a person. He was less and less like someone with human emotions. He made "that act" into a kind of duty that had to be carried out.

'Sometimes, after reading documents in the evening, he'd stretch his back and say, "Let's add on an evening class tonight." He looked

[1] The Gang of Four was considered 'ultra-leftist' and her husband was supporting them before their fall from power in October, 1976.
[2] Zhou Enlai died in April 1976, Mao died in September 1976, and the Gang of Four was arrested in October of the same year. After Zhou's death and before the downfall of the Gang of Four, people brought wreaths to Tiananmen in a silent protest.

exactly as though he were going off to hoe fields in Dazhai. What kind of passion is there in that!

'I think he just read the editorials of the two papers and one magazine[1] until he was an idiot. Those articles were so long and tedious they could flatten a man.' She drew a long sigh.

'You know,' he responded after a pause, 'I have the same feeling. People in the Cultural Revolution were brutal, crazy, and a good part of the reason is that they'd been sexually repressed. In the coming years, I feel this should be made a primary subject for research in the field of social psychology.'[2]

The two of them went on to talk seriously about life as though the passionate love-making that had just passed had been an illusion. Her neat hands had already made up the bed, smoothing it better than any regulation hotel staff could have done.

She said that she was not upset by being cheated by politics. 'What upsets me is waking up afterwards. There's a movie out called *Morning Always Comes After a Nightmare*, but there are, after all, different kinds of mornings. If it's cloudy and unclear, nobody knows how to arrange the day's affairs.'

She told him for the first time that she was thinking of leaving the country.

He, on the other hand, had recently been liberated[3] and so he was still charged with enthusiasm. He was puzzled as he gazed at her, trying to think of a way to lift her spirits: he realized that, except for her face, he hardly knew this woman at all. All of her life's experience was focussed in her black eyes. The sight of them made him think that labor reform may not have been the worst thing that could happen.

---

[1] There were only two newspapers and one magazine in China for the decades preceding the 1980s. The two papers were the *People's Daily* and the *People's Liberation Army Daily*, and the magazine was the *Red Flag*. The Chinese Communist Party used the editorial pages of these publications to announce policy changes: as the author says, to 'make directives and inform people of the correct line'. He adds that around half a billion people were supposed to read these, and often had to memorize them.

[2] The author holds this opinion strongly. He believes that sexual repression has contributed substantially to the psychological problems of the Chinese people.

[3] After rehabilitation in 1979.

Later that evening she said bitterly, 'We are a generation that has been messed over. They've messed over our thinking, and our lives, and even our destinies.'

FLIGHT PLAN

New York,
in a Chinatown restaurant with A, 1987

'WHO ARE "we"? We are the generation that has been messed over.'
He took a sip of cold coffee. 'Now I know how true that is. I gave
several off-the-cuff speeches at various universities in America –
through my very openness I wanted to show how we Chinese
do have freedom of expression. And now, behind my back, the
newspapers come at me with this. It looks like not only the Chinese
are being deceived, but also my American audience – it has no idea
what to believe.'

'The frightening thing,' she said, 'isn't that they have criticized
your novel, but that we have no idea what's coming next. All
political movements put the knife into literature first. But you know
that.'

She kept hold of his hand, and an observer might have thought
she was saying, 'Dear, won't you take me down to Bermuda? It's
such a marvellously sunny place – take me away from this gloomy
New York.'

He thought for a moment, then said, 'My intuition tells me that
for a while, at least, nothing much will happen. The problem isn't
whether or not something will happen, the problem is that the tone
of their criticism makes me afraid. The language is exactly as it was
before.'

To an onlooker he too might have been saying, 'Darling, it
doesn't matter whether we go to Bermuda or Jamaica, you know I
have to watch my money.'

'Go ahead and believe your intuition!' she retorted. She might
have said, 'I don't believe you don't have enough money – let's go!'

'Do you know what my first reaction was, when you called to tell me I was being criticized again?' He raised his eyes to hers. 'It was fear. Later, I thought, why should I be afraid? Why in the world should I still be afraid? After going through so much, and especially when I'm way out here in New York. The most frightening thing is that I can still feel fear.'

'I know,' she responded, 'and I also know that you aren't even afraid of death. What you're afraid of is being rectified and criticized.'[1]

He shook his head. 'We Chinese say, "There's nothing the Chinese can't accomplish, since we are not afraid of death." We take great pride in this, and I know it's true. The Chinese are not afraid to die, but neither are they coming up with any great achievements.

'Why? Because we fear something else, something besides death. What is it that we fear? What can be more terrifying than death? I haven't figured it out yet.'

'I'll tell you a story,' she said, 'which may explain why I finally decided to marry that foreign baby.' Her face turned solemn as she began – she was as good at conversation as C was at sex.

'One time when I was flying to Salt Lake City I sat next to a visiting scholar from a Chinese university. The two of us began talking to each other. He said that he once took a six-seater plane to a remote part of the southern United States. He went with several Americans on vacation, and they didn't bother to record the flight plan with the authorities. The plane ran into trouble just as it flew over a huge stretch of forest, and it looked like it was going to crash.

'Like you, the first thing this man thought wasn't that he might die – he wasn't afraid of crashing or dying. He was afraid that it would be days before anyone found his body and that his leaders would misinterpret his disappearance. The leader he had come with

[1] The author explains, 'These are commonly used terms in China. One is prejudged guilty of a social or political crime and one's life is often ruined as a result. The actual practice of being criticized is lengthy – a person might be brought before a group of criticizers twice a week or even every day for several months. Once the criticism is over, a self-criticism has to be written.'

was in Washington – would this man think he had become a political refugee? Would he think he had jumped ship, gone to work for some American research institute? After his body was found, how could he explain to the leader why they hadn't filed a proper flight plan? The leader would consider his death a result of lack of discipline and organization. This sort of thing occupied his mind as the plane went down.

'These fears are the result of the personality cult,' she continued, 'the stamp that our leadership put on each of our lives, to the extent that we really do put the thought of death aside. So when I came back from the trip to Salt Lake City, I told that old Western baby, "All right – I'll marry you!" I realized that only by marrying an American could I begin to escape, to get out from under the weight we Chinese have pressing on us.'

'If only it were so easy.' A wry smile played at the corners of his mouth. 'I'm afraid that you'd still be thoroughly Chinese even if you married a man from outer space.'

Her eyes widened as she feigned surprise. 'You're just saying that because you're jealous.'

'There may be a little of that in there too,' he admitted.

'Don't be like that.' She laughed, and her tone was soft and gentle as she increased the pressure on his hand. 'You're not about to get a divorce, are you?'

'Looks as if it would be too late now, even if I were.' He was genuinely sorry about this.

'That's just it. Whatever you do, you're always half a beat behind.'

FISHING PLATFORM

New York,
in a Chinatown restaurant with A, *1987*

EVENTS AND emotions follow the course of their own unseen logic. He decided that perhaps this outcome of their love was the most beautiful. Love-making had ended, but not the love itself.

He had once told her, 'Love has to end in tragedy for it to be beautiful', and he now realized that this was a lousy line from a third-rate Chinese movie. It was full of smothering affectation. Life had revealed many truths to him. He knew that the same thing seen from another angle can be just as valid.

This outcome between the two of them was the best, yet the outcome with C was the same. To have love-making continue for the rest of one's life, to have one's cock aching for love right up to the time it was pulverized – this too was certainly a desirable way to end. As long as there was love, it seemed that any outcome at all was fine.

Perhaps desire was the stronger emotion. Because of the constant physical contact, it was of greater concern to all involved. And so, on his deathbed, it would be C who came running to him from America. He could no longer use that small thing to try to connect their two lives, but she could still use a finger with a ring on it to stroke down his eyes in a final gesture.

He knew that when news of his death reached A she would be hurt, and he also knew that it would be her final hurt. The first and last heartache in a person's life have the same significance. She would say to his soul, 'I didn't come at the end because not long ago I had to bury the old Western baby. Going to two men's funerals in one year is too much for a woman to bear.'

He would nod his head. His final smile would be tolerant and forgiving.

He accompanied A to the subway station, passing clouds of that amazing white vapor. A light rain blew against them. They might have been in southern China but for the occasional thundering of the underground train. The dark night towered overhead with metallic solidity. Neither day nor night in New York allowed a person a shred of fantasy – this was a completely materialistic city. Bright neon lights lay across the wet sidewalk like some rich noblewoman who had fallen down drunk. Vigor and decrepitude seemed splashed all over the city, like a can of fresh orange juice poured out on the muddy streets of Chinatown.

He couldn't imagine why Joe's black maid loved New York at night.

A said she had to be going, without specifying exactly where. A vague finger pointed up Broadway towards the north, where she said she was staying. Tall buildings blocked the direction in which she pointed.

Only then did he realize she had come with her old Western baby. No-one else had been going to meet her at the airport. She had behaved as she should, been loyal to them both, or at least made both believe that she was being loyal. The woman he saw before him had been able to transcend national boundaries – she was truly an international woman.

She stroked his neck with one fingertip – he was uncertain if it was meant as a caress or a benediction. A fathomless ocean lies under the fingernails of a woman – no standard of measurement in the world can plumb its depths. Its seductive power lies in that unfathomability – the touch of one finger can make a man dizzy. For a moment, he felt the metallic night melt as gentle glances seemed to stroke his soul.

She asked him not to visit anyone, and told him not to talk too much. She said that she would 'pay close attention to how the situation develops'. This familiar wording made him think they were standing by a subway station in Beijing. She said that she would call him as 'new circumstances arose'.

'One should meet all changes with unchanging stillness, sit tight on the fishing platform despite the rising wind and waves.' This was the traditional Chinese way of meeting political movements. He must have heard this stoic philosophy a thousand times . . . and he stood up against it every time. New York was an accomodating city – the mainland of China had been allowed to extend to their very feet.

She began to stretch her chin up to him and he knew that she would soon stand on her toes. Not forgetting this movement of hers was proof that he could not forget her. He hugged her hard around the waist. When their lips met, he unexpectedly felt a slight parting of her mouth. It made him feel that he was, after all, loved.

GUNS

New York, 1987

HE STAYED at the subway entrance for a long time, until he noticed a taxi driver watching him closely. Tossing away his cigarette, he strolled aimlessly towards the north.

There was a gun store at the corner of the first cross-street he came to. Every sort of long and short gun was carefully arrayed behind its metal grill. He had passed this place before, the last time he was in New York, and had been drawn to the display window then as well. He remembered being surprised at how people think of death as the spirit returning, when here was death calmly watching them as they crossed the street. He seemed to be the only one around who looked on death as something serious, certainly the only one who felt that he'd been destroyed by wanting and being denied death.

As he saw the guns lying so comfortably in the window, he felt different parts of his body violently begin to twitch. He again felt the thin crispness of his own skull. Standing before this window, he realized that he suffered from an uncurable nervous fatigue.

The city radiated brilliance this evening – even the raindrops carried a world of color. Lying so sweetly and adorably in their custom-built cases, the gunbarrels seemed to soften in the colored light. It is at such a time, in such a place, that death tempts a man. Instead of being an escape from the world, death revealed itself as the highest state a life could achieve. The primitive models were cheap, but the fancy ones were lovely. They would make you feel that dying before their barrels would be a pleasure. He stared at the guns one by one, comparing, selecting.

If one is to die, why not die in luxury?

The passers-by in the rain were no longer in a hurry. Lovers strolled by the flowerbeds planted along the middle of the street. The bars and coffee houses were attracting people like magnets. It was the end of October and the trees were still untouched by frost – the night lights dyed their leaves a deeper shade of green. The cold rain carried with it the promise of snow.

He noticed that the glass of the display window had misted over and he thought with surprise that he must have started to cry. In a moment he realized, however, that it was only his breath panting in eager anticipation at the guns.

People were laughing, some were singing. Cars sped by. Walking on, he looked up and saw that all the windows of the tall buildings had their lights on. Gorgeous colors, too gorgeous for this world to allow, were rushing down on top of his head. He remembered that it was Hallowe'en.

He marvelled that people could be so happy – what festival of the living deserved such celebration? Pretending to be ghosts and demons and to be frightened by them might be fun, but it was a kind of fun he could not comprehend. It was always possible that people had tired of being human and had decided to see what it was like to be a ghost.

He was searching instead for a humam mask: he wanted to become a real man. Whether he was to live or to die, he wanted to stand straight like a human being.

Some ten days later when he returned to the Chinese mainland, he learned that the criticism had been a false alarm. It had not been 'our' newspapers but an American reporter who had been playing some kind of political joke. Friends now laughed at him for ever having wavered: 'You ought to have faith in the masses and the Party. Why should you want to die again?'

The side without power is always the side that is accused of being irrational.

It may have been a false alarm, but his fear had been real. Calm reality could now soothe his nerves, but it could not erase the memory of fear in his brain. Sending people to the execution ground to scare them would not have become a traditional means of punishment if the shock did not have a long-lasting effect.

Shock stays forever in a person's body, hardening over the years to become a focus of infection. One by one the infections grow until a person's entire body has been weakened, until he becomes so afraid that he jumps if he hears a cat fart.

We in China went through a period of entering into the communist ideology, we went through a period when we truly believed that one day could equal twenty years. For a time we surpassed America and caught up with England, for a time we were the only country with no internal or external debt. For a time we lived the most fortunate lives of any people on earth and we wanted to liberate the two-thirds of the world's population who still lived in misery. For a time we were the leaders of world revolution . . . For a time we were actually that excited, that proud, that fanatic. Today, looking back over the past, that childishness can be forgiven.

But the shocks that some of us experienced are now regarded as merely amusing.

Empty vanity can be forgiven – it is simply mistaken, like 'trying to pick morning glories in the evening'. But meaningless shocks place the responsibility on those who were shocked. We are told that it's our problem, that our nerves just aren't strong enough.

It seems the footnotes to history can all be found in that *Encyclopedia of Jokes*. It seems the best response to a shock is simply to laugh. But how can the mental condition of those who always had the barrel of a gun pointed at them be as placid or as amused as that of those pointing the gun?

When someone has fired an empty gun at you and then blamed you for being so scared that the urine and shit flowed down your legs, you don't join him in a round of laughter.

A car honked before sharply braking to a stop. He realized that he was crossing against a red light. The car still seemed to be shaking, as though it were the car and not he that had been frightened. A young white girl sitting behind the wheel smiled and motioned to him to hurry across the street. For a moment he couldn't figure out whether he should excuse himself to her or she to him. That's what frightened him – that the line between those scaring and those being scared was so unclear.

He made a noncommittal gesture and quickened his stride to get across the street.

It occurred to him that if he were killed in a car accident tonight on the streets of New York, nobody in the world would know the reason for his death.

WORDS

Joe's home in New York,
the evening after meeting A in Chinatown, 1987

HE COULD be destroyed, he thought, but not that book.

Several million copies had been printed and distributed, and they were now in the hands of several million readers. That book would not be like his other works which he had personally obliterated, one by one.

So many words, written with his own hands, had been torn up by those hands. Some had been buried in paddy fields, others had been burned, still others had been shredded and thrown into the latrine. If words had souls, the whole sky would be dancing by now, whirling with little stars like a cloud of mayflies. Each little star would be transparent and able to cry out.

He drew aside the curtains and opened the window. Joe had not yet returned. A light rain blew gently into the room. The entire apartment building resounded with its own solitude. Millions of lights shone in the distant darkness. There was no scenery here to enjoy – New York's landscape depended on one's own imagination. To a million different minds, New York took on a million different shapes.

But he was not interested in imagining the view – he wanted to focus on hearing those tiny words.

Notebooks he buried in the paddy fields would have crystallized by now. As he smoothed the dirt over them, he had heard their cries. Yet as he thought of them now they crumbled to dust and, like light snow, were windborne into the opaque sky. Other words which had been burned now licked the snowy sky bare with their flaming tongues, until all that remained in the sky was darkness. Even the lights flashing in the distance were gone.

He tapped the sill of the wide open window, distracted, not knowing what to do. When every flashing light had subsided, he was left with a sense of emptiness. A feeling of age and fatigue assailed him, making him sway with nausea. The ground under his feet seemed to float away. His former literary prowess, all his words, were gone. He knew perfectly well that words he now wrote were only the dregs of what he had once written. His intelligence, his inspiration and vigor had turned to ashes and compost, through the action of fire, water and garbage. Helpless, unable to return, his words were being blown to the East and West by the wind.

If words could remain in the ground for years, immutable, like a knife, a statue, a ceramic pot, what treasures our descendants could dig from these 9.6 million square kilometers!

The real intelligence of China's past thirty years had been hidden underground. People have recorded the essence of their thoughts and emotions in silence. They have used brushes, fountain pens, ballpoint pens, pencils, even bits of wood and fingernails. They have written under dim electric bulbs, by kerosene lanterns, by candlelight, they have written under the bedcovers with no light at all. Due to the difficulty of writing, their words have been truly condensed. Like the ancient written language of China, one poem might have required ten years of deliberation.

We can ridicule these geniuses now, for having nerves that were over-fragile. We can tell them that their fear was 'laughable'. To those of us who are still living, who have survived, each political movement was a false alarm. To those of us still living, the First and Second World Wars were also false alarms. Most of these people could have been rehabilitated after 1979. They should not, therefore, have thrown their very hearts into the fire or the water, or shredded them into the garbage. They should have been patient . . . and waited. They should have trusted the masses and the Party.

Who was it, though, who persecuted them so that they did not dare to trust? How can you blame earnest good people who had no chance to study the *Encyclopaedia of Jokes*?

He fell onto the sofa, depressed. He watched the cold rain become a mist inside the room. The air was so piercingly cold it turned into magic – he could have reached out and shattered it with his touch. The green outside the windows had dissolved to a muddy black, while hanging leaves of potted plants inside seemed to be dripping dark green tears. It was unclear whether that tick-tocking was the clock, or whether it was the tears dripping off the plants. The clock was not going forward but backward – time was tick-tocking him back to a previous death.

He held up his glass of whiskey and soda. The ice had melted, and tiny mysterious bubbles were floating up from its base. They were like periods in his notebook, struggling to emerge, to break to the surface of the water. The words themselves, however, had left no vestiges, no trace – all he remembered today were meaningless punctuation marks.

He rubbed his forehead. Age seemed to have swaggered across his brow. He yearned for youth – even behind bars his youth had shone. This time, if they threw him behind bars again, he feared he would not be pacing around in jail for long.

Could it be that all he was afraid of was insufficient time?

Years later, as he lay on his sickbed awaiting real death, he finally understood the correct answer to that question:

One should not ask what is more terrifying than death, but rather what is more important than life. He had never been afraid to die and yet had been terrified of political movements, those relentless movements deployed in China with such precision. Political movements could obliterate all that was more important than life.

Bit by bit, they could scrape away your dignity, your love and self-respect until, tyrannized, with your head already rolling on the ground, you would actually want to thank your executioner. You would still want to wish him 'Long Life!'[1]

---

[1] In 1989, the slogan 'Long Live the Thought of Chairman Mao' was still written in large characters on the walls at the main entrance to the compound in Beijing where the leaders of China live.

Heaven and earth do not age, the months and years pass without haste. When I am floating alone in the air, looking back down on the globe, I will find it unbearable to remember all of this. Raising my eyes, I will see the glittering Milky Way and the universe, I will see the sunlight and moonlight meeting each other. I will know that my previous life and future lives are now up to me. In the vastness of space, I will be unable to see any minute spiderweb markings – I will be astounded that there are no man-made rules here at all. I will have become my own god.

Without a physical body, love and even its memory will fail to move me. I will be enlightened, knowing that nothing in my past or future has any so-called value, and that nothing, therefore, is important or unimportant.

Then, only then, will I be able to look back, and call my terror 'laughable'.

PROFOUND NEW
PHILOSOPHY

Ningxia, China, 1988

WINTER DAYS draw near now that I am back in my own country –
the poplars of the high plateau have lost their leaves. A sudden wind
last night sent what remained of them rustling to the end of the
road. With my head on the pillow I heard the footsteps of time and,
although hurt and sad, I thought I heard in them some hope.

Memory is man's greatest burden, not the daily hardships that
he has to face. We have an old tale in China that says when a person
dies he must drink 'Old Lady Meng's soup'[1] before he can enter a
new womb to be reborn. This folktale epitomizes the ancient wisdom
of mankind: if men and women were not able to forget through
drinking that soup, how could they have hope, how could they bear
to be reborn?

Up the next morning, I decided to test a VCR bought in the
United States to see if it had been broken on the trip in its loading
and unloading. I unwrapped the machine and plugged it in, then
inserted a tape to try it out. The machine seemed to be operating
normally.

What appeared on its screen, however, was a blizzard of black
and white. The contents of my tape seemed to have been washed
away by a snowstorm.

I remembered that when I went through customs the official

---

[1] When a person dies in China, and walks along the road to the Yellow Springs, he passes
Old Lady Meng selling her tea. Drinking the tea enables a person to forget everything in his
previous life, so he can go on to be reincarnated. If a person does not drink the tea he is
obliged to remember and forever repeat his previous existence.

made me hand over the tape for investigation. I explained that this tape was made in China, not the United States – that I had taken it on my trip as part of a cultural exchange. In fact, it was a Chinese movie made from a script I wrote myself.

'Not good enough! Every single tape has to be checked!' Expressionless, the official added, 'Orders from up there!'

Three days later, I went to retrieve the tape from customs; today I discovered what they did to it. Apparently, what was on the tape made no difference – all tapes were erased in order to save time and trouble.

I glanced out the window and had to laugh. An early snow was beginning to fall. Everything in the past and now the present, including even the scenery of this small town, was being mercilessly erased by the technology of a modern machine. Customs officials were becoming masters of a profound new philosophy.

Can I deceive myself into thinking I can still write? Any words I put down are pallid in comparison with the singularity of my life.

The movie script had been about a rich father who left his son behind in China after the Revolution, and about the son's subsequent decades of hardship. In 1979, the son receives rehabilitation and restores his name, just as the father returns from America. The father wants to take the son back to the States, but he refuses. Among his many reasons for refusing, the grandest one, naturally, is patriotism. With such a noble theme this movie became a popular success.

Now not only was the movie erased, the logic behind the virtuous action of its main character was destroyed. All that remained on the screen were numerous seething black and white spots.

I still want to make something of those black and white spots, though. If I were to rewrite that script, how would I write it now?

MADAME

New York,
at the home of Madame on Long Island, 1987

WHAT FOLLOWS is not simply a story, but a record of what happened. It can be read as the revision of the movie script he wrote.

He sat quietly in the car as Joe drove onto the Queensboro Bridge from 59th Street. The car hurtled on across Roosevelt Island in the East River. Until they reached Interstate 495, he was musing about how his writing seemed to prophesy the future more than it related the past. In the limited time he had left, each of his stories seemed to be coming true. When he wrote the movie script, he would never have thought that today he would be visiting the lover of the main character's father. For a moment, he was uncertain if he was the main character or himself.

Joe pulled up in front of a large mansion on Long Island which was completely covered in ivy. 'We're here. This is it,' he announced, appraising the house and neighborhood.

As they got out of the car, the main character realized, from this point on, he would be entering his own fiction.

She received them in a large drawing room. She was the woman his main character's father had brought to America thirty years before. This woman had been the cause of the father's abandoning his own wife and child. He examined her curiously, thinking that she was exactly as he had imagined. It would be easy for him to assume his role.

She had appeared only once in the movie, flitting across the mirror of memory, and then she had been relegated to the wings. Unwilling to accept this treatment, however, today she burst onto the screen again. She drew aside the long jingling beaded curtain of time and stood compactly before him. They exchanged conventional greetings and were seated, then she said, 'And his bones? He may have died, but where are his bones?'

The bones she asked about were her lover's bones. According to the rules of the script, they should be the bones of the father of the main character, the capitalist who had emigrated to America before liberation. Reality had not accepted the rules, however, and instead of moving to America, this capitalist had died inside China.

He immediately felt both confusion and shame. He had been living inside his own head all this time, passing his days in memories and dreams to the point that he had mixed them up with fact. For three decades, it had been supremely easy for him to transform facts into memories, and for the memories then to produce dreams. As a result, memory, fact and dreams had been stirred together until they were indistinguishable. He felt he had to organize his thoughts before he could tell which door to enter.

After a moment's thought, he realized that the main character's father had sent this woman alone to America. The father had remained inside China. The capitalist in the movie who returned to the mainland to find his son was no more than a ghost, a shadow on a screen.

Having entered the proper door, he now felt suffocated. Reality can be overpowering when stripped of the comfort of dreams. Having come through the door, he recognized that there was no main character at all, let alone a father of a main character or that father's lover. He had to face the fact that he was himself the main character.

At what point do memories, dreams and reality meet? Or do some move forward and others backward along parallel lines, never able to converge at all?

'When a person dies, there has to be a skeleton and it has to be buried. Do you mean to tell me you don't even know where his grave is?' She was stubbornly sticking to a search for his bones – she felt that that rack of bones should belong to her. He felt that it was absurd for her to think bones were important when the person was dead. People living in different environments have radically different ideas. He had sickened of playing with bones.

Nonetheless, if he was that main character created by his own pen, then he should indeed have a father. Sitting here he began to consider that he ought, by all rights, to have a father.

The image of a father had seldom crossed his mind. Eight generations of his ancestors[1] had been hounded relentlessly in China. Each in turn had become the subject matter for his forced confessions. Ultimately all his ancestors, right up to his father, became nothing more than caricatures in politicized literature. Transformed into black Chinese characters, they were simply names that he no longer wanted anything to do with. They had also become names that made him afraid. He consciously and voluntarily rejected his own blood lineage and, as he did so, the blood in his veins ran cold.

Intense investigation of ancestors and intense criticism of tradition had resulted in the loss of both. Ancestors and tradition no longer existed: each person in China had become a flying kite whose string was cut. Dodging and cutting, each was on his own. If a hurricane were to blow up in China, the entire race would be lost.

But bones could not be blown about by the wind. The broken bits of his father's bones must be hiding somewhere, or else must be scattered so that they were everywhere. It was possible that when he was eating watermelon, or bread, or meat or eggs, he was also eating his father's bones.

He felt his hair rise as he imagined the possibilities.

Joe had explained the situation to him as they drove along. Since coming to America over thirty years ago, this old Madame had little to do with Joe's family. At Christmas or Spring Festival there might be a card, nothing more. 'The old Madame is plenty wealthy. The money your father left her has multiplied many times. Don't worry,' Joe added, 'you won't run into your little brother – he's doing business up in Boston.

[1] The saying is a common way of referring to ancestors in general.

'You should thank the American papers,' he went on. 'Unintentionally, they helped you find this relative. The article about criticizing you on the mainland gave some of your background, so after the old Madame saw it she started calling me. She must have called a hundred times!'

He was not even sure what he should call this relative. According to convention a new wife could be a stepmother only after the real mother had died. While his own mother was still alive, this lady had been called a 'little woman with whom arrangements had been made on the outside'. This string of words had come from the mouths of the cook and the driver that year: the childhood memory had stayed in his brain for a lifetime.

This 'little woman' had borne a child and that child must be his little brother. He was curious to meet this little brother, secretly feeling that a brother was a kind of second life – a second destiny that he himself might have lived.

All he remembered about his father's second house that year in Shanghai was that there was a wolfhound there named Deutsche. The dog had been delivered in a German car and the name stuck. He had played with Deutsche for a while, but two months after arriving Deutsche disappeared. In another two months he came upon the dog, lying on the living room carpet of a stranger's house. Deutsche still remembered him and excitedly leapt up to greet him, so he was allowed to take the dog into the garden to play. There were roses and calla lilies in the garden, and he thought it was strangely like a small piece cut out of his own large garden at home. Flowers that his father loved were planted everywhere.

He had none of his current rich knowledge of ambiguous male-female relationships then – he thought his father had simply taken him along on a social call. Whatever his father muttered that he should call her had been forgotten long ago. Many years later, while shooting that movie with script in hand, the director had asked, 'What kind of image should this woman project?' For in the script this 'little woman with whom arrangements had been made on the outside' had no name, no description, not even a line.

Thinking how these 'shoulds' had invaded everything, he answered, 'Whatever you think!'

So the director had carelessly grabbed a pretty young face from the stand-ins, who flashed by the camera and was gone.

Today the shadow of that flash had come to possess her own image, had filled out to become a three-dimensional being. She performed with considerable vigor, and even kept saying lines that she 'should not' say.

She said over and over again that she 'should' get that rack of bones.

Joe had explained that the old Madame was a spokesperson for American cats: she was engaged in a struggle on behalf of their sexual rights.

Wherever there are overseas Chinese in the world, there are bound to be mahjong and popular Chinese music. Together with tea, these form the legs of a tripod on which is supported our glorious Chinese culture. This Chinese Madame seemed impervious to mahjong and music, however. She was devoting all her energy to defending the reproductive organs of male American cats.

It seems that an American newspaper began a lively debate about the pros and cons of castrating male cats: was it a humane or an inhumane thing to do? The vigor of this debate and the earnestness with which it was followed were equal to political debates between opposing factions in China. The old Madame was firmly in the Protect the Cat Balls Faction.

She felt that, in the spring of their sexuality, cats had the right to pursue their lusts. As man's rights were God-given, so too were those of cats. Before God, man and cats were created equal. She therefore had contributed a large sum of money and had placed several large advertisements in major newspapers.

Joe explained that the old Madame seldom read the newspapers, but that 'the news of your being criticized happened to be in the same paper where she had placed an ad – looking for her ad for protecting cat balls, she discovered you.'

It was thanks not only to that American wire service but also to the balls of cats that he should now be meeting this character, this woman situated somewhere between a stepmother and a 'little woman'.

As Joe was talking, he was thinking: the Madame stayed a widow for over thirty years – she never remarried. Could it be that this heartfelt mission to preserve the sexual desires of cats was related to her own embarrassingly-hard-to-talk-about situation? At the same time, a man who could make a woman remain loyal to him, when she was free to do otherwise, must be a virile man indeed. He could not help feeling admiration for his father.

Awkward as it might be, he was sure there was some connection between his father and the balls of cats.

Joe called her the Old Madame, and he thought this was what he might call her also. 'Mother' or 'Aunt' did not seem quite appropriate. But from the moment he saw her, he could not make himself call her 'old'. He was used to seeing older women on the mainland and had formed a fixed idea of age: this woman did not fit that idea at all. She was more beautiful, for example, than the young actress the director had so randomly chosen to play her part. She had an enduring elegance which could be appreciated by all who saw her, even though she must now be approaching eighty.

She was that kind of woman. No wonder his father had given her all his wealth and sent her off to America – he would have done the same. There was truth in the saying, 'Like father, like son'.

The only thing to do was call her Madame. This was still a common form of address for older women in villages in China. It declared straight away that he had spent more than twenty years out in the countryside.

Madame scrutinized his face. She stared at him until his skin prickled. She said that his eyes were like his father's, as was his nose and his mouth, until he learned that everything about him was like his father. In the end, he thought that his father must never have died.

He had voluntarily rejected his bloodlines, but his bloodlines had not rejected him. Madame commented, however, that he looked much older than her lover ever had. 'He had a great deal more style than you. He had returned from being a foreign student at Harvard, and he never wore shirts without starched collars.' This made him more than slightly jealous, but he smiled and pretended to agree.

Oddly, Madame said his father had resembled Mao Zedong, which almost made him burst out laughing. 'And he acted like Mao Zedong, too, always doing inexplicable things. He was always praising Mao – he even pleaded on behalf of the Communist Party when the KMT's Military Union[1] got hold of some of its members. When Shanghai went under he refused to leave – he thought Mao Zedong would bestow some kind of official position on him. And now, just look – even his bones are lost.

'Why did they have to execute him?' she asked. 'Certainly not because he had relations with the Military Union. And yet, if he hadn't had relations with the Military Union, how could he have come to the aid of the Communist Party!'

With the elegant gesture a woman in the Shanghai of the 1940s might have used, Madame wiped a tear from her cheek. This theatrical expression of grief made him realize that over these years this woman had seen in her lover both the devil and the divine.

[1] The Military Union was the military intelligence organization under Chiang Kai-shek's Kuomintang.

AN ANCIENT, MUSTY BOOK

Home of Madame on Long Island, 1987

AFTER HE returned to China, he thought back to visiting Madame that time in America but the customs officials seemed to have seized half the images stores in his brain. Those that remained were indistinct, either under- or over-exposed. Many even seemed to have been double exposed. In the background was always a red house, wrapped in ivy, set on a broad expanse of green lawn. Now and then a graceful old lady rocked gently on a swinging chair in front of the house. In the image, a breeze would be sighing off the Atlantic, and a precious bird would be singing in the maples . . .

A clearer image was that of the three of them sitting in the drawing room. Fall colors outside matched furniture that seemed burnished with autumn gold. He was contemplating where the clouds off the Atlantic might climb onto the continent, and how the East River might connect and flow into the ocean. The sound of water's flowing wetness slapped softly inside him, as though the pages of an ancient, musty book were slowly being turned.

'I was eighteen years old when I met your father,' Madame said. 'I had graduated from high school but didn't have a job. My family was poor, so I went down to Chongqing from Chengdu. At that time, Chongqing was the joint capital. A relative introduced me to your father to be his secretary. Your father was treated like a gentleman from birth, he had servants to wait on him for virtually everything. He also had to do business, though, and at that time you could make a lot of money by moving things along the Burma Road. He had the wildest fantasies about accompanying the goods himself. His life was spent generating a new idea every second. You couldn't tell today what he might do tomorrow. Sometimes he'd say he wanted to go to Yan'an,[1] other times he'd say he wanted to go to America. He died because he had a character like that . . .'

She sat above him in a straight-backed chair, while he sat before her on a low couch. As he looked up at her he felt himself diminishing in her eyes, until he eventually disappeared. It was as though time had gone back almost forty years. He felt that he had lived enough, indeed was sick of living, but to her he was still only twelve years old. She talked on and on to this twelve-year-old, acquainting him with his father and through his father with himself. Didn't his father's equivocation between China and America foreshadow his own future?

He smoked continuously – at the outset he controlled the craving, then realized that no matter what he did, smoked, farted, dozed off to sleep, it wouldn't make any difference to this old lady. He could neither annoy her nor surprise her. To her, he fundamentally did not exist. What she saw before her was not a twelve-year-old him but his father. She even said that she enjoyed watching him smoke like his father.

'He only smoked Philip Morris. As soon as he woke up, he smoked a cigarette. Before going to bed at night, the last thing would also be a smoke. That's the reason he contracted tuberculosis.'

Small yellow flowers like chrysanthemums were withering in the garden, tucked around a camellia in full bloom. Through full-length windows the white swinging chair on the lawn could be seen. The moment he saw it he knew it would play the role of a character in his memory, for its appearance was exactly like the demeanor of its mistress: it was eternally waiting for someone to come and sit down.

He imagined that as the sun went down every evening, Madame would sit there and slowly rock back and forth. She had swung on that chair like a pendulum for thirty years. Time passed, but the

---

[1] Yan'an was the communist base from which Mao, Zhou Enlai and others conducted the civil war.

pendulum did not change. She would keep rocking until she was gone.

Starting with his father's tuberculosis, Madame began to describe his father's body, giving details down to his ribs. No wonder she had not aged, he thought, with all the nourishment provided by her memories. Others follow time forward as they rush into the future, while she followed it backward, moving further and further into the past. She went all the way back to the year she was eighteen and met her lover.

No political movements had occurred here to chop off her ties to her former life. History had not become a heavy millstone around her neck. The mention of the past here did not make a person tremble with fear, it was not something that perpetually had to be handed over to the organization. Her memories had, indeed, become more and more endearing. They had been painted with a layer of romanticism even though some of them were painful.

For all its claims to being a young country, America is actually one great garbage pile of history.

Joe was surreptitiously covering his mouth to yawn. This poor realist found it hard to get far from concrete subjects, real things. Soft dreams and memories made him impatient. He later said, 'The only reason I could make myself keep listening to her nonsense is because she's rich.'

It seems that even the recollections of the rich are worth money, whereas few people pay attention to the history of the poor. Because this woman had money, she also had power – power to keep talking whether or not anyone was interested.

'I'll never forget that time in Bijie when we overturned the car. Bijie is in southwest China where the Miao people live, although I can't say what it's like now. Then it was simply wild and remote. There wasn't anything in sight where the car overturned, no village or inn. All alone, using my own hands, I slowly pried your father loose from the car. That was the time his leg got crushed – from then on he was a much more peaceful man . . .'

She unconsciously looked at her hands and he followed her

glance. There was no trace of any scars left from digging out his father. She was an antique that had been personally fondled by his father but the sweat from his tubercular hands had been washed off long ago. Her fingers were long and white and looked even younger than her face. Their sleek smoothness reminded him suddenly of women who had cut their fingernails for him and also of women who hadn't.

He raised his head. From her high-backed chair, looking like a pharaoh's queen, she continued to relate her pharaoh's story. He was surprised to discover that for an instant she did indeed look like women he had loved.

And now he found his time and her time changing places. He grew old, while she became very young. With the eyes of a fifty-year-old, he took measure of this twenty-year-old Madame. The white ivory of her complexion, her figure, the shape of her face, her eyes, the hairline on her head which came to a point like the letter M, the texture of the hair itself – each met the standards of beauty that he set for women. Transfixed, he now knew he was not looking for his mother in every woman, but for what his father sought in every woman. He was searching on behalf of his father, that is, his father was directing his search from the netherworld.

Madame was right, he was merely his father, the continuation of his father. No matter which way he made love to various women, it would be just the same way his father would have made love to them. Whatever way his father made love to this woman sitting before him was just as he himself would make love to her. Without even closing his eyes he could imagine how his father played along the length of her body, brought her to submission, and in the end made her give allegiance to his sex. Things that he had done on women's bodies had been done, repeatedly and continually, since the beginning of time.

The delights of love could never be extinguished, orgasm followed on orgasm. To this day she remembered how she had extricated his father, that is to say, him, from under the flattened car. (He actually felt his legs begin to hurt.) She had not remarried for her entire life in order to remember the delights that his father – that is, he – had bestowed on her.

He was overcome by sadness. He now knew that he deserved all the punishment he had been given. Punishing him, labor-reforming him, looking down on him . . . was actually punishing, reforming, looking down on his father. And on his father's father.

Having been through re-education, he had long since considered his ancestors to be representatives of the old world's evil sins. Toward those representatives of the old world, who oppressed and exploited people he felt only contempt. It was because his country had such people that it was now as poor and backward as it was.

For decades he had been put through a force-fed education of hatred. To ask him to sit in this huge drawing room and listen to this woman, to set before him this final representative of the old world who talked endlessly of his father, was to place him in an impossibly unfamiliar world. Was she relating the past, or speaking of future myths?

He had not gone out of his way to meet this relative – it was she who pestered others until she found him. His body, that of his father, had rotted back there on his native soil, but another had sprouted from a branch cut off from his own hand and it continued to grow here in another country, until it encountered a person who demanded, 'Come here!'

Damn!

It seemed that the recent criticism of him was also correct. The voice of criticism had long ago entered his own breast, which was why, he now realized, he was so afraid of it. The denunciations in the papers were nothing but a continuation of his own unremitting self-criticism. Words revealed in the papers were things he knew at a glance – not because he had read them before but because their original text was engraved on his mind. His conflict with those who criticized was an outer expression of his inner contradictions; criticism was no more than the externalization of himself. A person who is not afraid of others can still be afraid of himself: this was the reason he was terrified.

On a brilliantly sunny day in fall, sitting in a comfortable room, listening to an adorable old lady talk, he had combined himself, his father, and his current criticizers: this proved that his one life was altogether too heavy! He had to escape all this to think for a while.

BONES

Graveyard of labor reform camp in Ningxia, 1965

Home of Madame on Long Island, 1987

THE DAY the troop leader dispatched me to lead my convicts to collect dead men's bones – bones that had supported this or that person in dark silence, inside, obscure, of no aesthetic value – I never dreamed that a dead man's bones could become collectors' items. If anyone had wanted mine then, I would have sold them for five pieces of bread.

Even less could I have imagined that many years later, I would be sitting in another country, watching clouds sift through sun on a lawn, listening to a charming old lady demand that I return her lover's bones. If I had known then, I would have collected a few extra in advance. Bones, like broken sticks, could be found everywhere in that wasteland. There were enough to satisfy the desires of all the world's bone collectors.

Madame is berating me for not taking care of her lover's bones. She sits on her high-backed chair but in my mind's eye she is rocking on the white swing, now and forever marking the pendulum of time. I realize that she exists in a timeless trance.

How can I begin to tell her that labor reform camps in China are not that rare.[1] That if they feel like it, camps execute people whenever and wherever they please – exactly the way people spit in China wherever they please. Heaven knows in which camp, on what small patch of land they executed him. Him: my father, the

---

[1] The author notes that, unlike in Russia, labor reform camps are scattered uniformly around China. All major cities have them, as well as all provinces – one does not have to be sent to Siberia to be sent to a camp. A camp just outside Beijing is called 'Tian Tang He' or River of Paradise. 'A very pretty name,' he says.

lover of this woman. Even if I had known where he was back then, I would have had to 'draw a clear line', pretend I didn't know him.

(As time passed, and the deaf and dumb pretense went on, what was fake became what was real. In the end, many of us became truly deaf and dumb.)

After telling me about the past, Madame started giving me her opinions of it. 'His bones are those of a good man!' she exclaimed. 'If I could only see them, I could recognize them at a glance. The lower section of his right legbone must have a scar – he had a compound fracture from that time the car overturned at Bijie.'

I've seen quite a few human bones but I never paid attention to scarred lower right legbones. Back then I was simply trying to meet my quota, stuffing bones into plastic bags as hard and fast as I could.

As I write these things today, my reader must think I am describing some kind of fairy-tale, but at that time it was all so rational, so logical, so altogether writable. To labor-reform convicts, digging graves and exhuming bones was just like digging a canal. Like harvesting crops, it was nothing more than another sort of physical labor.

An important-looking stranger accompanied the troop leader when we went out to the graveyard. Any cadre who was a stranger to the camps in those days had to be someone sent from above. At that lowest level of human life it was impossible, after all, for anyone to be sent from below. So I perked up my ears as we shuffled down the road and tried to hear what they were saying.

It turned out this cadre's rank was much higher than that of our troop leader – he had been sent by the provincial authority. The cadre said that the families of all the convicts who had died in the camp between 1958 and 1960 were now bringing a court case against the camp's leaders. They were bringing the case before the Public Security Bureau in Beijing, so it had to be heard.

They had been pressing charges since the start of the Socialist

252

Education Movement.[1] Before the movement, when others were in power, they had no recourse to the government.

'Our relatives have died,' the families were saying, 'and their belongings may have been lost . . . *but what about their bones?*' (How similar these voices were to that of Madame!)

The thought of citizens outside the camps was obviously not reformed. Convicts who died here had gone obediently to their deaths. They had not given the leaders any trouble, had not even left instructions on how to dispose of their meager belongings. The unreformed relatives who survived them were not so docile. In order to meet their demands, the leadership decided to present each litigant with a sack of bones.

I heard the troop leader say with some embarrassment, 'Do you suppose we'll know whose bones are whose?'

'So long as they're human bones, they'll do fine,' the stranger replied. 'First get the sacks hauled to the warehouse and stack them up. Then we'll notify the relatives to come and get them. When someone lets you know he's going to be coming, you should write his relative's name there on the sack.

'If you can't tell whose bones they are,' he added, 'how can they? The important thing is not to leave any out. If someone takes his bones back and finds a toe or finger missing, he's going to report to Beijing that these convicts were tortured before they died.'

Since this story proceeds so smoothly, so rationally, the reader can see it is not a fairy-tale. It is in complete accord with the logic of our politicized life.

We followed the troop leader and the stranger to the graveyard. The dirt road we walked along was the same one I came close to going down before, but then, going down that road meant that you wouldn't be coming back. Luckily, I missed the trip that time,

[1] The author says that relatives of the many convicts who died in camps during the disastrous years during and after the Great Leap Forward had no recourse to the government until members of that government had changed. The Socialist Education Movement began in 1964, according to him, and was aimed at government officials who had recently been in power. Taking advantage of this movement, relatives now dared to bring a court case against leaders of the camps. The case was brought to the central Public Security Bureau in Beijing, not the regional or provincial Public Security Bureau.

during my first stint in labor reform, so I had the opportunity to walk the road alive.

The clouds above us were strangely immobile. From the Main Troop all the way to the graveyard they hung stationary, dead, up in the sky. Insignificant details often came to my mind, like a white swing or those unchanging clouds, but half the actual plot is forgotten. I am always like an inexperienced child – and such a child must be beaten and criticized.

The graveyard was nothing but a vast sweep of uncultivated wilderness. It could have accommodated all the dead in the world. Innumerable lizards were scared by our line of fifteen men and they scampered wildly across the sandy yellow earth. They seemed to live quite well off the soil here – each one was plump and strong.

Thirteen convicts filed out to the graveyard, but looked around in confusion once they reached its boundless expanse – nobody had any idea where to start digging.

Fortunately the troop leader was not as stupid as the convicts. Pointing to a little sand mound, he ordered, 'Stop walking! Dig here!'

I have found that I have no memory of what I thought when the first skeleton came out of the ground. I've forgotten.

As a result, I feel I did that unconventional physical labor for nothing. Grave digging is not something every writer gets to do. If I had any thoughts at the time, then this novel would be more literary, less like those pale, stark bones from which all meat had withered away. Regrettably, I did not. I had no interest in philosophizing. All I wanted to do was fill my quota.

When we were assigned to dig dead men's bones it was as though the troop leader had assigned us to dig potatoes. This is one thing that I do remember clearly: the assignment came with a quota. Each person, each day, was to dig up ten full skeletons. Who knows how they arrived at a figure of ten. If we did not complete the quota, we didn't eat, and not eating was a terrible punishment.

The troop leader stood on top of a sand mound (under which were undoubtedly plenty of bones, rather like potatoes), and he shouted, 'Listen here, all of you! You're to get every bone in a skeleton. You're not to leave out so much as one toe. The whole thing gets dug up and put in the bag: whoever misses a bone pays for it with one of his own.'

As captain of the convicts, it was I who asked, 'How will we tell which one of us dug up the bones that are missing a toe? How are we supposed to mark the skeletons?'

'Whoever packs the bag makes a mark on it. See here?' He held up one of the large plastic bags that we had carried to the graveyard on our backs. 'Every plastic bag has this cotton tag attached. Whoever packs the bag writes his name on the tag.' He pulled a pencil from his pocket and waved it in the air.

The plastic bags were brand new. They were then still very much a luxury item, glassy and transparent yet soft as cotton. The troop leader went on to educate us: 'See these bags? Don't forget, letting you lousy convicts use such beautiful things to stuff bones in is due to the beneficence of our Mao Zedong.'

Later, after the job was finished and we were heading back to the main troop, I saw him slip two bags out of the remaining stack. He folded them and tucked them into his shirt. So I too, without much trouble, stole one to use under my sleeping pad back in the cell. There is nothing better than plastic to keep out the damp. I slept on that bag right up to my second release.

Many years after that, travelling outside China for the first time, I saw those same large plastic bags on a street in Stockholm. I learned that they were used to collect the city garbage. Seeing my glance as he accompanied me on a tour of the city, my host remarked with irritation, 'Yes, that's a problem. All our sanitation work here in Stockholm has been taken over by immigrants.'

'I wasn't interested so much in who was doing the work,' I responded, 'as what containers they were using for the job.' My host commended the exquisite powers of observation of the Chinese people.

I am still trying to recollect what my thoughts were when I dug out that first skeleton. I feel that it is a vitally important detail.

Because of China's new crematoriums, I'll probably never again see bones concentrated in one place on such a scale.

In order to save land, India's method of corpse disposal has spread to China. Mao Zedong is said to have taken the lead in advocating this, and to have signed the official endorsement of cremation. He may have signed it, but he didn't apply it to himself: even today he sleeps in that huge mausoleum.

The rest of us, however, are bound for the incinerator. My own pile of flesh and bones, complete with the scars of a lifetime's encounters – from being bound and shackled, scratched by women, from general wear-and-tear – will pass through the process of drying to burning to ultimate obliteration. Emerging from its husk, my soul will take flight, and wing its way toward an unknown destination.

The soul has no meat covering it and no bones inside. It has no need to wear any clothes. Naked, it is in a most convenient form to make love any time it wishes.

This may be one reason I am so fond of death.

MAGIC MIRROR

Graveyard of labor reform camp in Ningxia, 1965

MY CURRENT thoughts are written above. At that time I thought nothing of it. For some things my memory is oddly clear, for others, it is just as oddly missing. I seem to have forgotten the stench long ago, the dung beetles and maggots, the fibrous quality of the remaining flesh. I don't feel I'm to blame for this – it's only natural. The beauty of an artist's creation is often different from the true face of his subject.

After the troop leader had finished his haranguing, thirteen labor reform convicts spread out over the land. Each was thinking of nothing but how to meet his quota, for the quota meant a lunch and a dinner. If all went well some rest time might be added in. We hoped, therefore, that the dead would be plentiful, that the corpses would be abundant inside a single grave, like potatoes flourishing in one place. One shovel, and up would come a basketful.

> *The sun goes down behind western mountains*
> *as rosy clouds fly.*
> *Soldiers from target practice return to camp,*
> *return to camp . . .*

A convict struck up a song, the beat was lively, the tune happy. It was a popular song, full of the spirit of revolutionary optimism. That bum must have found a pit where plenty of the dead had been buried together. His bones must be positively set out in lines, just waiting for him to reach down and pick them up. This fellow was bound to fulfill his day's quota in a single morning.

That time in Atlantic City in the Atlantic Hotel, when C told me that I looked like a kind of Hamlet, I marvelled that a warm current suddenly ran through my body. It was just like the feeling of being resurrected.

Hamlet had noticed, so long ago, how we convicts dug those graves. He had said, 'Has this fellow no feeling of his business, that he sings at grave-making?'

Horatio did not have to change his lines, 'Custom hath made it in him a property of easiness.'

And Hamlet responded, 'Tis e'en so: the hand of little employment hath the daintier sense.'

Yes, Hamlet had been right: my hardened hands were those of a laborer, my nerves were no longer sensitive. He was a prince, he had hands 'of little employment', and so he could find it in his heart to say, 'Here's fine revolution, and we had the trick to see't. Did these bones cost no more the breeding, but to play at loggats with 'em?'

But Hamlet is a dead ghost, whereas I, looking like Hamlet, feel I have been resurrected.

I had none of the emotions of Hamlet back then. The only thing I was curious to know was where all the flesh had gone, all the meat that once separated bone from yellow earth. Could the outer shell of a man be shucked off so easily? So that Zhang Three could be made to serve as Li Four? So that, in the midst of their grief, Li Four's family could be comforted by the bones of Zhang Three?

No two faces in the world are alike – a person's face cannot be reissued. Each is born with its own separate blueprint. Those who create people, be they devils or gods, must be exhausted by the engineering feat they face. And yet extinguishing a person's face is supremely easy – it is pointless to have creators do it. To save time and effort, best to wait for someone else to come along and do the job.

They had not dug actual graves to bury the corpses. They had folded the bodies so their heads faced their feet and simply stuck them into small depressions in the ground. Then they shovelled dirt and weeds on top and that was that.

The corpses had returned to the state in which they left their mothers' wombs: they were bare, without a stitch on. As in the Zen saying, they had 'come and gone naked, without a care'. Several years later, when we convicts arrived, we hadn't expected that the job of filling our quotas would be so easy. We were delighted. The dead slept soundly, on their backs facing the sky, not once having changed position. Although not quite dead when buried, perhaps merely in shock, they had accepted the responsibility of death and had well and truly died.

I gradually worked out a general procedure of bone packing: starting first with the skull, then the vertebrae, then the collarbone. I worked on through to the shoulder blade, the upper arm, the ribs, the breastbone, down to the toes, not missing a single crushed bone. After this particular labor, each of us could qualify as an anatomist.

If there was still some muscle adhering to the bones, that made it all the easier. Our job of picking up human bones became like picking up dead fish in a dried-out marsh.

Some of the corpses had been gnawed by wild animals and pecked by birds, so that the bones were scattered like a stack of rotten firewood that has tumbled down. We were too lazy to work on this kind of skeleton, and would use it only for spare parts when needed. If a relatively complete skeleton was lacking a toebone or a shinbone, we'd pick one up from somewhere else and toss it in.

When A, in that hotel in southern China, said that we are 'a generation that has been messed over', I immediately thought of those many bags of bones.

I remember giving her a little smile then. The problem is that my smile is always the same, no matter what I intend it to mean. To her, the smile seemed to be ridiculing her, although I had no desire to ridicule the world or anyone in it. The smile made her think that I disagreed with her conclusion, so I hastened to say, 'No! I agree completely with what you say. It's true, even the bones of our generation have been messed over. Who knows if the very bones supporting our muscles are really ours.'

While I said this, I was considering that single-smile problem – it was probably a symptom of nervous facial paralysis. Thinking back very carefully, I decided that my single-smile sickness must have settled on my face at the time I collected those bones.

Embracing this or that beautiful woman now, with my face buried in her lovely neck, I am often reminded of a scene from *The Dream of the Red Chamber* – the episode when Jia Rui looks into the magic mirror and sees a skeleton in it.[1] I have decided this is something Cao Xuejin simply wanted to write – it couldn't possibly have any connection with reality. No man can feel terror at the outside beauty of a woman simply because he has seen through to the skeleton underneath. Certainly no man could be so terrified that he would die. On the contrary, it's because I have seen so many bones that I seek the beauty of the skeleton's wrapping of flesh.

I am loving a slender woman. Caressing her breast, I feel the softness of her breastbone. If I listen I can hear her ribs, like the soft creakings of sofa springs. Nonetheless, I am as infatuated as ever. Since the time I was employed in that most unusual occupation, I have developed the ability to see both sides of the Wind and Cloud Mirror. My courage in loving comes from seeing all the way through things.

[1] This is a famous chapter in the eighteenth-century novel by Cao Xuejin. The character Jia Rui is hopelessly infatuated with a woman named Phoenix and is given a magical mirror by a Daoist priest in order to be cured. Jia Rui is told to look only at the back and not the front of the mirror. He looks at the back and sees a terrifying skeleton and is angry that the priest may simply have intended to scare him. So he turns the mirror around and looks at the front, and sees in it his beloved Phoenix. She beckons to him and he joins her in rapturous love-making. He turns the mirror around four times in succession, after which he is weak from passion. Two men suddenly appear in his imagination and, with a cry of submission, he is carried away. Servants hear the cry and enter the room to find him dead and the bedcovers soaked with semen. The mirror is later retrieved by the Daoist priest.

A LONG, BLACK BRAID

Graveyard of labor reform camp in Ningxia, 1965

THE SKELETON I could never forget had a long, black braid growing from its skull.

It was approaching noon when a middle-aged labor reform convict cried out, 'Quick! Come see! There's a woman over here!' In the dry, barren desert even the spoken word 'woman' could lubricate a man. Convicts who had not seen a woman for years swarmed over to him from the various patches they had declared their own. If one was unable to see a woman, the sight of a woman's skeleton was almost as good, especially this one, which could hardly be more naked.

I was the last one to make it over to the side of her pit and she had already been fully exposed by digging. She slept peacefully in her tiny bed, as though drunk or insane. She must have died quite early, perhaps in 1958 when this camp's convicts began to die in groups. The flesh of her body had gone cleanly, as if the bones had just emerged from a bath. The bones the yellow earth had so long concealed were now delectably pure and white. An ink-black braid wound down from her skull, three feet long with not a hair out of place. It ended just between her legs. On the end of the wavy braid was a smartly tied blue ribbon.

The skin of her head had gone, the braid alone remained. This was a direct refutation of that famous quotation by Chairman Mao: 'If the skin is not kept, what will support the hair?' She seemed to want to draw support from this orderly braid in expressing a protest from her former life. But the yellow earth had covered her muffled shout and, when at last she was excavated, the braid proved she was female and said nothing more.

The troop leader and the stranger were both surprised when they walked over. The stranger grunted, 'Very good', then held his nose. It was unclear if he had meant to commend the woman or her bones, for he turned to the troop leader and revealed that among those bringing accusations were several families looking for female corpses. The hair on this skull would help prove that this had been a woman.

The rarer a thing is, the more it is valued – he ordered me to pack this skeleton particularly carefully. I was to specify the word 'woman' on the plastic bag, so that if anyone came along looking for a mother, sister, or daughter, this evidence-bearing skull might take her place.

Such an elegant head of hair, combed and plaited even till death, was something that was worthy of respect. After the troop leader and the stranger had gone, we thirteen convicts circled around her, and lowered our heads in silent tribute. Regretful glances were cast where her breasts and her 'Yin place' had been. She gazed at us with two emotional eyes of yellow earth, so intently that I will never be able to forget their look. Every time I part ways with a woman I have loved, I see those same eyes on her face – eyes that are so lost, and so hopeless.

Since I have seen such a skeleton, I know that a woman's beauty lies not in her flesh but in her bones. Indeed, the Chinese have long praised the charm of beautiful women by saying, 'Her charm penetrates her very bones.' The creator of this sentence was devilishly clever. The flesh of the body has a sentence placed on it – it must age, unlike unchanging bones, which can inspire an infinite number of dreams. You can imagine onto a set of bones whatever flesh you wish.

My true enlightenment came only after death, for it was only then that I began loving women's bones rather than their bodies. I saw the universe afloat in pure white bones – catching them among the meteorites was like catching butterflies among the flowers.

As the bones of that woman and I were exchanging eye and eyebrow signals from one another, a convict suddenly began to thrash around on the ground. His face was an ashen white, and he shouted in pain that his stomach hurt. This man was a round, chubby thief. He had stolen the cow of his commune and been sentenced to five years. The silence of dead bones had not seemed to frighten anyone, but these shouts from a living person made us jump with fear.

With 'seven mouths and eight tongues' the convicts debated what to do: it was clear this man was being repaid for the blasphemous things he'd said as she was being dug out. (One convict started to repeat those words, and got only halfway before fearfully covering his mouth and spitting on the ground several times.) Just then an opportune breeze came skimming along the ground, blowing some sandy soil with a gentle rustle onto her bones. The sun was shining down from the center of the sky, and now clouds at the horizon came to life. They raced toward the sun as the agitated cries of a bird started up from nowhere, and every one of us was so terrified that our hair stood on end.

I took advantage of this chance to play the devil. 'This will not do at all!' I said sternly to my comrades. 'It must be that her soul refuses to leave. It has come before us now to make its power felt. We had better kneel down immediately and do obeisance to her, otherwise she may wrap around one of us and jinx him for the rest of his life.'

Thirteen grown men knelt in awestruck fear and trepidation. From a distance, the atheist troop leader and the stranger had a good laugh.

Yet among those thirteen convicts only I, the most devout, was affected by her spirit in the end. That spirit became more and more radiant as time washed away the dirt. Sometimes it was like deer-hoof grass, creeping along the ground, its flowers like little clocks silently releasing their fragrance from its braid. The braid too was like deer-hoof grass, since both drew their nourishment from things already dead. Sometimes her spirit seemed like lightning in the night, seen in one flash and then not again. When I looked around a crowd of people, it might have receded to a deep corner of my mind. This year in Paris when I saw the chestnut trees blooming, I saw her braid again in their long flowers. I was amazed that it had turned white, until I remembered that both of us were already approaching old age.

Braids are sadly out of fashion in the 1980s, seldom seen on the streets or in the stores. I ask the woman I am loving to comb back the elegant hair from her shoulders and, every evening, to make it into a braid. I tell her that I have decided to devote the rest of my life to her, but only when she braids her hair do I feel our love-making is complete.

And she does indeed braid her hair every night: it becomes a signal to me that she wants to make love. I am drawn to her as she gazes in the mirror while singing a song and braiding – drawn not as to a stage but as to the grave. Each night I am amazed at the fresh beauty that covers her long, white bones. For me, the graveyard has become a place of reincarnation. I can begin to feel that the world has no evil to speak of, that all evil is finally transmuted into good.

And so, with an easy conscience, I begin to make love with her, after playing with her braid to arouse my desire. Like me, she is finally resurrected one night, and I am finally able to see her smile. I watch her blue ribbon waft through the sky like a small flag for freedom.

I should confess to her, apologize to her: I have been messed over but I have also messed over others. She moved so easily through space, with the charm of a shy young woman and no sign of a limp or stagger, and this was all the more proof that my men and I had done our work well. I sifted her out of the earth with great care, getting even the fingernails that might have scratched a lover. I stuffed every bit of her into the plastic bag. The troop leader and I then shared in the same crime, for I wrote on the bag the one word, 'woman'. Who she had been, what her name was, all of that was gone when she later became somebody else's daughter or wife. Disturbing the purity of her past sullied her silent protest from the grave.

And so, without a home, she floated aimlessly through the sky. In windless outer space she lacked even the breezes to prop her up.

I flew toward her to woo her, but eyes of yellow earth stared at me as she shouted, 'Go away! You cowardly ghost, you lousy accomplice!'

Gripping the pen to write this novel, I can see the meat of the dead under my fingernails. Back then, I threw people's bones about at random. Lord only knows how many people I messed over.

PARROT TALK

Long Island with Madame, 1987

Beijing, with mother during Cultural Revolution, 1968

CHINA HAS many ways of proclaiming that the old world is dead. Any one of them can bring to mind the sight of dandruff on my mother's shoulders.

Madame was saying to me: 'No, your mother knew absolutely nothing about your father. There were long periods of time when they didn't even speak to one another. How could she possibly expect to represent your father? All she thought about was playing mahjong all day. She would sit at the table for days on end, until her legs were swollen.'

As a child, I had never noticed that my parents spent long periods without talking to each other. Heard today, this stale information was something new. America is such a marvellous place that family secrets can be hidden and preserved here. Several hundred years' worth of bedroom secrets from all over the world are maintained, swimming just under the surface like fish in a frozen pond. When the ice melts a little they begin to come to life, jumping and ultimately thrashing through to the water's surface. But to what purpose, and for whose benefit?

I secretly evaluated Madame as I sat before her, weighing her up for my father. Was she worth it? Was this woman worth destroying family feelings?

The sun over the Atlantic had gradually shifted several degrees, so that the shadow of Madame was now quietly thrown against my feet. Folded together with her high-backed chair, she resembled a Chinese character lying on the furry yellow rug. She also resembled an old castrated male cat, crawling steadily towards me.

I unconsciously drew back my feet, afraid that they could not take the weight of the shadow. My mother had been a beautiful woman from a well-known family, while Madame must have been mere jasper from a poor house. As my father, I found it hard to judge their relative worth.

When I was released the second time from labor reform, I turned north from the deaf doctor's home, and headed for the dusty, windy, ochre northern capital, Beijing. It had been ten years since I had been there. Now, during the Cultural Revolution, I went again to see my mother. I found that she had aged a hundred years.

As she herself said, she had 'been through a great transformation'. From malnutrition, poverty, and suffering, dandruff covered her thin shoulders like a layer of snow.

Today, the still-attractive Madame sat arrogantly in this large mansion on the coast of the Atlantic. She sought the bones of her lover, while I visualized the dry white hair of my mother. The juxtaposition brought home to me the unjust whimsy of the world. The tricks of history may be laughable to some, but the chrysanthemums had already withered and no other blossoms would be coming to take their place in the cold.

Madame seemed to feel that she had to criticize my mother. 'She didn't feel anything for your father – where was she when his leg was crushed? Back in Chongqing at the mahjong table! It was hard, but I carried him on my own back to a peasant's hut that night. Although your father had lost consciousness, he was still murmuring your mother's name . . .' Madame began to cry.

Joe laughed later as he said, 'Hundred-year-old vinegar sure is sour!'[1] But I envied my father for being loved for so long, and also respected Madame for being able to love for so long. The value of this hundred-year-old vinegar was priceless, I felt, since I myself lacked the strength to be jealous at all.

Travelling north to see my mother in 1968, everywhere I looked I saw hosts of fiery red slogans. They were written on huge sheets

[1] To 'eat vinegar' in Chinese means to be jealous.

of cloth and draped from windows and over streets. I saw countless red flags fluttering, saw countless great Mao badges pinned on the breasts of Chinese. I noticed that regardless of what one was purchasing in a store, one first had to raise an arm and shout, 'Long Live Chairman Mao!' Otherwise, the person behind the counter might think that your currency was counterfeit.

I had just climbed out of a grave and was raising my eyes to a brand-new world, but this did not resemble any new world promised in books. It looked more like descriptions of a Central European country before World War II. I could not decide at first if theory[1] had died or if, like myself, history had been resurrected.

With this new world as a backdrop, I walked through a small lane in Beijing, with my hundred-year-old mother on my arm. She was carrying a shopping basket made of bamboo. In it were two leaves of Chinese cabbage and one radish. She was saying happily that she had run into extraordinary luck that day: 'First, you came home, and second, the queue for vegetables wasn't too long!' She had gone from hearing the cook's daily recitation of the bill to queuing in the streets with a basket over her arm, and she had actually thrown herself gladly into this change. She had even written her transformation into a short passage known as a 'Statement of What I Have Learned from Reform', and given it to the neighborhood committee to post on the newspaper wall.

Every person in China, down to the smallest baby, has been nailed with a class attribute. There is nothing in China, not one blade of grass, not one tree, that has not been painted with a political hue.

I saw the defeated sun of the old world reflecting off ruined buildings of the new, saw the crumbling nineteenth-century walls in a small lane being pasted with countless crimson slogans. As my mother and I walked down that phantasmagoric lane, I watched it aggressively press in on people.

[1] 'Theory' refers to the communist ideology.

Stopping before one huge banner with its slogan (and all the slogans were so afraid of death that they prayed for eternal life), my mother turned to stare at me with unfamiliar eyes. 'It's been ten years,' she said. 'I wonder what reform has done to you?'

Some pigeons were circling in the air above the small lane: the radius of their flight had naturally been dictated by the revolutionary committee. As I heard their circling cries, I honestly wondered whether my mother hoped I had reformed well or had not reformed well.

My mother said, 'I, too, am reforming. I've already become someone who earns her own living.' She raised her hands to look at them, much as Madame did years later, but my mother's were covered with tiny blue veins. 'I know,' she continued, 'that your life was difficult out there in the labor reform camp, but here on the outside, life was even harder. Knitting sweaters for people, all I earn is around fifteen *yuan* a month. I sometimes wanted to steal food to have something to send you.'

My mother spoke quickly and her eyes went nervously to the enormous banner slogans. It appeared that she had reformed well but not too well.

I saw the dandruff on her shoulders shining like gold in the defeated sunlight. And then I suddenly heard the old world split apart. It came crashing down on my mother's head as the dust of tiles and shattered bricks sifted onto her thin shoulders.

In the midst of the ruin of her world, all I said was, 'Don't worry, Mama. I don't believe the Chinese people can let things go on like this.'

I felt my lips tremble as I said it. For years, parrots, not humans, had been giving us our language classes. I was already unable to express my own feelings and opinions. Why couldn't it go on like this? What, after all, was wrong with its going on like this? The parrots themselves could not give me the answer: they couldn't handle language that was too complex.

And yet my mouth had to leap across the abyss, even if my eyes couldn't see the other side.

Later, with years of accumulated wisdom, I knew why it could go on: it was not that others were messing over Chinese, but that Chinese themselves actually enjoy being messed over. They are like children who enjoy getting tossed high in the air before being suddenly swung down to the hip.

After the Cultural Revolution, everybody developed foresight and became a prophet. My mother, however, was the only one who deserved the name, for she knew enough to select the perfect time to die.

When the Great Cultural Revolution began, a crowd of cadres came running from all parts of the motherland. With official documents clamped under their arms, they were led to her home by the people's militia. They wanted to investigate problems related to her husband, a man who had been dead for almost twenty years.

She had been amazed that the Great Cultural Revolution was not like revolutions in books or movies, or even like the one she had experienced herself. Hanging aristocrats from trees, confiscating belongings of counter-revolutionaries – these were conventional, to be expected in a revolution. But it surpassed her understanding that they should show such interest in a criminal who had died so long ago. Only gradually did she realize that the investigation was for the purpose of implicating her husband's surviving friends.

An old woman who had come so far down in life that she now made a living by knitting sweaters in an alley had been recognized as a living record of a name-list from the old world.

'He was already dead,' she said to me of my father, 'so whatever they said about him was all right by me. I never tried to argue with them at all.' She had lived under a revolutionary political power for years, and did not, like Madame, consider a dead man's bones to be lovable. Towards living people, however, she maintained ethical standards passed down from an older order.

She told the cadres, 'These are things that happened years ago, so I'll have to think hard and remember any questionable things about these people. As soon as I've thought it out, I'll write it down for you, word for word.'

By the time the cadres, eager and excited, returned to her dilapidated room to hear what she had to say, she had already, coldly and happily, said goodbye to the world of men.

The last words of this prophet were: 'I know nothing!'

THE GAMBLER

Long Island with Madame, 1987

Beijing with mother, 1968

YET MADAME now said that my mother really did not know anything.

'She knew nothing about either your father or his friends – all she knew was how to win in mahjong.'

Madame's asperity increased whenever she mentioned my mother, even though events she spoke of had taken place thirty-five years before, and even though two of the three parties had died. The nature of a female can be seen in this – it's an incomparable misfortune to be loved or hated too deeply by a woman.

If I had to choose between my mother or Madame, I would naturally support my mother. Those cadres should have crossed the Pacific to interrogate *this* woman, I thought bitterly. I tried to imagine what Madame would do if they walked into this drawing room with their dossiers. Dressed in crisp green army uniforms, they would be enjoying the benefits of travel at public expense. The image faded, but not because the scene was impossible – the world was simply perturbed enough without adding to its troubles. 'The trees wished to be still but the wind wouldn't stop blowing.' Hadn't articles criticizing me again appeared inside China?

A more conceivable scenario was to have Madame and my mother change places. If my mother had been the one to cross the Pacific in 1948, then she might now be protecting the reproductive organs of male cats. She might be the one raising presumptuous demands for bones. In effect, Madame was the continuation of my mother, so by this time my mother and I would also have lacked a common language. Only those who have spent their lives in China can see that one another's thought processes are rational. Chinese who have been away too long behave almost as if they're insane.

It was better, therefore, that my mother stayed on the mainland. At least she was sane until the day she died.

I returned to her small room fifteen years later and was amazed to find it unchanged. Only the newspapers pasted over the windows had been redone, and now boasted a 1983 Beijing *Daily News*. Red headlines announced a great day of celebration. The new occupant of the room, an old man with a white beard, emerged to ask me who I was. I told him I was looking for the woman who once lived here, and I described my mother in detail.

'Do you remember her?' I asked, as the white-bearded old man frowned in thought.

After looking me carefully up and down, he stated definitively, 'No such person! I've lived here close to twenty years,' he added, 'and I know all the old ones and all the young ones. Mister, maybe you've returned from some other country?'

'No,' I said. 'Fifteen years ago I was arrested in this very room.'

In order not to disappoint the old man I offered him a foreign cigarette.

'No such person,' he had said but yes, there was still such a room. Back then, the small room had been filled with warmth. The love remaining in me had been carried from far away and buried here like a handful of dust.

The Chinese scholar-tree before the house was just as it had been. My mother said that every spring it was thick with white flowers. 'You haven't come at the right time, I'm afraid, a little earlier and I would have mixed some with flour and steamed them for you.' I told you that I had already eaten that dish for a long time, that for the past ten years I had sampled every wildflower and grass there was. I'd become a modern 'St Shen Nong.'[1] I could make the

---

[1] Shen Nong is the god of agriculture in Chinese folklore, credited with teaching Chinese how to cultivate plants and also with beginning the science of Chinese pharmacology.

bitterest herbs into delicious dishes: pig-eared grass, shepherd's purse, Chinese mugwort, purslane.

'And,' I added, licking my lips, 'I usually try to have them in a "cold mix".'

'And what is a "cold mix"?' my mother asked with interest. 'What spices do you use in that?'

'A cold mix,' I explained, 'is made by plucking a plant from the ground and sticking it straight into the mouth. To do it properly, the plant should never be washed: washing is said to reduce the chlorophyll by half.'

My mother laughed, praising me for reforming so well. I proposed that she write what I had just told her into the statement of What I Have Learned from Reform. Who could tell, it might help the neighborhood committee decide to remove her capitalist hat a bit earlier.

Gravely responsible now, my mother responded, 'That simply wouldn't do. Your accomplishments in reform are yours, mine are mine. One cannot be substituted for the other, let alone put together and adulterated. That would be cheating the government and cheating the party.'

Each of us was at ease speaking this common language, communicating what we had learned from reform. The walls of the room as well as the windows were pasted with newspapers at that time. Large red characters of 'The Revolution' and many cockroaches surrounded us as we talked. I was serenely oblivious to the familiar sight. I sat before my mother, helping her wind yarn. Her hands stayed still while my elbows rocked back and forth, mother and son a perfect match. I was already over thirty years old, but as long as my mother was alive my heart was young.

She was worried about my getting married. Everything about me, in fact, was of concern to her. This concern was the basis of my bad habit of relying emotionally on women. My hurts, my happinesses, all had to be placed on some woman, as though the feelings would not otherwise have a foundation. They would be left dangling in the air, with nowhere to land.

And so I wove romantic stories for my mother, created tales of what went on in the labor reform camps. Needless to say, I didn't talk of death or bones, but made China's camps into something like Europe's Monte Carlo. One gambled with one's life there and it is true there was danger, but one also met princes, wealthy women, famous movie stars and countesses. I smiled as I said the words, 'One could really die, it's so much fun!'

My stories convulsed my mother with laughter. She took all my lies to be the truth: she wanted to make a son who had sunk to the status of a convict into a son chased by women, a son she could be proud of. She never imagined that the woman in my stories was nothing but a long braid attached to a skull.

At times she would put aside her ball of yarn, stop the constant motion of hands, and give me lessons on how to love. Nineteenth-century people are as familiar with the art of courting as leaders in this new world are adept at the art of power – adept, that is, at inciting the masses to struggle against the masses.

The art of seduction can be more complex and more enduring than any of history's revolutionary schemes: it can be a field of true scholarship.

It was at a cocktail party in Paris that I decided to pursue Natalie. I rubbed my hands in anticipation, preparing to use everything that my mother had taught me. I felt this was an obligation I had to fulfill for her. I had woven many love stories about my life on the labor reform State Farm, but none had the flavor of Paris and a Parisian woman. This disappointment was surely making her un-easy, down there in her grave under the nine springs. She had wanted her son to conquer one woman after another – I could still remember her eager concern as, winding her yarn, she wished me success.

This interest made her look younger. It made the old world float momentarily from its ruins in the ocean, to leap in crystalline light from the tops of the waves.

On the day that I died, at the age of sixty-five, I realized that my role had been the same as that of Madame's male cats: both of us were entrusted with the souls of old widows.

I went straight for Natalie's Citroën when I emerged from the cocktail party. I spent the night in her apartment – it was as easy as could be. Natalie asked, 'How did you know I was waiting for you?' I answered, 'Because my mother told me so. I noticed your eyes on me at the cocktail party.'

After love-making, Natalie spread out my palm to read it. She told me she had learned the art from a gypsy. She spent a long time looking, then shook her blonde hair back from her shoulders. 'This Chinese man is complex!' she said. 'You seem to have a person in front of you and another person behind.'

I smiled as I told her, 'Your use of the Chinese language is slightly wrong: the proper phrase is "you have two souls".'

When I died, however, I knew that her Chinese had been correct.

Madame was clearly impervious to reason. She was someone who merely lived off her interest: she sat quietly rocking in the white swing all day, waiting for her stocks to go up. Black Monday on Wall Street had not yet happened – if Black Mondays never occurred she would have nothing to worry about.

She said she had no desire to go back and see China. 'Unless they find your father's bones,' she added. I shrugged and told her that was impossible. 'Impossible! I've heard that the police system on the mainland is airtight. If they decide to, they can definitely find them.'

She did not let up on this theme as the three of us ate dinner, but gradually switched from tales of her pharaoh to the twentieth century. In turn, I told her that China had seen great changes since 1979, that I now had my own place to live and the Organization had allocated me a car.

But Madame was more stubborn and shrewder than my mother. She turned abruptly to my novels and demanded, 'What kind of novels do you think you've written? As soon as I read about you in the paper I sent someone to Chinatown to buy two of your books. After a few pages all I could do was yawn. If it hadn't been by you, I couldn't have kept on reading. It was all hungry stomachs, harvesting rice, some kind of reform through labor . . . if labor is so holy, why is it they still want to criticize you? I simply can't figure it out.

'Don't go back!' she concluded. 'Take advantage of the opportunity and stay here. Move your wife and child over later. Why should you want to go back? To give them another chance to criticize you? You're lucky they haven't hounded you to death already after so many years. Like your father, so rectified that they can't even find his bones . . .'

Yes, Madame was shrewd but my mother was different – she was a woman deeply conscious of what should be, of what was right. She died carefree, without the slightest mud dirtying the water. She did not begrudge my father his bones, did not even care about the disposal of her own. Getting rid of her entire skeleton was like going to the beauty parlor to have her fingernails clipped before mahjong.

When I was small I used to hear my mother's partners praising her gamesmanship. She had the bearing of a great general, smiling and self-possessed even after heavy losses at the table.

The gambler had finally lost – she finally knew that the Organization had won the entire game. But as she retreated she took time to crack a joke, a joke on those officials with their dossiers in Beijing. 'My gambling money was gone long ago,' she said, 'Why don't you take my old bones with you and use them as chips!'

MASS DICTATORSHIP

Paris with Natalie, 1988

*Jail in Ningxia,
after trip to see mother in Beijing, 1968*

Long Island with Madame, 1987

AT THE MOMENT my mother was leaving the gaming table, I was being placed in a mass dictatorship troop.

Linking the new term 'mass dictatorship troop' to an old one, the 'Paris Commune', gives it a broad kind of internationalism. It gives the term a nice classical revolutionary tinge.

When I told Natalie about the 'Cultural Revolution', I mentioned that from 1968 to 1969 I had been in such a troop. Her blue eyes widened as though I had been sent to outer space.

My arm was around her waist as I said, 'Don't be so surprised. If you want to get to the root of the Chinese revolution, it comes right back to you French.' I pinched her breast in retaliation.

'You can imagine how. Robespierre died, for example – a mob of people pushing him up on the platform of the guillotine. Today the mob cut off this head, tomorrow that one, until an upsurge of wholesale guillotining began. This was what we would call a spontaneous mass dictatorship in China.

'In 1871, you Parisians developed this into violent revolution. Later, after twists and turns, it was transmitted to China, but along the way the revolution got rubbed out. By the time it got to us, the violence was all that was left.'

'Why should the masses want to dictate to you?'

She had seemed to understand but she could still ask this idiot question, something only a Western female might ask. If I were to tell any Chinese girl that I had been 'mass dictated', she would never ask why, she'd just give me a knowing smile.

'Why! Why!' Angry now, I told her, 'Because I was an easy target. I had papers certifying I'd been released from the camps!'

Several days before my mother died, my eyelids began to twitch uncontrollably, as though two birds inside my eyes were struggling to get out and fly away. My eyebrows were like the string of a bow that every so often gave a twanging sound.

A Quotation of Chairman Mao pasted on the wall of the jail said, 'If you don't beat down all reactionary elements, they will not fall.' But my eyes read it as 'Even if you beat down all reactionary elements, they will not fall.' The slogan 'Be frank and we will be lenient, resist and we will be tough', became, in my eyes, 'Be frank and we will be tough, resist and we will be lenient.'[1] Two years later, when I met the young girl named Lan-lan, I understood how she could turn 'Long Live Chairman Mao' into 'Long Live somebody else'. She had not intended to commit any crime, it was just that her tongue had been temporarily tied in knots.

My eyes were twitching when the team leader of the mass dictatorship troop arrived with a cable. He said that he had excellent news for me. 'Your capitalist reactionary element of an old mother has died! You can now draw a clear line between yourselves!'

This man had been quite fat before, but now he seemed emaciated. He was not only as thin as a gravestone, he had begun to change shape, like some grotesque image in a distorting mirror.

I told him that it was better she was dead, yes, better dead. If alive, she would simply have had to go through more hard times. 'But she wasn't a reactionary,' I said. 'She threw her heart into supporting Chairman Mao.'

[1] This slogan was used frequently by Deng Xiaoping in the weeks following June 4, 1989, in order to persuade people to turn themselves in.

'How can a member of the capitalist class dream of supporting our Great Leader?' the team leader asked haughtily. 'That's preposterous.'

I pointed out that she hadn't run to America before Liberation. 'That's proof that even back then she honestly believed in Chairman Mao. She actually thought that he might confer the title "enlightened personage" on her.'

'Now I see!' the team leader exclaimed. 'Of course she didn't go to America. She planned to go underground and wait for heaven to change.

'She must have been dreaming!' he added. 'Her real crime was not running off to America!'

Only then did I understand my mother's crime, and why she had to climb the scholar-tree every spring to pick flowers for food.

My eyelids stopped jumping and my eyebrows went back to being normal. Later, no matter what shock or terror I faced, I never blinked an eye. Even when a gun was pointed at my brain.

But from then on too, my eyes began to terrify others. Most women closed their eyes when they made love with me. Although that lovable actress kept hers wide open as she awaited orgasm, her line of vision was clearly focussed on the back of my head. She was looking at what Natalie had called the 'person behind me'.

When I was a child and my mother and I stood looking at rows of ancestor pictures, I remember that she said in fright, 'Look at their eyes!' Later my eyes came to look like those of my forebears, but theirs were malicious because they murdered people while mine were malicious because I had been murdered myself.

I know that my mother died serenely because she didn't leave me with any last wishes. While Madame was an irrational, tongue-scorching old nag, my mother had a perpetual youth glowing inside. She was a high-class gambler, willing to lose everything on one throw of the dice. She would never equivocate, never try to keep two feet on two different boats. She would either go to America, or she would stay in China. Since she had stayed, she would put heart and soul into self-reform. With hands that were accustomed to mahjong tiles, she would raise the flag of 'from each according to his ability'.

And so, as I sat musing in front of Madame, I felt fortunate in the end not to have had her as my mother. I was glad not to be my little brother – it had been a lucky biological fluke. When Madame died, she would leave behind one thousand and two requests, more, anyway, than in the Arabian Nights. She would want her stocks looked after and the ivy trimmed, and she would want to continue the search for the long-lost bones (she would never rest in peace until they were found). She would want to let me know how to handle her own bones (should they be buried safely in the public cemetery in Long Island, or taken back to the home town, Chengdu?). Even watching a show at the Moulin Rouge in Paris, I would never be able to feel at peace.

The distinction was not between the refinement of a lordly house and the false-jade feeling of a minor one, it was between sharply different world-views, developed from different styles of life.

So finally, right in her face, I gave Madame a noticeable yawn. I felt I had experienced nothing new this time in America. On the contrary, I had been surrounded by the past. I was exhausted by passing through all this historical dust.

It was a good thing the criticism had arrived to give me some stimulation.

NOBILITY

Beijing, 1968

Written from Paris, 1989

HAVING BROUGHT my novel to this point, I am uncertain how to continue. It is not that I equivocate between truth and lies this time; I am also not, as C once said, trying to make the truth more beautiful. No, I am trying to decide how to lie in a way that weaves a seamless heavenly robe. I must make everyone content.

My writing has provoked unfavorable response before. The movie script mentioned above is an example. Some felt that the son should accept his inheritance, then use the foreign exchange to support the motherland's Four Modernizations.

To such people, the son behaved according to a new code of ethics in China, a code that said that leaving China means you don't love it, staying means you do. The problem was that it was the Organization that felt this way, and a number of my countrymen who were trying to emigrate suffered as a result.

One has to be very careful when weaving a story in China. It must be so tightly constructed that not a drop of water can get through.

If the story has anything to do with money, then it is imperative that one relate the full history and the source of that money. (The reason Mark Twain isn't widely read in China is that he never gave sufficient details about Tom Sawyer's treasure. Balzac's works are long-standing best-sellers in China, while Kafka and Joyce are read in very limited literary circles.)

If you miss a few details and finally confess, 'The story was all a figment of my imagination', you will find you've aroused the fury of the masses: 'You swindler! You led us through all these joys and sorrows for nothing!'

Chinese readers like stories that describe real people and events. Made-up details have to be placed in a believable setting. This is both admirable and frightening, for if your readers are moved by what you write they will do anything to learn about your personal life. A writer has no privacy to speak of in China. His personal life is so open to public criticism that he is sometimes driven to divorce. Or, out of fear of further criticism, he is unable to divorce.

I ran into another problem with the movie script: writing a tragedy became impossible the moment I wrote of leaving China and inheritance. The mood of the book changed and took on overtones of comedy. The Chinese want to leave China more than almost anything else. Of course, an inheritance is wanted by everyone in the world. If you allow your hero either, however, your story will not only not accord with reality, it will have a negative impact on sales.

Denying him both has its own drawbacks. 'It's the same old thing,' critics will say. 'This despicable writer has been rectified until he's half dead, and yet he still won't get out of here. He stubbornly insists on staying in China.'

Before I've even finished it, I already know the fate of this book. In Madame's eyes it will be another novel not worth reading: it's all getting into bed here, getting out of a grave there, and it never does give the whereabouts of her lover's bones.

To average readers, who want only love-making and death, they've hardly got hot under the covers when the main character is thrust into icy moonlight. This will be distinctly unsatisfying.

'The End!' But I am not willing to end it yet.

I must tell you what happened one afternoon in Beijing before I was arrested and taken away.

I was sitting on a stool, holding my mother's hand. Her hand was weak, hot and dry, like the wind over the desert. She often coughed, bringing up green bile and spitting it into a tin can. She was lying on a bed made of planks of wood. A thin cotton mattress set off the thinness of her body. A gust of wind could have lifted the mattress and sent the two of them sailing through the sky.

She felt chilled, although it was summer and the scholar-tree flowers had gone. She shivered in harmony with the movement of the tree's shadows falling through the window. She seemed to feel that she still had a long time to live, though. Her eyes flashed a vigorous interest in life.

She lay on the planks giving me a lesson in love, and with the etiquette of the British upper crust. The course in love was superb, but the etiquette had been so flayed by Dickens that there was scarcely any skin left. Nonetheless, I played the game.

This daughter of a senior diplomat in the early years of the century, this woman who had once been tutor to a select group of brilliant students in school, now had to submit a weekly report to the Organization on 'what a poor street knitter has learned from reform'. During this most excellent revolutionary situation, however, she was still instructing her son on the proper deportment for entering the courts of Europe. I gradually realized that she was really riding on a cloud – that the wind had blown in and carried her away.

I built a number of flood-dikes when I was in the camps, and learned that river water never looks back. A drop of water passes the Great Thousand Worlds and doesn't pause a second to enjoy the beauty of their banks. It knows that hidden rocks lie ahead, but it plunges on to flow into the wide ocean. Unless steamed away by the sun to become a cloud, it gives no thought of returning to Paradise Lost.

I was arrested two days later. Two women from the street committee arrived with a people's militiaman. Madame had been right: even during the upheavals of revolution the police system in China is very tight. The reason they gave for arresting me was that I had dared to sneak into the Great Capital after I had been released from a distant labor reform camp. They were obliged to return me immediately.

'Your old mother has to be cleared out of here too!' A razor-thin woman from the neighborhood raised sharp eyebrows as she said, 'How can she qualify to live in the same city as Chairman Mao!'

My mother was calm, and told me, 'You go on back. Arrange a convenient place for me to live, and I'll be there soon. Believe it or not, I would enjoy living in a farming village.'

She had never been to one in her life, but I knew that wherever she lived would be fine with her.

Not long ago, here in Paris, I accompanied a young Chinese man on a visit to the Louvre. His family background was proletarian and he was a member of the Communist Party. He had been a student at the school of workers, peasants, and soldiers. After the visit we walked over to the open square by I. M. Pei's pyramid. With the light rain of Paris falling on us, he raised his head to the sky and said with emotion, 'I've learned one thing only from this entire museum: without a nobility there is no art. I mean nobility in the broadest sense, true nobility. A country that cannot produce a nobility of the spirit is a country that is doomed.'

'You're right,' I said.

WHOREHOUSE

New York, 1987

JOE'S SPIRITS revived as soon as he walked out from under the dense mat of ivy. It was already approaching midnight in New York, and he was waking up. He was a night creature, the same breed as owls and bats. The night I arrived in New York, he told me, 'By day I'm a lowly insect, but at night I become a dragon! I've been reading about what goes on behind the scenes in communist countries, and have learned that Stalin, Mao and I have something in common. We all like to work at night. If I don't come home at night, don't worry – you go ahead and sleep.'

It was probably what Joe said as we drove back that night that made me decide to go to such a place. He said, 'Don't worry, they're scared too. They're as afraid of getting communicable diseases as you writers are of losing your creativity.'

This was the one and only sentence he had uttered that had any literary grace – all the rest were unbelievably vulgar. Writers and prostitutes do have one thing in common: they have to keep smiling as they're worn down by life.

Joe pulled the car over to the curb at 59th Street. 'Have you thought it over or not?' he said, as the car slowed to a stop. 'If you want to stay, you don't have to put yourself out – you can have a lawyer do it.

'According to American laws, to apply for political asylum you have to prove that if you return to your country you'll be politically persecuted. The proof is ready-made in your case, namely that news release from Beijing. Now, I know an American lawyer who lives near here, near Central Park. You can't get to him during the day, but I know him well enough to go to his home.

'If you've decided you don't want to stay, then I want to take you to a certain place I know to relax. I'm bored to death listening to that old Madame talk all night.'

It was an hour when New York seems to come alive. All the cars in the city were on the move. They tore madly through the streets, as though New Yorkers were all homeless, and had to spend their lives racing around. The city was alive with white lights, green lights, red lights, but there was no moon shining in the sky. New Yorkers don't see the moon, which is why their suicide rate is so high.

Joe gripped the steering wheel: 'Will it be forward, to Central Park West? Or south to lower Manhattan?'

Cars were competing to catch the light at the cross-street before us – it was like watching a flock of sheep I used to herd racing across a gully. The green light turned and I suddenly shouted,

'Go south! Take me to lower Manhattan!'

Then, for some reason, I smiled a huge, crazy smile. In his overseas Chinese, Joe said, 'That smile's enough to kill a man.'

I followed Joe up the stairs and we ran into two burly men in front of a closed door. One was black and the other was white. Four slightly deranged eyes measured the two of us up and down. Joe pressed the doorbell without paying any attention – in two seconds the lock snapped and the door opened. So far, this seemed supremely easy: you didn't even need to say 'Open Sesame.' We filed into the room and found ourselves in darkness.

Joe held my elbow as he felt his way to the front of a counter. In the dim light behind it I could make out the seated form of a dignified Asian woman. 'Write down any old English name,' Joe now instructed. 'David? Scott? Chimpanzee will do.'

Reassured by the darkness, I felt a kind of going-to-the-execution-ground determination setting in. I remembered that there is an American state where people go to be checked for AIDS, and many people put down the name of a President when they register.

So I sputtered out in English, 'I'm called Luonade Ligen.'[1]

[1] Ronald Reagan.

The Asian woman was sufficiently old to have lost her sense of humor. Expressionless and with great care she wrote the name I had given into her large book. It probably already had a Winston Churchill and perhaps a Khruschev. As Joe paid, I saw the burly man on the screen of a small TV up in the top corner of the room: they weren't guests, but guards, and the realization made me feel both safe and insecure. A brief spasm attacked my stomach.

Joe pulled aside a thick curtain and I discovered about ten half-naked women lounging behind it. Some were lying, some were sitting, some were standing in the dim light. Joe asked if I wanted to drink something first or if I would like to start straight away. I said that this didn't seem the place to enjoy a cup of tea.

'Well then,' he said, glancing over the women, 'take your pick.'

'That one!' I said.

My choice was made by destiny, for I hadn't had time to compare. I had handed myself over to what Easterners call Fate, to let it make the choice for me. When I pointed a finger, she was simply the one behind it.

She stood and walked toward me without hesitation, and only then did I realize that she was much too short. She seemed like a tiny bird that had just left its nest, that was just beginning to flap its feeble wings. She gave me a smile – the little bird had a seasoned smile that displayed the teeth of a tiger.

Joe looked questioningly at me. 'You can choose again, if you like. Don't you think the one in the white negligee is a little better?'

I smiled at him – it was the smile of someone staking everything on a single throw. For me, the visit was not simply aimed at sex. It was also to have had this experience, to have known the meaning of it once in my life.

'She's the one,' I confirmed.

The little bird led me by the hand. Her joints were large and rough. 'These are the hands of the working people' I thought, as a sentence from Chinese novels came into my head. She led me to a changing room and quickly removed my clothes. They came off smoothly, her hands so skilled that she was like a butcher taking apart a lamb. I looked down, trying to see her face. Her skin was slightly dark, her eyes large and black, she had a full forehead and a wide, moist mouth. She was concentrating on her task. She was not Korean, I decided, and also not Filipino or Thai.

This was the first time I had ever let a woman wash me. Everything that happened that night was, of course, happening for the first time. I tried to mask my confusion with humor and tolerance, using everything my mother had taught me about entering high society.

Stark naked, I faced a stranger who was also stark naked. Yes, the important detail was that she was a stranger. She used a fragrant soap to lather and rub down my body. The water was warm but I felt no warmth from the little bird's hands. My only sensation was that she treated me just like an object – even before I treated her like one.

She was particularly intent on washing that place and used some other solution in addition to soap. Her concentration on this was like a hygienically fastidious woman who cleans her chopsticks vigorously before eating in a common restaurant.

I felt stupid and clumsy, felt that there was no room here for putting into effect all my substantial knowledge of the art of seduction.

The little bird used a large towel to dry my dripping body. I finally had some faint sensation: that the towel was soft. It was, indeed, softer than the hands – a high-grade towel was stimulating me rather than a woman. She led me to a small door, pulled it open, pulled the towel off my body and stuffed me inside.

It was a steam sauna. Joe was already there. He was perched on its wooden frame, naked, with sweat rolling down his body. The two of us sat in silence, facing each other. The small room was full of hot steam which turned out not to be uncomfortable. I tried to think of things to say to pass the time, and finally asked him the name of the place.

Joe said it in English and then translated for me – in Chinese this place would be called 'Eastern Beauties'. 'All the women they employ are Asians, and the only customers they'll take are Asians. With AIDS giving the world such a scare, Asians seem to have some kind of racial superiority.'

'Is this where Jenny used to entertain?'

'Jenny? Which Jenny? Oh, you mean that Korean woman. No, it isn't.'

'You seem to have forgotten her already.'

'Not at all. But I only remember the names of business clients – I never remember the names of women. How could I keep all those names in the back of my mind? By the way, don't forget to give Jing Hui a long-distance call – she phoned yesterday, very concerned about you. She said not to worry, if the worst comes to the worst, you could always stay here in the United States.'

'All right, I'll call her in the morning. You know, I think you should go back to San Francisco to look after her. She's living by herself there and it gets pretty lonely.'

'You don't know everything. Jing Hui is the kind of woman who's too cloyingly sweet. I discovered I got too lazy, living with her. But her sort would be just right for you.'

'Do you mean to say I'm lazy?'

'Sure – writers are always lazy buggers. All you do is lie on your beds all day, thinking up things to write.'

'Joe.'

'Yeah?'

'After this is over, you go on home. I'll get back myself on the subway.'

'Why?'

'No real reason.'

'Comrade, the last subway went long ago.'

'Then I'll call a taxi.'

'Why should you? Why shouldn't we go back together?'

'No, let's see each other again after the sun comes up. I want to be by myself to think for a while.'

'Whatever you say! You mainland comrades can be funny sometimes.'

The little bird dried my sweaty body again, then put her arm around my waist as she led me to a small room. A pseudo-antique kerosene lantern stood beside the bed, giving the room the appearance of a cave.

'Please wait. I will go wash myself – OK?' She said this in English.

'Yes, of course, OK.' She disappeared, leaving behind a smile which seemed more like a shadow in the gloom.

I stretched out on the narrow bed. A pack of cigarettes and an ashtray on the bedside table were the only other things in the room. I opened the pack with a practiced hand and lit myself a cigarette.

'Since you're here, be at ease – let nothing worry you.' This homily from Chairman Mao actually came to mind in such a place. I had chanted it continually in 1960, when I was so near starvation I almost didn't get out of the corpse-shed. Bitterness washed over me as I found myself using the phrase now for comfort.

I knew that I was beginning to revolt, beginning to cast off the brainwashing of the past thirty years. But I found that I was powerless. This decadent act was all I could use to assert my own control, my own sense of superiority, my opposition.

All the beautiful words, all the lofty language had been co-opted by the criticizers. The use of language itself had been monopolized by those with power. Going outside the boundaries set by those who criticized meant that one must be willing to descend into the mire. There was no alternative: everything in my mind had been put there by them.

But this step I was taking also proved to me and to the criticizers that the criticism of me had been correct.

The little bird came fluttering back after about ten minutes, a large white towel wrapped around her glowing body. I tried to think of something to say, a way to tell her that I was not in the practice of making love purely for the sake of making love, of limiting love-making to the physical motions. I consider myself something of a romantic in love-making, a poet, and so I said to her, 'Please tell me, what is your name?'

'Lucy.'

This 'Lucy' and my 'Ronald' were probably about the same.

'Can I ask how old you are?'

'Twenty-two.' She took off the towel as she approached the bed.

'Where do you come from?'

'Vietnam.'

'. . . Vietnam.' The smile of a fatalist flickered across my face. 'So that means we're "comrades in addition to being brothers", doesn't it?'[1]

'What?'

It was hard to believe, but she did not know this term that every man, woman and child in China knew so well – this phrase expressing great friendship toward the people of Vietnam.

Even in labor camp, the moment Vietnam or the Ho Chi Minh Trail was mentioned, this phrase would spring to the mind of every convict. The only translated work of Vietnamese literature that hundreds of millions of Chinese were required to read in those years was a piece entitled, 'Letter from the South'. Even labor reform convicts in China felt an instinctive obligation to support the Vietnamese in the Anti-American War.

Who could have guessed that as soon as Vietnam's liberation had been won, millions of Vietnamese would try to flee the country? That a tiny bird like this would be able to flap her tiny wings and make it all the way across the Pacific?

By bizarre chance, both of us were refugees to this cave, this place called Eastern Beauties. Was this the only place in the world that was willing to give the two of us a perch?

'Nothing, never mind.' I was disappointed. 'Have you been in America long?'

'Six months.' She indicated with her hands that I should turn

---

[1] This phrase was used by the Chinese to describe their Vietnamese allies during the years of Chinese support for North Vietnam in the war. Since 1979, when Chinese troops fought a border war against the Vietnamese, the phrase had been used ironically inside China.

over. 'I will make you comfortable.' She began to massage my shoulders.

'I believe you,' I said.

'Comrades in addition to being brothers.' And now here we were in America, the country that had been our common enemy. The two of us were using the enemy's language to speak to one another.

Many Americans had not yet healed the psychological wounds of the Vietnam War, but we two were preparing to 'get comfortable' and make love right here in their country. The minds and hearts of Easterners are indestructible – I couldn't help smiling, just thinking about it.

She spread her legs to straddle my back as she massaged. Her laborer's hands were surprisingly strong, but after the conventional treatment she began substituting her tongue. I felt it run from my ear down my back. Slowly, I felt the stirrings of desire. Lying face down on the bed, I reached my hands back to feel her legs, but where she should have been moist I discovered that she was bone dry, as dry as two dried Jinhua hams hanging in a store window.

Deflated, I wanted to turn over and look her in the eyes. When I did, she stared back blankly, not knowing what to do. Trying to increase a sense of emotional engagement before making love, I said to her, 'You look just like a girlfriend of mine.'

'Really? That's good.' The tone of her voice and her expression were flat. Her strong hands seemed to hold down any feelings I might have had.

After a moment, she put her head down and again set her tongue to work. I closed my eyes.

'*Ping!*' came the sound of a gun shot.

The sound split through the deep recesses of my memory. Dozens of China Pinks instantly blossomed before my eyes. Incomparably fresh, the blooms opened one after another. The bullet was never fired, but its sound had caught up with me.

Terrified, I began to sweat. The sound of my panting was added to hers, although mine was not from pleasure and hers was from professional exertion. Stimulating sexual desire in me was her job.

Her tongue seemed to wrap around my whole body as I felt myself melt inside her mouth.

This only increased my sense of frustration. By the time my sweat cooled, I knew that I couldn't summon the strength to make love with her again.

In making love with other women, the shot had always rung out after the act, whereas in this situation, with this kind of woman, the shot had come before. This was not a shot signalling the start of a race – it had clearly been fired in warning.

Moody now, I pulled away. She put on her green bikini and helped me with my clothes. I saw a complete lack of comprehension in her large eyes, and also a sort of waiting, of hoping. There was no hint of ridicule in them – it was all the same to her whether I couldn't, or wouldn't, make love. As I finished dressing I realized that she had kept the key to my locker. In the ten minutes she'd been away she had probably opened it and gone through my passport. At least she now knew I was Chinese.

I took more from my wallet than the amount Joe had recommended and gave her a one hundred dollar American bill. I tucked it into the brassiere of her bikini.

Her face widened in its first sincere smile. 'Welcome to come back again!' she said.

She reached up to kiss me, and I replied, 'I'll be sure to come. Goodbye.'

A fresh snow was brewing in the night sky of New York. Winds careened down from tall buildings to attack streets full of dirty litter. I leaned my head back to look at the sky and shouted two words with all my might:

'The End!'

✖ V ✖

MUTTON SWEETMEATS

Paris, writing to C, 1988

New York with C, 1987

Village in northwest China, Chinese New Year, 1989

YOU DID NOT come to Paris, but you called me long distance every day. I was amused, at first, by the thought of our voices travelling over the Atlantic. Soon the calls grew tiresome, and I began to suspect your motives when you started calling in the middle of the night. I felt that in my lifetime I had been monitored enough.

This book is now finished, and it is partly due to those calls that I was able to complete it on time. I might otherwise have spent my time running around France with Natalie.

I remember the day you raced back from South America and appeared before me in Joe's New York apartment. Surrounded by the fragrance of yellow soybean meal, we discussed my decision to return to China. You begged me to stay in America, said that there were indications that China would soon be starting another political movement. You ridiculed my old-fashioned patriotism.

That evening you also ridiculed the literature being written in China, which, you said, can have no hope so long as it's formulated rather than inspired. You even ridiculed women on the mainland, saying scornfully that their breasts 'look just like fried eggs'.

Only when you said that did I manage to smile. You then asked me again why I wanted to go back.

I told you to look at the top of my head – to see if it had a bloody hole. You cradled my head in your arms, and said, 'No, it appears to be a complete and perfect skull.'

'That's right!' I responded. 'And as a result I feel I still owe those people a hole and I feel they owe me the bullet. Only when that debt is settled will I be at peace. I must go back to get the bullet that belongs to me!'

You may understand more after reading this book. I didn't, for instance, tell you about the Eastern Beauties back then. If you had known, you would have scolded till 'dog's blood flowed from your head'. Going there actually had a salutary effect: I emerged from that place knowing that I had lost the ability to be depraved. I also knew that I had lost the ability to start a new life, and that the reason was that the bullet had lodged too deeply in my brain.

When I see a gun aimed at me out there, I begin to shake. There is a blood relationship between that gun on the outside and the bullet that is already within. The gun has only to point at me for the bullet inside to explode – it is unimportant whether or not the trigger is pulled.

And it does not matter where I try to take refuge – the gun knows exactly where to aim. The connecting line between gun and bullet is like a barrier that has been set across my life: it keeps me from creating, from achieving, and it also prevents me from doing anything wrong.

You took me to the airport when I left, and at the boarding gate I saw the hopelessness in your eyes. It was as though you were taking leave from someone who had died. Today we both know that the article criticizing me was a false alarm and that for years false alarm has followed false alarm. But, with the bullet in my brain, I have shaken with fear all this time.

Since the sound of that gunshot hasn't changed, however, I have gradually grown accustomed to it. It now both terrifies me and stimulates me. My soul did not land in the wrong place after all, for only in China could I have been offered such a challenge. The challenge has given me vitality that has lasted a lifetime, to the point where I have the strength to die.

If my soul had landed in some country like Switzerland, or Iceland, everything would have been too easy – I would almost certainly have become obese. You once admired my figure and said it was unusual at my age. And I thought to myself that there are two good ways to stay in shape: endure starvation when you are young, and fear when you are middle-aged.

As you kissed me goodbye at the airport, you said, 'I hope you find the broken fragments of your soul.'

The minute I entered the 747 of the CAAC[1] flight, I began to search in all directions for the gun. Never mind that the Chinese stewardess gave me a welcoming smile.

On the fifteenth day of the first month of the lunar calendar of this year, I hid myself away in a small mountain village in northwest China.

The purpose was to write the final sentences of this book. I stayed at the home of an old lover, a woman who once played the main character in one of my novels. In the quarter-century since we parted, she had been married to three men and borne six children. The children were grown-up, the youngest was working in a county enterprise. With nobody left at home, she lived on her own.

I sat cross-legged on her *kang*. The bricks were heated to a comfortable temperature below me. This manuscript was spread out on a small *kang* table before me. There was no electricity in the small village, nor a telephone for five *li* around. At first, she prepared a kerosene lamp for me, but it was too reminiscent of the cave at the Eastern Beauties. When I asked if there was anything else, she suggested lighting a candle.

'Fine,' I said. And so she lit three candles.

Tonight she came quietly in to collect my supper bowl. She had cooked noodles for me, flavored with generous chunks of mutton. 'I remembered that you like to eat mutton sweetmeats,' she said. 'So I bought some – I'll make them for you tomorrow.'

'Fine,' I said. She went out to wash the sweetmeats and soon after I heard the splashing of water.

[1] The national airline of China.

299

As I worked on the manuscript, I gathered together the fragments of my soul.

A dog barked with lazy interest as the sound of a tractor engine approached the town. The village livened up briefly when people climbed into the tractor's cart. I had heard during the day that there would be a celebration in the county seat tonight, and I wondered if villagers kept up the tradition of lighting lanterns at this festival time. When it sounded as though everyone had sat down, the tractor put-putted slowly into the distance. Silence returned, and from the outside room I once again heard the trickling of water.

The wick of the candle sputtered a moment. The candle was a local product and not too well made. As I raised my eyes to look at the wick, its yellow flame somehow warmed my insides. I felt that I wanted to ask for forgiveness and that I wanted to pardon others too.

Do not condemn me any more. Even if those with the guns put down or are forced to put down their weapons in the future – and I do not dare to hope for this – I will willingly return the hole in my head. The bullet is forever pressing on a nerve in my brain.

The sounds stopped outside the door. In a moment, she lifted the curtain and stepped inside. She leaned over to sit on the edge of the *kang* and said, 'It's late. You should sleep.'

'Fine,' I said.

We spread the bedding, a sheepskin pad over a mattress of dogskin. 'A thin cover should do,' she said, 'a thicker one might be too heavy.'

'Fine,' I said.

She stood beside the *kang* for a moment, then asked quietly, 'Do you want me to stay with you?'

And I said, 'Yes.'

Unhurriedly, she took off her clothes. In the candlelight, I saw that her breasts and stomach sagged. I saw that she was covered with folds and wrinkles. She threw me a glance and an apologetic smile. 'You see, this is what has become of me. What was it that made you come here?'

'Maybe it was my patriotism, eh?'

'What?' she said. 'What did you say?'

'Never mind. I said that if I hadn't come to you, I wouldn't have been at peace.'

She climbed under the covers and pulled them up around her chin. 'Going to keep writing?' she asked.

'No,' I answered, 'I have finished. It's written.'

'Then sleep.'

'I'll sit here for a moment, to think.'

'Then blow out the candles,' she said. 'Don't waste them.'

'Fine,' I said.

As I blew out the candles, one by one, moonlight from the high mountains came streaming through the window.

I sat with my legs crossed and closed my eyes. She looked young and beautiful to me, under that moon.

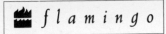 **flamingo**

Flamingo is a quality imprint publishing both fiction and non-fiction. Below are some recent titles.

Fiction
☐ The Things They Carried *Tim O'Brien* £4.99
☐ Matilda's Mistake *Anne Oakley* £4.99
☐ Acts of Worship *Yukio Mishima* £4.99
☐ My Cousin, My Gastroenterologist *Mark Leyner* £4.99
☐ Escapes *Joy Williams* £4.99
☐ The Dust Roads of Monferrato *Rosetta Loy* £4.99
☐ The Last Trump of Avram Blok *Simon Louvish* £4.99
☐ Captain Vinegar's Commission *Philip Glazebrook* £4.99
☐ Gate at the End of the World *Philip Glazebrook* £4.99
☐ Ordinary Love *Jane Smiley* £4.99

Non-fiction
☐ A Stranger in Tibet *Scott Berry* £4.99
☐ The Quantum Self *Danah Zohar* £4.99
☐ Ford Madox Ford *Alan Judd* £6.99
☐ C. S. Lewis *A. N. Wilson* £5.99
☐ Meatless Days *Sara Suleri* £4.99
☐ Finding Connections *P. J. Kavanagh* £4.99
☐ Shadows Round the Moon *Roy Heath* £4.99
☐ Sweet Summer *Bebe Moore Campbell* £4.99

You can buy Flamingo paperbacks at your local bookshop or newsagent. Or you can order them from Fontana Paperbacks, Cash Sales Department, Box 29, Douglas, Isle of Man. Please send a cheque, postal or money order (not currency) worth the purchase price plus 22p per book (or plus 22p per book if outside the UK).

NAME (Block letters)_____

ADDRESS_____

_____

_____

While every effort is made to keep prices low, it is sometimes necessary to increase them at short notice. Fontana Paperbacks reserve the right to show new retail prices on covers which may differ from those previously advertised in the text or elsewhere.